Lucian trusted no one.

If not for his wealth and name, they'd all be gone in a second. He'd learned that the hard way.

What about Megan? The beauty seemed to radiate goodness. He could almost believe she truly cared about helping this town. Was it real? Or a clever act designed to make him lower his guard?

He resented this present circumstance that was beyond his control. As empty as his life in New Orleans had become, it was familiar.

Frustration surged. If not for this young lady, he would've already put the house up for sale and be out of this backwoods town.

"Let me make myself clear, Miss O'Malley. I plan to do everything possible to find a way around that stipulation."

Anger flashed in her eyes. "And let me assure you, Mr. Beaumont, I will do everything I can to fight you."

He blew out an aggravated breath. He was beginning to wish he'd never heard of Gatlinburg, Tennessee. And Miss Megan O'Malley.

Books by Karen Kirst

Love Inspired Historical

*The Reluctant Outlaw
*The Bridal Swap
 The Gift of Family
    *"Smoky Mountain Christmas"
*His Mountain Miss

*Smoky Mountain Matches

KAREN KIRST

was born and raised in East Tennessee near the Great
Smoky Mountains. A lifelong lover of books, it wasn't
until after college that she had the grand idea to write
one herself. Now she divides her time between being
a wife, homeschooling mom and romance writer. Her
favorite pastimes are reading, visiting tearooms and
watching romantic comedies.

His

Mountain Miss

KAREN KIRST

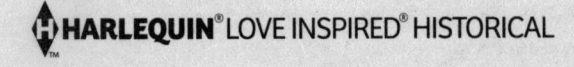

™ LOVE INSPIRED BOOKS

ISBN-13: 978-0-373-82961-3

HIS MOUNTAIN MISS

www.LoveInspiredBooks.com

Printed in U.S.A.

I will turn their mourning into gladness;
I will give them comfort and joy instead of sorrow.
—*Jeremiah* 31:13

To my parents-in-law, Pavel and Julie Turon,
who have brought such joy into my life.
I'm blessed to know you both. I love you!

A big thank-you to my editor, Emily Rodmell,
for all her hard work and dedication.
This series wouldn't be possible without you!

Chapter One

May 1881
Gatlinburg, Tennessee

"Who are you, and what are you doing in my house?"

Jolted out of her concentration, Megan O'Malley dropped the books she was holding, and they thumped to the gleaming wood floor. She twisted around to face the unexpected visitor whose voice she didn't recognize. Odd, she hadn't heard the doorbell. Mrs. Calhoun normally announced company.

The stranger standing in the parlor's wide entryway was definitely not a local. Even dressed in their Sunday best, the men of Gatlinburg couldn't come close to imitating this man's elegance. Glossy black Hessian boots encased his feet and calves. Muscular thighs stretched the dove-gray trousers he wore taut, and underneath his black frock coat, the silver-and-black paisley brocade vest hugged a firm chest. The snowy white, expertly arranged cravat at his throat resembled a work of art.

Nothing was out of place. No lint on his coat. Not a single speck of dust dared cling to the mirrorlike surface of his boots…which was why his hair seemed to her untamed. It was glorious hair, really, thick and lustrous and wavy, the dark brown layers kissing his forehead in a manner that must irk him so.

His eyes, she noticed at last, were watching her with marked suspicion. He did not look pleased.

His black gaze raked her from head to toe and back up again, his frown deepening at the sight of the flower circlet adorning her loose curls. Megan experienced a spurt of self-consciousness. In preparation for the children's story time, she'd dressed the part of a princess, complete with a flowing white gown and fingerless lace gloves.

Unsettled, she clasped her hands behind her back and adopted what she hoped was a casual smile. "Hello, I'm Megan O'Malley. You must be new in town. Is there something I can help you with?"

He didn't deign to answer. Instead, he surveyed the airy room as he stalked towards her, circumventing the wingbacked chairs arranged in a semicircle about a plush Oriental rug. Fit and athletic, he exuded an air of command. Of authority. He struck her as a man accustomed to giving orders as opposed to taking them.

A wrinkle formed between his brows. Haughty brows, she thought. His was an arrogant beauty, with razor-sharp cheekbones and a harsh jawline. His nose was unremarkable, medium size and straight. The fullness of his mouth and the small dimple in his chin offset the harshness of his features.

When he stopped very near, his sharp-edged gaze cut into her, demanding answers. "Would you be so kind as to tell me what you're doing in my grandfather's house?"

A great trembling worked its way up her body. *This* was Charles's grandson? It couldn't be, could it?

"Lucian?" she whispered.

He sketched a bow, his gaze narrowing. "*Oui.* Lucian Beaumont, at your service. I take it you were well acquainted with my grandfather?"

"Charles was a dear friend of mine."

Sadness gripped her. How she missed the gentle, insightful older man, their lively conversations about life and love, music and books. Theirs had been an unlikely friendship brought about by a mutual love of literature. To Megan, he'd been a substitute grandfather.

"I see." And yet, it was perfectly clear that he didn't. Resentment came and went in his expression. "He passed away nearly three months ago. Why are you here?"

"I could ask the same of you." She met his gaze squarely, a rush of indignation stiffening her spine. "Why did you wait until now to come? In all these years, why didn't you visit Charles just once?"

The rift between Charles and his daughter, Lucian's mother, Lucinda, was common knowledge among the townspeople. He'd been dead-set against Lucinda's marriage to New Orleans native Gerard Beaumont, had rashly threatened to cut her out of his life if she went against his wishes. A threat he'd lived to regret. After their elopement, Lucinda and Gerard left Tennessee and settled in New Orleans, never to return.

A muscle in his jaw jumped. His already cool manner turned glacial. "That is none of your concern, Miss O'Malley. As to what I'm doing here, I happen to be the new owner of this house. And despite my repeated inquiries, you've yet to tell me what you're doing here." He gestured to the chairs and the books scattered behind her.

The story time! The hand-painted, gilt clock on the

fireplace mantel showed ten minutes to five o'clock. She glanced out the window overlooking the front lawn. The children would start arriving soon.

Turning her back on him, she bent and hurriedly began to gather the books she'd dropped. "Every Friday afternoon, we have story time for the children. They'll be here any minute."

To her surprise, Lucian crouched beside her, his tanned hands deftly assisting her. "Children? Here?" They reached for the last one at the same time, his fingers closing over hers. A frisson of awareness shot through her, and she was suddenly conscious of his knee brushing hers, his bold, sweet-smelling cologne awakening her senses. Megan had the absurd notion to lean closer and sniff his clothes. Instead, she snatched her hand back. His eyes as black as midnight, he held the book out to her, waiting.

Flustered, she took it from him and pointed to the cover. "*The Princess and the Goblin* is our story for today. In case you haven't noticed, I'm the princess." She touched a finger to her crown of daisies.

"I noticed." He held her gaze a moment longer. Then, with a fleeting touch on her arm, he assisted her to her feet. "How long has this been going on?"

"About a year," she said, hugging the books to her chest. "Your grandfather wholeheartedly approved."

"So this was your idea?"

"Yes."

His open assessment put her on guard. He didn't know her, yet he regarded her with a healthy dose of distrust.

"Here are the refreshments, Miss Megan." Mrs. Calhoun entered the room with an oval tray piled high with strawberry tarts, stopping short when she spotted Lucian. Her mouth fell open. "Oh my!" Her gray brows shot to her hairline. "You look so much like Charles did when he was younger that I was momentarily taken back in time. Mr. Lucian, I presume?"

Setting the books aside, Megan took the tray from the older woman's hands and placed it on the credenza beside a crystal pitcher of lemonade. Turning, she caught Lucian's arrested expression before he smoothed all emotion from his face.

He regally dipped his head. "I'm afraid you have me at a disadvantage, *madame*. I—"

"Of course you wouldn't know me." She chuckled as she mopped her brow with a handkerchief. "I'm Madge Calhoun. My husband, Fred, and I came to work for your grandparents when your mother was just a baby. We live in the little house on the back side of the property. I do the cooking and cleaning, and Fred maintains the grounds."

"I see."

Her expression clouded, the lines about her eyes becoming more pronounced. "I sure was sorry to hear of Lucinda's passing. And now Charles… I keep expecting to hear him coming down the stairs asking me what's for dinner. Hard to believe he's gone."

At his low hiss, Megan's gaze darted to Lucian. A flash of regret on his face, of deep-seated pain, mirrored what was in her own heart. Was his grief entirely for his mother? Or did he—too late—understand what he'd given up by refusing to mend things with his grandfather?

The doorbell chimed. "Oh, our first visitor." Mrs. Calhoun stuffed the handkerchief back into her apron pocket. "It's probably Ollie Stevenson. He comes early in hopes I'll relent and give him a treat before all the others get here. Of course, I never do, but he's a persistent little fellow."

As soon as she'd gone, Lucian turned to Megan, his voice low and urgent. "How many children are coming?"

"On a good night, we have about twenty."

"Twenty." He visibly swallowed. "And how long will they stay?"

"About an hour. Why do I get the feeling you don't like children, Mr. Beaumont?"

"In my world, children do not normally mingle with adults. I've little experience with them."

"And yet—" she smiled sweetly "—you were once one yourself."

His lips didn't so much as twitch. "Miss O'Malley, I will absent myself for the duration of your…story time. It's obviously too late to cancel. However, I'd like a word with you immediately afterward. There are matters we need to discuss."

He pivoted on his heel and strode out of the parlor before she could respond. Cancel? Matters to discuss? Somehow, Megan sensed she wasn't going to like what he had to say.

The children's excited chatter, punctuated by Megan O'Malley's lilting voice, ultimately drove Lucian out the back door and into the flower gardens. He strode along the winding stone path, past gurgling fountains and whimsical marble statues and wildflowers in every imaginable shape and hue, unmindful of his destination. His chest felt too tight. He needed air. Distance. In that house, unwanted emotions crowded in without his consent, nipping like rabid dogs at his tenuous hold on his composure.

He abruptly swung about to glare at the two-story, gabled Victorian, the late-afternoon sun bathing its yellow exterior in soft, buttery light. The stained-glass windows glowed like fine jewels. White wicker chairs situated along the porch invited a person to sit back and relax, to enjoy the view of the blue-toned mountains rising above the valley.

Had his mother sat and rocked on that very porch? Explored these gardens?

Reaching out, he fingered the velvet bloom of a purple hyacinth. Of course she had. Lucinda had been born in one of the upstairs rooms, had spent the first eighteen years of her life here. Until his father had happened into town and turned her life upside down. He frowned. No good would come of revisiting his mother's unhappiness and regrets. Releasing the petals, he turned and continued walking in the opposite direction of the house, purposefully moderating his steps.

He concentrated on his breathing. Blanking his mind, the heavy feeling in his chest slowly began to recede. The air here was fresh and clean. Pleasant, even. A far cry from the humid, salty tang of New Orleans, the rush of the mighty Mississippi and steamboat blasts and lusty cries of the dock workers. His home.

Over the course of the past year, Lucian had learned to avoid his darker emotions, to push aside grief and loss instead of dealing with it. A coward's way, he admitted. But it meant survival. And right now, that was his only goal. To keep his head above the waters of disappointment and disillusionment that was his life.

This house and all it represented threatened to suck him under. He could not—*would not*—allow that to happen. He would sell it to the first reasonable bidder, no matter if it was at a loss. Money was not the issue here. Ridding himself of this burden was. The sooner the better.

Quiet footfalls against the stones registered behind him. Megan O'Malley.

Wearing that filmy, bridal-like gown, with flowers intertwined in the white-blond curls hanging nearly to her waist, she seemed to him a sort of woodland fairy, as insubstantial as a dream or a figment of his imagination. He blinked, wishing her far from here. But she kept coming, her movements graceful and fluid. She was beautiful, radiant even, with dewy-fresh skin that invited a man's touch. Inquisitive eyebrows arched above large, expressive eyes the color of the sea. Straight, flawless nose. Lips full and sweet like a ripe peach.

In New Orleans high society, Megan O'Malley would be a much sought-after prize. Thankfully, he'd learned his lesson where innocent-seeming beauties were concerned. He was immune.

The determined jut of her chin gave him pause. Made him wonder if she was going to prove an obstacle to his plans.

Boots planted wide, he clasped his hands behind his back. "Story time over already?"

"I cut it short today. I saw the last child out myself, so there's no need to worry you might bump into one later." Amusement hovered about her mouth, but her eyes were watchful. "So, what do you wish to speak to me about?"

He gestured to the metal bench to his right. "Would you like to have a seat?"

"No, thank you. I'd rather stand."

"As you wish. Miss O'Malley, I'm not sure exactly what sort of arrangement you had with my grandfather, but I'm afraid it must come to an end. You see, I'm here to oversee the sale of this property, and in order to do that, the house must be kept in excellent condition for potential buyers. I can't have strangers, especially children, traipsing in and out doing who knows what sort of damage. I'm sure you understand my predicament."

"Actually, I don't." Her pale brows collided. "Charles assured me that the children, and indeed the townspeople, would always have access to his home. In addition to the weekly story times, we host once-monthly performances open to the community."

"He meant while he was alive—"

"No." She shook her head, curls quivering. "He meant *always*. In those last months when he was growing weaker, he spoke of how he wanted our endeavors to continue after his d-death." Her blue eyes grew dark and stormy, her distress a palpable thing.

Lucian couldn't help but be suspicious. What had been her true motivation for befriending the old man? Had she assumed that, because of the rift in their family, neither he nor his father would come to claim the house? That after Charles's death, she would have unlimited access to it?

"Must you sell?" She stepped closer, tilted her head back to gaze imploringly up at him. "Charles wouldn't have wanted it to go to strangers."

"What he wanted is no longer relevant," he retorted, years of animosity born of rejection rising up within him. His only grandfather hadn't wanted anything to do with him, so why should he care about the man's wishes? "I am the owner now, and I will do as I see fit."

Sidestepping her, he stalked back towards the house to order his valet to unpack enough clothing for the next week. Hopefully, that was all the time it would take to find a buyer.

"What kind of unfeeling man are you?" Megan called out after him, voice shimmering with indignation.

Lucian stopped dead in his tracks. Pivoted on his heel. Smiled a cold smile. "Unfeeling? How I wish that were the case! For without feelings, one could avoid a plague of problems, wouldn't you agree? Good evening, Miss O'Malley."

He left her there in the garden to see herself out, lips parted and eyes full of reproach. If he felt a pinprick of remorse for his less-than-stellar manners, he shoved it aside. This wasn't about her. This was about unloading emotional entanglements. He couldn't allow her or anyone else to distract him from his goal.

Chapter Two

Megan hesitated before the imposing mahogany-and-stained-glass door, her finger hovering above the doorbell. Gone was the eager anticipation that had marked her past visits to Charles's home. Now there was only sadness. And dread. That Lucian Beaumont's behavior had marred her pleasant memories of this place stoked her ire.

In her left hand, she clutched the missive that had been delivered to her cabin shortly before lunch. What could he possibly have to say to her? He'd made his intentions plain last night. Charles's wishes meant nothing to him. Though it was a stretch, she could somewhat understand why he wouldn't care about helping her or the townspeople. They were strangers, after all. But Charles was family. His only grandfather.

A grandfather he hadn't bothered to come and meet, despite repeated invitations to do so.

Recalling the anguish in her friend's eyes as he spoke of his failed attempts to bring his daughter and grandson back to Gatlinburg, Megan blinked away tears. Nursed the grudge she'd harbored towards his estranged family. Knowing what she did, she shouldn't be surprised by Lucian's selfish disregard of everyone else's needs but his own.

The door swung inward, and there stood the object of her turmoil, looking coolly refined in a chocolate frock coat, tan vest and pants, and the ever-shiny black Hessians. Her gaze was drawn once again to his hair, the dark, unruly waves at odds with his neat clothing and stiff manner.

His black gaze bored into her, making her want to squirm. "Miss O'Malley, I see you received my message."

Walking past him into the entrance hall, she was glad she'd chosen to wear one of her best outfits, a deep blue fitted jacket with layered skirts that skimmed the tips of her boots. Her mass of curls, too heavy to be piled on top of her head, was restrained at her nape with a matching ribbon.

"No princess attire today?"

"No, that was strictly for the children's benefit."

Glancing up, she caught him gazing at her hair with a look akin to disappointment. She blinked and it was gone. Must've been a trick of the light.

"I see."

There was that phrase again. She gritted her teeth, fairly certain Lucian Beaumont did *not* see the true picture at all, his outlook tainted by cynicism.

"You wished to see me?"

"Actually, Charles's lawyer is the one who asked for you. He arrived this morning from Sevierville and wishes to speak with us about the will." He motioned for her to precede him. "He's waiting for us in the office."

"But Charles never indicated that I'd be included. I can't imagine why he would've done such a thing."

Lucian's steady gaze assessed her. Perhaps gauging her sincerity? "You indicated the two of you were close. Most likely he wanted to leave you some things to remember him by. Your favorite books, for instance."

Megan's thoughts were a jumble as they passed through the hallway to the rear corner of the house where the office was located. She hadn't spent much time there, as she and Charles had preferred to use the library or, weather permitting, the back porch or gardens. Like the rest of the house, this room was richly appointed with dark wood furniture and plush throw rugs. However, there were personal touches here. Artifacts from his travels littered his desk. Photographs lined the bookshelves. Even his scent lingered in the air, a blend of sandalwood and lemon. For the second time that afternoon, Megan blinked away moisture gathering in her eyes.

"Mr. McDermott," Lucian addressed the man standing at the window, "may I introduce Miss Megan O'Malley?"

The distinguished older man smiled a greeting as he moved behind the desk. "How do you do, Miss O'Malley? I'm pleased you could join us. Won't you have a seat so we can begin?"

She looked to Lucian, who indicated she take one of the two chairs facing the desk. On the low table between them rested a silver tea service.

"I had Mrs. Calhoun prepare a pot of Earl Grey," he commented as he lowered his tall frame into the chair beside her. "Would you care for some?"

"Yes, please." Hopefully the warm liquid would ease the sudden dryness in her throat. But when she attempted to pour herself a cup, her trembling hands managed to spill the brew, splashing it onto the tray and table. "Oh," she gasped, embarrassment flooding her cheeks.

Half expecting Lucian to react with irritation, she caught her breath when he stilled her attempts to mop it up with his large hand covering hers, slipping the napkin from her suddenly nerveless fingers to do the job himself. Then he poured her a second cup, adding sugar and cream when she indicated her preferences.

"Here you are." His enigmatic gaze met hers briefly as he settled the cup and saucer into her hands. "I believe we're ready now, Mr. McDermott."

"Charles summoned me here approximately six months before his death to add a stipulation to his will."

Beside her, Lucian went as still as a statue. Tension bracketed his mouth. "What sort of stipulation? I was under the impression from your letter that the house is mine."

Mr. McDermott nodded. "Indeed, it is, Mr. Beaumont. However, there's a condition attached." His thoughtful gaze settled on Megan. "As you are aware, he and Miss O'Malley were involved in various community projects. Charles felt strongly that these should continue under her guidance after his death."

Megan quickly swallowed her mouthful of tea and set it aside before she dropped it on her lap. The storm brewing on Lucian's face was on the verge of being unleashed, tempering her anticipation. This was not going to be pretty.

"Get to the point, McDermott," he practically growled.

"If you do not allow her to continue use of the house as stated in the will, you will forfeit and ownership will transfer to Miss O'Malley."

Megan's mouth fell open.

Lucian clutched the chair's armrests, knuckles white

with strain. Megan sensed his control on his temper was slipping. "That's ludicrous!" he pushed through clenched teeth. "How am I supposed to sell it, then? What potential buyer would agree to have their house available to the whole town?"

"Not many, I agree—" the lawyer began gathering his papers into a neat pile "—but then, Charles didn't intend for you to sell it. He wanted to keep it in the family."

"She's not family," he gritted out.

"True, but it was plain to see he cared a great deal about her. If you refused to honor his wishes, at least it would go to someone close to him. Mr. Beaumont, I got the feeling that your grandfather wanted you to stick around for a little while. Maybe he thought the town would grow on you and that you'd decide to stay."

His grip on the armrests tightened. It was a wonder the wood didn't snap in two. "That will never happen."

Standing and rounding the desk, the lawyer shook her hand and nodded at Lucian. "Yes, well, it would seem the two of you have much to discuss. I'll let myself out. Good day."

Battling outrage and disbelief, Lucian shoved to his feet, paced to the fireplace and leaned his weight against the marble mantel, his back to the room. He'd known the old man was controlling and manipulative, but this... Closing his eyes, he forced himself to take deep, calming breaths. The tightness was returning to his chest.

He didn't have to hear Megan's approach to sense her nearness. The faint scent of roses wafted over. "Lucian—"

He stiffened at the soft, irrationally pleasing sound of his name on her lips.

"Mr. Beaumont," she began again, "I had no idea

what Charles was planning. I realize this will make things difficult—"

"You mean impossible," he interrupted, turning to face her. "He's made it impossible for me to sell this house." He fisted his hands. "I don't know exactly what he expected me to do. I have a life waiting for me back in New Orleans. I can't stay here indefinitely."

Her brow furrowed. "I can't claim to know his reasons, but I'm certain it wasn't his goal to make things difficult for you. That wasn't his way."

"Oh, wasn't it? He certainly made things difficult for my mother when he cut her out of his life."

He'd witnessed her tears, the brokenness caused by Charles's need to control those around him. Even now, he was attempting to control Lucian from beyond the grave. Unbelievable.

"Is that why you never came?" she demanded, eyes brimming with accusation. "Because you couldn't forgive him for what he did to your mother?"

"How could I forgive someone who wasn't sorry?" He didn't tell her Charles hadn't wanted him here. It was too painful to put into words.

"But he *was* sorry." She took a step forward, intent on convincing him. "He regretted pushing her away, I know it."

For a second, Lucian got lost in her impossibly blue eyes. She seemed to sincerely believe what she was saying. He, on the other hand, wasn't that naive.

"It hardly matters now," he pushed out. "They're both gone. And I'm left here to deal with the whims of a manipulative old man."

She bristled. "Since you're obviously so eager to leave, why don't you?"

"You'd like that, wouldn't you? Me out of the way so

you can be free to come and go as you like? That was probably your goal all along. Why else would a young lady like yourself willingly spend time with a man three times her age?"

The color waned and surged in her cheeks, and when she spoke, he had to strain to hear her. "Your accusations are not those of a gentleman, sir. Charles was a fine man. Good and wise and generous. He was like a grandfather to me, something you couldn't come close to understanding."

Whirling away, she strode from the room with her head held high. Lucian sagged against the wall. What was supposed to have been a relatively short and simple visit to East Tennessee was proving to be anything but.

At the conclusion of the church service, Megan and her sisters, Nicole and Jane, joined their good friends, Cole and Rachel Prescott, in the shade of a sugar maple's sprawling branches. The Prescotts' one-year-old daughter, Abby, grinned at Megan and extended her arms, wanting to be held. The sweet little girl had captured her heart the moment she was born. Megan supervised her from time to time, and she liked to think of herself as a favorite auntie. Taking her from Cole, she hugged her close. It wasn't Abby's fault that her dark hair and eyes reminded her of a certain haughty gentleman.

Her heart squeezed, remembering Lucian's hurtful words and the blazing suspicion in his eyes. She'd spent a restless night, reliving their conversation again and again. He was a hard man. Arrogant and close-minded.

"So what do you think Mr. Beaumont will do?" Concern marked Rachel's expression.

Megan shrugged. "I don't know. He doesn't want to stay, yet he won't agree to leave me in charge." She gave a dry laugh. "And the last thing he'd want is for the house to go to me. He doesn't trust my motives."

Cole's hazel eyes turned quizzical. "What motives would those be?"

"He thinks the only reason I spent time with Charles was to ultimately gain control of the house, like I'm some kind of opportunist."

Fifteen-year-old Jane placed a comforting hand on her shoulder. "We all know that's not true. Despite his advanced years, I found Charles a delight to be around. He always had interesting things to say." Sometimes Jane and Kate, their cousin Josh's wife, had accompanied Megan on her visits.

Rachel nodded, pushing her heavy sable waves behind her shoulders. "The man is obviously hurting, and he's lashing out at you."

"But he doesn't even know me," Megan exclaimed, inexplicably bothered by this stranger's poor opinion of her. "He just assumes the worst."

Cole placed an arm around his wife's shoulders. "His attitude has nothing to do with you, Megan. Something in his life has skewed his thinking. If he spent a little time with you, he'd quickly come to see his error."

Megan wasn't so sure. Lucian seemed to *want* to believe her capable of such underhanded behavior. And anyway, it wasn't as if he was going to stick around long enough for it to matter. The only time the two of them would be spending together would be to figure out this mess.

Seventeen-year-old Nicole, who'd been leaning against the tree trunk with a bored expression, straightened and brushed off her bottle-green dress. "I'm starving. Can we leave now?"

Megan was used to her younger sister's sour attitude, but it had gotten steadily worse since their mother, Alice, and Jane's twin, Jessica, had departed last week for Cades Cove. Their oldest sister, Juliana, was due to deliver her first baby any day now. Of course, they'd all wanted to go, but there simply wasn't enough room in her sister's cabin. Too many people milling about would overwhelm the new parents, anyway.

She aimed a reproving frown her way. "If you'd rather not wait for us, you're welcome to go on ahead."

Jane, ever the diplomat, offered to go with her.

Megan watched the two girls, so different in both appearance and temperament, head arm in arm down Main Street. Then her gaze encountered her friend, Tom Leighton, striding in her direction wearing a determined look.

With a smile at Rachel and Cole, she returned Abby to their arms. "I guess I should go, as well. I'm keeping you from your lunch."

"No, you're not—" Rachel smiled as she spoke "—but I can see a certain gentleman is intent on snagging your attention. Whenever you need to talk, our door is always open. Come over anytime."

"Thanks, I appreciate that."

Megan watched the couple stroll to their wagon, Cole holding Rachel close to his side, his smile bright enough to rival the sun. She was thrilled to see her friends happy at long last. Cole and Rachel had very nearly lost each other, but God had brought them back together in their darkest hour.

"Megan, I'm glad I caught you."

"Hello, Tom." She smiled at the tall and lean barbershop owner, genuinely happy to see him. His easygoing personality made it easy to relax in his presence. "How are you, today?"

"Better now that I'm talking to you." He grinned, dimples flashing. "Josh invited me to join you for lunch at his parents' house. Care to walk with me?" He held out his arm.

She felt a flash of momentary irritation. Her cousin Josh insisted on pushing his best friend and her together, and she didn't like it one bit. While Tom was an extremely nice man, she wasn't interested in more than friendship. There was no spark, only casual affection.

Growing up, she'd envisioned a dashing hero, her own personal knight in shining armor sweeping into her life and fulfilling all her childhood dreams. Older and, she hoped, wiser at twenty years of age, she realized the impossibility of those expectations. No man could be *everything* she needed and desired. God alone could be her all in all. Still, the romantic, idealistic side of her hoped for a man who would challenge her, thrill her, cherish her.

So far, that man had yet to materialize. She was beginning to fear he never would.

Suppressing a shudder, she met Tom's hopeful gaze. "I'd love to, but I'm going home for lunch."

"Are you sure I can't change your mind?" His smile held a tinge of disappointment.

"Not this time." She wasn't in the mood for a crowd today, even if it was family. Her mind was too full of Lucian Beaumont.

"All right, but at least let me walk with you part of the way." He lifted his hat and fluffed his brown hair, a habit that left him looking like a ruffled little boy. An adorable one, at that. How could she refuse him?

Placing her hand in the crook of his arm, she smiled her thanks. His conversation managed to distract her, at least until they passed the turnoff for Charles's house.

What was Lucian doing right this minute? Had he decided how he was going to handle the stipulation?

Friday would be upon them before they knew it. If he was not planning on honoring Charles's wishes, she needed to know sooner rather than later. The children deserved to be told ahead of time, as did the people preparing for the poetry recital coming up. She would visit him first thing in the morning, she decided. No reason to delay what would surely be an unpleasant confrontation.

If Lucian Beaumont thought he could run roughshod over her and this town, she would soon prove him wrong.

Chapter Three

Rounding the curve in the tree-lined lane leading to Charles's house, Megan was presented with an unobstructed view of the gardens spreading out behind it. Against the backdrop of gray skies, the lush grasses seemed greener than usual, the vibrant flower patches more vivid. Tree branches swayed in the rain-scented breeze.

And there, in the midst of everything, sat the lord of the manor. Eating his breakfast and perusing a newspaper as if he hadn't a care in the world. And looking entirely too at home, she thought peevishly. He was a worldly-wise gentleman, wealthy beyond belief and accustomed to the conveniences of city life. He didn't belong in her quaint mountain town.

Determination spurred her across the lawn.

When he noticed her approach, he set aside the paper and stood up, his expression carefully neutral. "To what do I owe the pleasure of this visit, Miss O'Malley?"

His voice, like sweet tea and molasses rolled into one, shouldn't please her, but it did. His accent was deeper than hers, almost like a song with its French undertones. She wondered what it would sound like if he was actually happy.

She stopped a distance away, the round, white metal table between them. "We don't stand on formality here. Why don't you call me Megan?"

"As you wish, Megan. Please, call me Lucian." His eyes seemed to impossibly darken. He gestured at the food spread out on the table. "Have you eaten? You're welcome to join me."

His invitation was born out of politeness, no doubt ingrained from birth. It was clear he didn't really wish to dine with her.

"No, thank you. I've already had breakfast." If you could call a cup of coffee breakfast. She couldn't eat when she was nervous.

"Some tea, then?"

"Yes, thank you."

Coming around to her side, he scooted out the chair for her and poured her tea, stirring in cream and two spoons of sugar.

"You remembered," she blurted.

"Yes" was all he said as he placed it in front of her.

When he was seated, he rested one arm on the table, the other fisted on his hip in a relaxed position, waiting for her to explain the reason for her visit. His black gaze was too direct, sharp, for her to be at ease. His masculine appeal didn't help matters.

Smoothing her skirts, she took a calming breath. "I came this morning because I'd like to know what you've decided about the house."

"I haven't yet."

"Until you do, are you going to allow the story times to continue?"

"Do I have a choice?" he responded evenly, one dark brow arched.

Megan truly didn't want to goad him, to argue, so she said nothing. Sipped her tea.

"Tell me, *mon chou,* why is this so important to you? Reading to other people's children?" His gaze swept her curls, which she'd again restrained with a single ribbon. "Dressing like a princess?"

"What did you call me?"

Lucian looked startled, as if he'd made a slip. He waved it aside. "Later. For now, I'd like to hear your answer."

Perhaps Kate knew French and could tell her what he'd said. An heiress from New York City, she must've learned other languages.

"Living off the land is hard work. As early as four or five years of age, children begin helping with chores. Depending on each family's situation, there can be little time for a child to relax and just be a child. In addition to this, many families can't afford books. Since Charles has a vast collection and ample space, he and I decided the children would benefit from a weekly story time. Not only would it be fun for them, but also educational." She leaned forward, warming to her topic. "Books expand horizons. They entertain, inspire and enrich lives. I enjoy reading to them. Dressing the part merely adds to the experience."

"And the strawberry tarts and lemonade? What purpose do they serve?"

She smiled then. "Incentive for them to sit still and listen. Treats are reserved for those children who behave."

"I see."

That phrase again. She wanted to shake him.

He was studying her, obviously trying to decide if he believed her. No one had ever doubted her sincerity before. It was not a pleasant feeling.

A raindrop splashed on her arm. Then another. She glanced up at the rain-swollen clouds overhead. "I think we're in for a shower."

The drops began to fall harder and faster.

Lucian surged to his feet and, circling the table, took hold of her hand. "Let's make a run for it!"

"The dishes—"

"Forget them," he ordered as the clouds opened up, releasing a torrent.

Tugging on her hand, they made a dash for the back porch, surging up the slippery steps to stand, breathless and soaked to the skin, beneath the sheltering roof. The rain pounded the earth in an unrelenting assault. Lucian dropped her hand. His unfathomable gaze met hers. His hair was plastered to his head, his face slick with rainwater. Megan shivered. Her white eyelet blouse clung to her body, as did her robin-egg-blue skirts. Before she could guess at his intentions, he'd shrugged out of his coat and stepped close, settling it across her shoulders and pulling it closed. His heat and exotic cologne enveloped her.

"Th-thank you."

"Are you warm enough?"

She nodded, suddenly tongue-tied.

Several wet strands clung to her face, and before she could brush them aside, his fingers were there. Warm and featherlight. His fingertips skimming her cheek set off sparks, shimmers of light through her body. Her breath hitched.

What was happening to her?

She didn't like this arrogant man, his polished manners and jaded view of life.

Thank goodness he moved away so she could breathe again. Resting one hip against the railing, he stared solemnly out at the rain. Without the formal coat, he looked more approachable. The white shirt molded to his athletic build, his biceps straining the thin material where he'd crossed his arms.

Stop staring, she chided herself. His outward appearance may be attractive, but it hid the darkness he held inside. The turmoil she'd glimpsed on his face the few times his control had slipped. Who was he, really? All she'd ever known was that he hadn't cared enough about a lonely old man to make the journey to see him before he died. That was hard to forgive.

Lucian's instincts were normally right. People in his circle tended to be shallow and self-centered, motivated by greed and the lust for power and increased social standing. He trusted no one. Not even his so-called closest friends, for he knew that if not for his wealth and the Beaumont name, they'd be gone in a second. He'd spent a lot of years wishing things were different. Eventually, he'd come to terms with the state of affairs.

Until Dominique. The seemingly innocent, sweet-natured girl had resurrected his hope, his longing for something real and pure. He'd thought she was different from the conniving, scheming vipers trying to win his favor. He was wrong. In fact, she'd turned out to be worse. Much worse. And he'd fallen for her act—hook, line and sinker.

Shoving the humiliation aside, he focused on the blonde beauty beside him. Megan fairly radiated goodness, the depths of her sea-blue eyes clear and honest.

Listening to her impassioned speech a moment ago, he could almost believe she truly cared about helping the children of this town. Was it real? Or a clever act designed to lower his guard?

"How did all this come about?" He circled a finger in the air. "With Charles, I mean."

"It started with a simple invitation to borrow books," she said as her features softened into a smile of remembrance. "He was a bit reclusive, your grandfather, coming to town only for church services and an occasional visit to the mercantile to catch up on local news. It was there that he overheard me complaining that I'd read everything I could get my hands on more than once, and that I longed for new reading material. He remarked that he had a houseful of books. I was welcome to borrow as many as I liked.

"My first few visits, he left me to my own devices. Then one day, he seemed particularly down. I joined him in the parlor—uninvited, mind you—and we wound up talking for hours. He wanted to be a writer. Did you know that?" Huddled inside his overlarge coat, her pale hair clinging to her skin, she looked small and vulnerable. Sadness tugged at her mouth.

"No, I didn't." He forced himself to look away from her, to watch the continuing storm that mirrored the one inside him.

It sounded as if she and Charles had shared a special bond. Of course he hadn't been privy to his grandfather's dreams, his likes and dislikes, or anything else remotely personal. He had never even met the man! The spurt of jealousy took him by surprise.

Why should he care? Charles had written his mother and him off years ago. They had ceased to exist in his grandfather's mind. This will stipulation only served to prove Charles's dislike, one final thrust of the dagger. It hadn't been enough to ignore Lucian during his lifetime. He'd had to go and complicate matters with this house, just to underscore his loathing.

"He tried his hand at poetry," she continued, "and he even penned a couple of short stories. I think it kept the loneliness at bay, if temporarily."

He chose to ignore the censure in her voice, the unspoken questions.

"Lucian, your grandfather was a good man. He—"

"Stop. I do not wish to discuss him anymore today."

"But—"

"Megan, don't." He shot her a warning glance.

"Fine." She jutted her chin. "Then how about we address the poetry recital coming up?"

"Poetry recital?"

"You know, when people stand up and recite poetry by rote?"

"I know what it is," he told her drily. "How many people are we talking about?"

"We average between twenty-five and thirty."

He sighed. Thirty strangers parading through his house. He didn't like it. Resented this present circumstance that was beyond his control. As empty as his life in New Orleans had become, it was his home. Comfortable and familiar. Predictable. He knew what to expect from those around him, and they him.

Frustration surged. If not for this young lady, he would've already put the house up for sale and been well on his way out of this backwoods town.

"By all means, proceed with your plans as you've always done."

Surprise flickered.

"But let me make myself clear—I plan to do everything possible to find a way around that stipulation."

She jerked her head back. Anger flashed in her eyes. "Why am I not surprised? You don't care about the children or the people of this community." Yanking off his coat, she thrust it at him, and he fumbled to catch it before it fell to the floor. "You care only about yourself—" she poked him in the chest "—what you want and what you need. Well, let me assure you, Mr. Beaumont, I will do everything I can to fight you on this."

Then, to his shock, she pivoted and dashed out into the rain. Though it had slacked off, the rain was still steady. Did she plan to run the entire way home?

"Megan!" He rushed to the top step. "Wait!"

He wasn't sure if she heard him or not. She didn't hesitate, didn't slow down, just kept going. Across the grass and down the lane, until she disappeared around the bend.

Shoving his hands through his hair, he blew out an aggravated breath. The woman was a danger to his sanity. And control? Hah! She had him so mixed up, he couldn't tell up from down.

He was beginning to wish he'd never heard of Gatlinburg, Tennessee.

Chapter Four

Lucian couldn't in good conscience allow Megan to leave without some sort of protection from the elements. Ignoring the fact he was dripping water all over the floors, he went inside in search of his umbrella. Seizing one propped against the wall, he tossed his coat on the hall table and hurried back out into the rain. There, at the end of the lane, was a flash of white and blue.

As he sprinted across the sprawling lawn, bits of mud splashed up on to his boots. His pristine, clean-as-a-whistle boots. And since, in his haste, he hadn't bothered opening the umbrella, his vest and shirt were now soaked. He ground his teeth together. If the woman had an ounce of sense…

Drawing closer, he noticed she'd slowed, her head bent and shoulders hunched. Her heavy skirts impeded her progress. His annoyance evaporated at once, and he was glad he'd followed her.

"Megan, wait!"

She ignored him. Still angry, obviously. The woman certainly had spunk. She didn't fawn all over him like the young socialites in his circle, which he found refreshing. It was growing tougher to stomach their batting eyelashes, coquettish smiles and honeyed words. Their thinly veiled attempts to garner his favor.

Megan, at least, gave the *appearance* of being straightforward with him.

Opening the umbrella, he caught her upper arm and moved to bring them both beneath its cover.

"What are you doing?" she demanded, eyes still smoldering and chin lifted in defiance.

She was strikingly beautiful, even more so when angry. With his finger, he outlined her chin, dislodging the water droplets. "Has anyone ever told you that you have a stubborn chin?"

Her lips parted. "Actually, you're the first."

Lucian dropped his hand. He really needed to stop touching her. He wasn't what one would consider an affectionate man. In fact, Dominique had complained at his lack of attention. Accused him of being an ice sculpture. He'd shrugged off her comments.

So why would he be any different with Megan? Why did he feel compelled to connect with her every time she was near?

Releasing her arm, he offered her the umbrella handle. "Take this. It doesn't look like the rain will let up anytime soon."

Her pale brows rose. "You followed me in order to give me this?"

His smile was grim. "Despite popular opinion, I'm not completely unfeeling."

"I—" She paused, her brow furrowed. "Thank you."

When she shivered, he pressed the handle into her hand. "You should go. Too much longer in this weather, and you'll become ill. Good day, *mon chou*."

He pivoted on his heel before he touched her again

or made another inane remark about her person. *Not smart, Beaumont.* As the cool rain slid over his skin, he reminded himself of his purpose. He couldn't allow Megan to distract him, or worse, trick him into giving her control of the house.

As soon as he got out of these wet clothes, he was going to sit down and draft a letter to his lawyer. One way or another, he would find a way to rid himself of Charles's house and all the emotional baggage that went with it.

Friday afternoon, Jane handed Megan the basket of tea cakes. "Are you sure you don't want me to come with you? What if he's hateful?"

Megan touched the red silk jacquard scarf tied about her head. It was a bit too snug, but she didn't want to take it off. The kids would enjoy her pirate costume. She could only imagine what Lucian's reaction might be. "Lucian can be difficult, that's for sure, but he isn't hateful."

Infuriating, yes. And bewildering. The man made it practically impossible to stay mad at him! Scooping up the umbrella he'd loaned her, she recalled their exchange and how his nearness, the intensity of his black eyes, made rational thought impossible.

"Would you mind opening the door for me?"

Clearly not convinced, Jane complied. "When will we get to meet him? Do you think he'll come to church on Sunday?"

"Oh, I hope he does." Nicole looked up from her latest sewing project, violet eyes shining. "From the way you described him, Megan, he sounds like a dream. Just think, a wealthy aristocrat in our midst. All the way from Louisiana!"

Megan couldn't help but smile at her younger sister's enthusiasm. Nicole was enamored with the idea of big-city life. As soon as she had enough money saved, she planned to open up a clothing boutique in the city of her choice.

Not Megan. She loved East Tennessee, the mountains and streams and forests. The peace and quiet, the fresh air and space to roam. To daydream. She couldn't imagine being content anywhere else.

She hesitated in the open doorway. "How about I ask him outright whether he plans to or not? That way your minds will be at ease." And hers, as well.

"Yes, do!" Nicole urged.

"Only if he's in an agreeable mood," Jane cautioned.

Lucian, agreeable? She didn't expect him to be, not with her and the children invading his territory. *I can handle whatever he dishes out. I have to. For the kids and the town.*

"I'll see you both later." She turned and headed out into the late-afternoon sunshine, soaking in the hum of life all about her. Birds chirping. Squirrels darting up and down the trees on either side of the lane. The breeze swelling through the tree canopy far above her head. Ah, spring. Her favorite time of year. If only it could last forever.

If only Charles was still here. Waiting for her and the children with eager anticipation, his weathered face smoothing into a welcoming smile, the loneliness in his eyes fading for the short time they were there. It was highly unlikely that Lucian would welcome them. If anything, he would take himself off to another part of the house in order to avoid their presence. That was fine by her. Why wouldn't it be? She didn't care one way or another.

However, standing on his front porch a quarter of an hour later face-to-face with the man, she realized that was a lie. Lucian Beaumont was not the sort of man who inspired indifference. Quite the opposite, in fact. The strong emotions he invoked within her were foreign to her experience. Sure, her sisters and cousins sometimes irritated her, but they'd never made her furious enough to want to punch something. And yes, she was naturally curious, but she'd never been driven to discover the inner workings of a person's mind. And never, ever had she felt this crazy, inexplicable, overwhelming attraction to a man.

Well, you're just going to have to control yourself, because he is not hero material. Far from it.

"Here's your umbrella." She thrust it at him, uncharacteristically flustered.

He, on the other hand, appeared coolly poised in a deep blue cutaway coat and vest, a brilliant sapphire tiepin nestled in the folds of his snowy white cravat. Black pants and his Hessians completed the ensemble. Way too formal for the occasion and even for the town, but she supposed that was the way he was accustomed to dressing in New Orleans. And he pulled it off beautifully, she had to admit. Masculine and formal. In control.

Except for the hair. There was no taming those luxurious, dark brown waves that insisted on falling forward to rest on his forehead.

"Merci." He stepped back to allow her entrance, his intense gaze sweeping her scooped-neck white blouse, full black skirts and wide black belt that accentuated her waist. "Where's your eye patch and wooden leg?"

"Isn't this enough?" She pivoted in the entryway and indicated her scarf.

After looping the umbrella on the coat stand behind him, he settled his hands on his hips and appraised her appearance. "You need an eye patch. The wooden leg, not so much, but definitely some gold jewelry—loot from the legion of ships you've besieged." Amusement shone in the depths of his eyes.

Was he *teasing* her? Her palms began to sweat. "I'm, uh, fresh out of gold. Sorry."

"That's too bad." He tipped his head towards the basket dangling from her fingers. "May I take that for you?"

"No, thank you." She tightened her grip. She didn't want him to discover the tea cakes now and forbid the children to have them. Better to wait until the book had been read to pass them out. He wouldn't be around to intervene.

"As you wish." The amusement faded, replaced with a subtle knowing.

His open scrutiny unleashed a flurry of butterflies in her middle. "I always come half an hour early to set up the chairs and get my books in order. May I?"

"By all means." He motioned for her to precede him into the parlor on their left. Megan stopped just inside the room.

"I took the liberty of arranging the chairs for you."

"Oh."

"This is the way it was set up last week." He stood close beside her, his exotic scent stirring the air. "Did you prefer it done another way?"

"This is fine. I—"

"Well, hello there, Miss Megan." Mrs. Calhoun entered the parlor bearing a tray of delicate-looking pastries and fresh strawberries. "Doesn't this look delectable? I was all prepared to make a batch of sugar cookies when

Mr. Lucian suggested I do something special. I'm so glad he did. The children will enjoy these."

Mouth hanging open, Megan's gaze followed the older woman's movements. *Lucian* suggested? But—

Mrs. Calhoun spotted her basket and pointed. "Oh, what do you have there? More goodies?"

"Y-yes." She avoided looking at Lucian. "My sister and I baked tea cakes."

"That's wonderful," she said, bustling over to take it from Megan, "they'll go fast." To Lucian, she said, "That Jane O'Malley has a way with food. Her twin, too. Whenever there's a church social, folks flock to the table to try and snag a sampling of their desserts. There's never enough to go around, though."

When they were alone once more, Megan finally looked at him. Spread her hands wide. "I don't understand. Why are you being so…agreeable?"

Folding his arms across his wide chest, the corners of his mouth turned down. "Just because I don't happen to like the situation I find myself in doesn't mean I should make things difficult for you. What did you expect I would do? Blockade the door?"

"No, not that." She shook her head. "But neither did I think you would help me."

His dark brows winged up. "My grandfather didn't?"

"He was too feeble to do any heavy lifting," she said defensively. "As to the other preparations, he left everything to me and Mrs. Calhoun. Which was fine by me," she rushed to add.

Dropping his arms to his sides, Lucian's expression turned pensive. "I must inform you that I've written my lawyer asking him to find a way around the stipulation."

She wasn't surprised. Still, disappointment spiraled

through her, as did a prick of anxiety. "I doubt he'll be successful."

But what if he somehow found a way? A loophole of some sort?

"We'll have to wait and see, won't we?" His gaze flicked to the window behind her. "For now, it appears you have an early arrival."

Turning, she spotted Ollie Stevenson trudging up the lane, gesturing and talking to himself. She suppressed a mischievous smile. "Would you care to greet him? I have to retrieve my book from the library."

"Me?" He followed on her heels. "How about I go and get Mrs. Calhoun?" A slight undercurrent of anxiety wove through his words.

With a dismissive gesture, she shot over her shoulder, "She's busy getting the drinks. Don't worry, Ollie doesn't bite. Not often, anyway."

Leaving him behind, she heard him mutter something about her enjoying this. A thrill lightened her step. Upsetting Lucian's reserve could become addictive. Good thing he couldn't see the wide grin splitting her face.

Lucian had initially intended to secrete himself in Charles's study for the duration of the evening. Those plans changed. Megan knew children made him uncomfortable and yet she'd purposefully left him to face the unpredictable creatures alone. Well, two could play at that game.

One arm propped against the mantel, he couldn't stop a satisfied smile as he recalled her dumbfounded reaction to his announcement that he'd be sticking around to observe story time. If her frequent, darting glances his direction were any indication, his presence made her nervous. Good. Served her right.

Ollie, the precocious, persistent seven-year-old whose earlier stream of chatter had given Lucian a headache, kept raising his hand despite Megan's calm assurances that there'd be time to ask questions later. He had to hand it to her, the woman had a seemingly endless supply of patience. And she was an adept storyteller. Her lilting, musical voice pulled one into the adventure, her enthusiasm transferring itself to the audience.

Watching her, Lucian's gaze was naturally drawn to her white-blond hair. Rays of waning sunlight slanted through the window to glisten in the loose curls, and his fingers itched to bury themselves in the silken mass. *Careful, Beaumont. She's as pretty as a picture, for sure, but you've no idea what lies beneath the surface. Remember Dominique.*

How could he ever forget? She'd convinced him of her sincere affection, had even claimed to love him, while all along she'd been biding her time. Holding out for the true prize—his father. Why settle for the son of a shipping magnate when she could have the man with all the power?

His chest seized up, and he absentmindedly rubbed a flat palm over his heart in an effort to soothe away the discomfort. The smothering sensation had started not long after his mother's death a year ago. Had worsened a few months later with Dominique's trickery. Being in this house didn't help. There was no escaping his grandfather's indifference and worse, the constant reminders of his mother and the fact she was lost to him forever.

When he glanced up and caught Megan looking at him with concern creasing her brow, he dropped his hand. There was nothing to worry about. At least, that was the family physician's conclusion, who'd declared Lucian fit as a fiddle. Mentioned something about anxiety and getting more rest. Right. Lucian wasn't one to sit around. When he wasn't working in the shipping offices or attending social functions, he was at the country estate, hunting and fishing and assisting his staff with repairs and the like. Lately he'd entertained passing thoughts of leaving the city behind to take up permanent residence there. But the prospect of rattling around in that big manor all alone stopped him from seriously considering it.

Just then, a small hand slipped into his, startling him out of his reverie.

Straightening, he stared down into the pixie face of a little girl he'd noticed simply because she reminded him of Megan with her long blond hair and big blue eyes.

"I'm Sarah." She didn't smile, only studied him with a seriousness that unnerved him.

Lucian glanced around the parlor, belatedly realizing Megan had finished the book. She and the parents were assisting the children swarming the dessert table.

"Uh, hello."

What did one say to a child? Her warm fingers clutched his, and he marveled at their fragility. If he had to guess, he'd say she was about five or six.

"What's your name?"

"I'm Lucian."

She scrunched up her nose, which only made her look more adorable. "Huh?"

Squatting to her level, he repeated, "My name is Lucian."

Reaching out, she touched the tip of her finger to his sapphire tiepin. "That's sparkly. I like pretty things. Can I have it?"

He cleared his throat to cover a chuckle. There was no guile in this little one's eyes, merely simple curiosity. "Well, I doubt you would have use of it. It's for gentlemen, and you are a lady."

She seemed to ponder that for a minute. He held his breath, wondering what he'd say if she insisted. He had no experience with this sort of thing.

"Are you Mr. Charles's son?"

He jerked his head back at the unexpected question. "No. I'm his grandson."

Tilting her head, a tiny line appeared between her fine eyebrows. "Mr. Charles was a nice man. Are you nice, too?"

Lucian sucked in a breath.

"Sarah," Megan said as she appeared at their side and placed a gentle hand on the little girl's shoulder, "wouldn't you like a treat? They're going fast."

With a nod, Sarah slipped her hand from his and hopped to the table without a backward glance. Lucian stood, grateful for the intervention and wondering what Megan had seen in his face that had induced her to take mercy on him. Could she read his moods that easily?

"She didn't intend to make you uncomfortable."

"I know." He watched her at the table, solemnly debating what to put on her plate. "Is she always that serious?"

A heavy sigh escaped her. "She's had a rough year. Her ma died in childbirth, as did the baby. Her father hasn't coped well."

Lucian's mouth turned down. Such a tragic loss couldn't be easy for a young child to process. His gaze returned to Megan to find her studying him with an inscrutable expression. One pale brow quirked.

"So, are you?"

"Am I what?"

Her voice went soft. "Are you a nice man?"

He exhaled. "That's impossible for me to answer, Megan."

She stepped closer, smelling of roses and, more faintly, strawberries. He clasped his hands behind his back, away from temptation.

"Well, I'll answer it, then. I think you *are* nice."

His jaw went slack. Pleasure reverberated through him, followed quickly by misgivings. "I'm astonished you'd say that, considering."

"You're simply acting under false assumptions concerning your grandfather." Her blue eyes darkened. "And me."

"Is that so?" He fought the pull of her innocent appeal.

"Don't go all haughty on me," she challenged, not in the least fazed. "We're going to have to discuss this sometime." Her mouth softened as genuine confusion settled on her face. "I'd really like to know why you didn't come to see him. You don't strike me as someone who'd deliberately hurt another person."

Lucian didn't often find himself without a ready response. Megan thought he was nice? If that was her true opinion, then she was one of the most charitable women he'd ever met. So was she really that bighearted? Or just very clever?

Chapter Five

Megan could tell she'd shocked him. No doubt he wasn't accustomed to anyone questioning his behavior, especially females. New Orleans socialites likely tripped all over themselves to gain his favor, to be linked with such a man as he—wealthy, influential, articulate, *gorgeous*. Not her. She may be a romantic at heart, but she wasn't about to allow herself to be impressed by superficial charms.

She wanted to know the man beneath the brooding reserve and smooth manners. His innermost thoughts and feelings. His motivations. And she wasn't sure if that was possible, or even wise.

Abbott and Ivy Tremain, grandparents of one of the kids, took the silence stretching between them as a sign to interrupt.

"Mr. Beaumont," Abbott interjected, thrusting out his hand, "it's an honor to finally meet you."

As Abbott introduced himself and his wife, Lucian shook his hand and nodded to Ivy. "Likewise. Please, call me Lucian."

Was Megan the only one who noticed the tension

jumping along his jaw? She mentally kicked herself. She shouldn't have brought up the volatile subject while the house was crawling with guests.

"Lucinda, Ivy and I grew up together. Your mother was a delightful girl. Fun to be around."

"Oh, yes." The attractive brunette nodded with a nostalgic smile. "She was as sweet as could be. Growing up, she never caused Charles a bit of trouble, and so we were all taken by complete surprise when she up and ran off with Gerard. Terrible time, that was."

Megan's stomach dropped to the floor. Lucian's face appeared carved in stone, his eyes as black as the forest on a moonless night. Beneath the blue coat, his shoulders went rigid.

Oblivious to his turmoil, Abbott continued, "Charles was never the same after that, was he, my dear?"

She shook her head sadly. "He missed her something fierce. I know a lot of folks around here hoped she'd come back and visit, but she never did."

"But we're glad Charles's grandson is here, at long last," the older man said with a grin. "How long are you in town for?"

Megan held her breath. Would he tell them about the will stipulation? If he did, the whole town would be buzzing about it within the hour.

"I'm not certain." Their gazes locked, but she couldn't tell what he was thinking. "For a couple of weeks, at least."

"Good, good. It's awful nice of you to continue your grandfather's traditions. The children really enjoy themselves when they come here." Abbott cocked his head at Megan. "This young lady is a gifted storyteller."

Lucian's dark brows met in the middle. "Yes, she certainly is."

Now, why didn't that sound like a compliment?

"She's going to make some lucky man a fine wife someday," Ivy piped up. The sly wink she sent Lucian's direction made Megan long to run for the door. Her cheeks grew hot. She kept her gaze trained on the colorful rug beneath her feet.

"I believe Tom Leighton's already figured that out," her husband joked.

Enough humiliation. "If you'll excuse me, I should go and help Mrs. Calhoun with the cleanup."

Leaving them to their conversation, she attempted to bury her embarrassment by seeing to the children's needs, wiping crumbs from sticky fingers and chocolate-rimmed mouths, refilling drinks and trying to ensure the furniture didn't get soiled. Though she refrained from looking directly at Lucian, she noticed many of the parents had drifted over to chat with him. She swallowed back concern. Was it too much to hope no one else brought up the subject of his mother?

A frown pulled at her lips. What if he found this evening so unpleasant that he did decide to blockade the door next time?

No. She sincerely believed that, despite his intentions to thwart Charles's wishes, Lucian was a good man. Misguided, definitely. A bit selfish and stubborn, maybe. But didn't everyone have faults? His actions tonight had softened her opinion of him. He didn't have to lift a finger to help her, but he'd anticipated her needs and acted accordingly. He'd suffered through Ollie's onslaught with fortitude, nodding at all the right times and answering the boy's questions with careful consideration. Watching his gentle interaction with Sarah, Megan's heart had squeezed with a curious longing. A longing she didn't dare examine.

Lucian is not responsible for these feelings, she assured herself. *It's just that, with both Juliana and Josh reveling in wedded bliss, you're dreaming of your own happy-ever-after.*

Besides, Lucian Beaumont didn't strike her as a man who believed in such a thing. He wouldn't willingly be any girl's knight in shining armor.

Lucian bade good-night to the last guest and, closing the door, sagged momentarily against it. He'd survived his first story time. While this evening had had its trying moments, there'd been interesting ones, as well. What surprised him most was how friendly everyone had been. It seemed Megan was alone in feeling betrayed by his absence all these years.

Going in search of her, he found her scooting a heavy wingback chair across the thick multihued rug towards its rightful place beside the settee. He strode to intercept her.

"I'll take it from here."

"That's all right. I'm used to doing this without help."

He placed a stalling hand on her shoulder. The warmth of her skin beneath her blouse, the slender grace of her, prickled his palm. He had the ridiculous urge to knead the stiffness from her muscles. "I don't mind. You've been on your feet for most of the night. Why don't you sit and rest for a few minutes?"

Her red scarf askew, she reluctantly nodded and, moving away from his touch, settled on the settee. Her hands folded in her lap, her gaze followed his movements as he quickly replaced all the chairs. The lamplights cast a cozy glow about the room, which, with its navy-blue-and-green accents and dark walnut woodwork, gave it a masculine feel that was echoed throughout the house. He wondered if it had ever had feminine touches, or if Charles had removed all reminders of his late wife and his absent daughter.

When he'd finished, she asked, "How do you think it went tonight?"

Standing in the middle of the rug, arms crossed, he gave her his frank opinion. "I think the kids are fortunate to have someone who's willing to give of their time and energy on their behalf."

Her chin went up. "I enjoy it." There was force behind the words.

On this point, he didn't doubt her. He'd seen her nurturing touches, the easy care of the children as if they were her own. Affection like that couldn't be faked.

"I know you do."

Surprised relief flickered in her eyes before her lashes swished down, cutting off his view. She began to pluck at the ruffles on her skirt, her trim, shiny nails winking in the light. "I noticed many of the parents made a point to introduce themselves to you. Was everyone… welcoming?"

The hitch in her voice lured him closer. *She must be thinking of the Tremains and their guileless comments.* He eased down beside her on the cushion, a respectable twelve inches away, and rested his palms on his thighs. "They were indeed."

Welcoming and genuinely glad to meet him. Effusive in their praise of Charles. He'd had trouble reconciling the man they'd described as *good as gold* with the cold, unfeeling grandfather he'd envisioned all these years. The discrepancy troubled him. If Charles was the man they made him out to be, why had he ignored his own family? If he regretted the rift he'd created with his pigheaded stubbornness, why hadn't he come to New

Orleans and attempted to make amends? It wasn't as if he couldn't afford to travel. And his health problems hadn't presented themselves until recent years.

He looked up to find her studying him, trying to decipher his thoughts.

"I received several supper invitations," he continued, "as well as a request to come to church on Sunday."

Interest bloomed in her expression. She angled towards him. "Will you come?"

"I haven't been to church in more than a year," he admitted. "My mother and I used to attend services together. Then she became ill, and I..." He shook his head, reluctant to think of his beloved *mère* and her swift decline, the bloom of health stolen from her without warning and without mercy. His wealth had garnered her access to the best medical care available, yet in the end, it hadn't mattered. No amount of money could've prevented her death.

His utter helplessness had nearly destroyed him.

"I understand how it would've been difficult for you to go, especially since it was something the two of you did together."

Megan's compassion threw him off-kilter. He'd gotten precious little of it back in New Orleans. In the face of his grief, his friends and acquaintances hadn't known what to say, so they'd avoided the subject altogether. And his father, well, he'd been relieved at his wife's passing. Gerard was finally free of the unsophisticated mountain girl he'd made the mistake of marrying all those years ago. To him, her love and adoration had been a burden. An embarrassment.

His hands curled into fists. Shoving down the familiar anger and bitterness that thoughts of his father aroused, Lucian nodded. "I couldn't bring myself to go alone. Besides, all those years I'd gone in order to make her happy. After her passing, there didn't seem to be any more reason to go."

Megan's brow furrowed in consternation. "What about deepening your relationship with God? Learning more about His Word?"

"Relationship? With God?"

"Haven't you ever shared with Him what's on your heart? Your hopes, dreams, failures? He already knows, of course, but He wants us to express it through prayer."

He'd prayed before, on occasion, but it had been brief requests for help. Nothing like what Megan was talking about. "You speak as if God cares about the details of your life. I don't see Him that way. While I believe He exists and that He created this world for our use and pleasure, I find it difficult to imagine He'd bother Himself with our problems."

"David wrote in Psalms, 'O Lord, you have searched me and you know me. You know when I sit and when I rise; you perceive my thoughts from afar. You are familiar with all my ways. Before a word is on my tongue you know it completely, O Lord.' Does that sound like a God who can't be bothered with us?"

The gentle curve of her smile, the utter lack of judgment in her eyes, compelled him to be truthful. "It sounds like you're much better acquainted with the Scriptures than I am. In fact, I can't recall the last time I opened a Bible." He thought of his mother's black Bible tucked safely in his trunk, a tentative link that eased somewhat the ache of her absence.

"It's not too late to start," she said encouragingly.

His gaze fell on a small portrait on the side table, one he hadn't noticed before. Standing, he stepped around her and picked it up, fingers tight on the gilt frame.

His grandparents, Charles and Beatrice, in the prime of their lives. And his mother, who looked to be about eight years old, dressed in a simple dress and her dark hair in pigtails. She wasn't smiling. No one really did for portraits. But her eyes were clear of the familiar shadows, and curiosity marked her rounded face. How might her life have been different—better, freer, happier—if Charles had handled the whole situation differently?

"Tell me something," he said quietly, still staring at the images. "Did my grandfather believe as you do?"

"Charles loved the Lord," she answered, matching her tone to his, perhaps sensing the turn of his mood. "He tried to model his life after His teachings, a life pleasing to Him."

Replacing the frame with a bit more force than necessary, he pivoted to glower down at her, unable to mask the cold fury surging through his veins. "Then surely God wasn't pleased with his coldhearted treatment of his own daughter. And what of his only grandchild? He didn't even acknowledge my existence! Isn't there something in there about loving your neighbor as yourself?"

Surging to her feet, Megan adopted a fighting stance—shoulders back, chin up, hands fisted. A not-so-friendly pirate. "And what of your mother's behavior? She refused Charles's numerous pleas to return. He desperately wanted to meet you, Lucian. How could she deny him that? How could you?"

He snorted. Sliced the air with his hand. "What are you talking about? What pleas? The night before she married my father, Charles warned her that if she went through with it, not to bother coming back. Ever."

"Charles apologized more than once for his past behavior. He sent letters begging her to come and visit. To bring you so that he could spend time with you. Show you around town, introduce you to all the townspeople, take you fishing. She flat-out refused. Charles didn't tell me why."

Lucian turned away, shoved a frustrated hand through his hair. No. No, this couldn't possibly be true. His mother wouldn't have hidden such a thing from him.

"I don't know anything about any letters," he ground out.

He startled when her fingers curled around his biceps, a slight pressure. "Lucian—"

The chime of the doorbell derailed her train of thought. "Would you like me to get that for you?"

"No." He straightened, and her hand fell away. "I'll get it."

He didn't recognize the brown-haired, green-eyed man on the other side of the door. "Good evening. May I help you?"

He looked to be about the same age as himself, maybe a year or so younger, and was dressed like the local men in casual pants, band-collared shirt and suspenders. While his expression was pleasant, his eyes were assessing, his fingers crushing the brim of his hat he held at his waist.

"Evenin'. The name's Tom Leighton. I own the barbershop on Main." He stuck out his hand. "You must be Charles's grandson."

He shook his hand. "Lucian Beaumont."

"Pleased to meet you." His gaze searched the entryway. "Is Megan still here? I came to walk her home."

"Yes, she is." Lucian stepped back and motioned him inside. "She's in the parlor."

Following Leighton, Lucian ignored a twinge of dislike. He had absolutely no grounds for such a reaction. He didn't even know the man. *It bothers you that he appears to have a relationship with Megan.* The banker let slip earlier that Tom Leighton saw Megan as a prospective wife. Question was, how did she feel about that? Did she want to marry the barbershop owner? Were they courting?

As the two exchanged greetings, Lucian watched her expression carefully. Was her smile a bit forced? Her eyes a little tight? Or was he being ridiculous? He puffed out an irritated breath. Definitely ridiculous.

He had absolutely no romantic interest in this woman. Or any other woman, for that matter. The misery of his parents' mockery of a marriage had carved deep scars on his heart, creating within him an aversion to anything resembling an intimate relationship. He would not repeat their mistakes. He would marry because it was expected of him to produce heirs and further the Beaumont legacy. For duty and social connections, not fickle emotions or fleeting attraction.

He'd had a near miss with Dominique. Had begun to entertain the notion that perhaps pure love could exist for him, that he wouldn't have to endure a marriage that was more business arrangement than anything else. Thank goodness she'd revealed her true nature before his heart had succumbed.

Watching Megan, he reminded himself of his charted course. She was a diversion, and, albeit delightful and intriguing, one he didn't want or need.

"Tom!" Megan wasn't sure why his arrival had disconcerted her. It wasn't unusual for him to show up to walk her home. She'd been so immersed in the conversation with Lucian, deeply attuned to his turmoil, that the interruption had thrown her.

"I had a couple of late customers. I wasn't sure if

you'd still be here." He seemed a touch nervous, which was unlike him. He lowered his voice. "How'd it go?"

"Wonderful."

Surprise flitted across Tom's face. "Really?"

Movement beyond his shoulder meant Lucian had entered the room, holding himself back, his dark gaze hooded.

Stepping to the side in order to include him, she touched Tom's arm in a silent request for him to turn around. "You've met Lucian already?"

He nodded curtly. "Yes."

The two men regarded each other in silence. She glanced askance at her friend. He was normally talkative and friendly, even with strangers. Why was he acting like this?

She cleared her throat. "Tom is a close friend of the family. We've known each other practically from birth. He and my cousin Josh used to take great pleasure in tormenting me."

Laughter erupted from Tom, and, ignoring her arched brow, he slung an arm around her shoulders. "Like hiding frogs in your lunch pails." Tucking her close to his side, he grinned at Lucian. "Made her so mad, she could hardly speak. But she'd eventually cool off and talk to us again. Megan and I know each other *very* well, almost as well as an old married couple. We have a lot in common."

"Sounds like it," Lucian responded drily.

Stunned and irritated by Tom's familiarity, his insinuations, Megan shrugged off his arm as unobtrusively as she could. "Well, I believe we should be going." Before he embarrassed her further.

She paused before Lucian, wishing they could've finished their conversation. Hating to leave him to deal with his confused anguish alone. Longing to reach out and comfort him. He seemed in desperate need of a hug. "Thank you for everything."

He stared at her for so long that Tom approached and took hold of her arm.

"Ready?"

She jumped, having forgotten for a split second that there was anyone else in the room besides the two of them. "Y-yes, I'm quite ready. Good evening, Lucian."

His nod was almost imperceptible, his low drawl a caress. *"Bonne nuit, mon chou."*

It wasn't until they'd reached the end of the lane that she rounded on Tom.

"Why did you do that?"

He held up his palms. "Do what?"

"You know perfectly well what." She jammed her hands on her hips. "Why did you try to make Lucian believe something about us that isn't true?"

Grasping her upper arms, he peered down at her with an intensity he rarely displayed, making her stomach clench with dread.

"I can't deny that I *want* it to be true. Surely you know by now how I feel about you, Megan." His green eyes blazed with conviction. "I would like to court you properly."

Megan squeezed her eyes tight. What could she say that wouldn't hurt his feelings? She'd been so careful not to encourage him!

"If you don't open your eyes, I'm going to take it as an invitation to kiss you."

"Don't you dare!" Her eyes popping open, she wriggled out of his grasp and strode briskly down the lane. He easily kept pace with her but didn't speak, allowing her time to sort through her response.

When she stopped at the split-rail fence that signaled the beginning of her property, he stopped, as well, expectant.

"I can't think about this right now." She took the coward's way out, opting to delay what would be an extremely difficult task, one that would alter their friendship forever. Feeling lower than pond scum, she rushed ahead to explain, "I'm in charge of my sisters while Momma is away, you know. This is the first time in the twins' entire lives that they've been apart, and Jane is having a tough time of it. Nicole is even more unpredictable than usual, and now I have the issue with Charles's house to contend with. I'm sorry, but I—"

"It's all right." He held up a hand. "This wasn't the best time to spring my feelings on you, but I'm not sorry it's finally out in the open. Take all the time you need."

His consideration made her feel even worse. "Thanks, Tom," she murmured, toeing the grass with her boot.

"Just remember, I'll be waiting."

With a slight smile and a tug on his hat's brim, he turned and walked back the way they'd come, headed to his farm on the opposite side of town. Sagging against the fence, she watched until the shadowed lane swallowed him up. *I don't know what to do, God. I need to be clear with him about my feelings, but I can't bear the thought of wounding him. He's been such a dear friend.*

Friend. That's all he'd ever be. All she'd ever want him to be. Tom was easy to be with, funny and interesting, as well as dependable and an all-around great man. But he wasn't the man for her.

Thoughts of Lucian crowded in, prodding her. Sure, he could make her tremble with merely a look. Release a storm of butterflies in her tummy with the slightest touch. Stir her heart with emotion. Despite all that, he wasn't the one for her, either.

Chapter Six

Lucian missed his predictable life. His comfortable routine. Coffee and croissants in the estate gardens, mornings at the waterfront overseeing his family's shipping offices, afternoons devoted to social responsibilities and evenings dining and dancing with the upper crust of society. Every day was pretty much the same, and he liked it that way.

The inactivity here was killing him. Too much time on his hands. Time to think.

Megan's assertions had circled through his mind like ravenous vultures until the wee hours of the morning. The prospect that his grandfather hadn't been indifferent, had actually yearned to meet him, weakened the grip of resentment in his soul. But it also brought heartache and disillusionment. For if Megan was right, that meant his mother had lied to him. He couldn't bear to entertain such an idea, so he forced his thoughts elsewhere…to another tangled coil.

Tom and Megan. Megan and Tom.

He kept picturing them in his parlor, tucked together like two peas in a pod, all the while wanting to protest that *he* should be the one holding her—not some back-woods mountain man. Okay, that wasn't exactly fair. Tom Leighton seemed nice enough, appeared to honestly care about her.

These feelings have nothing to do with Megan, specifically. You're accustomed to women throwing themselves at you, and now that you've encountered one who doesn't, you don't have a clue how to react. She's a challenge, that's all. One he wouldn't pursue, for both their sakes. Not only were they from disparate worlds, they had different expectations where relationships were concerned. A man would have to be blind not to know Megan O'Malley craved what many other women in the world craved—love and romance and happy-ever-after. He'd seen it in her eyes, that starry, hopeful light not yet dimmed by betrayal or misfortune. She wanted it all... adoring husband, bouncing babies and a cozy home. He wasn't prepared to give that to anyone, especially her.

He still hadn't made up his mind about her. Whether she was the genuine article or an exceptional counterfeit.

His fingers closed over her reticule.

He'd noticed the lacy, beribboned article lying on the entryway table this morning. Megan had left in such a hurry last evening that she'd accidentally left it behind. He'd toyed with the idea of allowing his valet to return it to her, but in the end, his curiosity about her home and family had won out. Getting directions had been a simple task. As Charles Newman's grandson, the locals accepted him more readily than he expected they would a complete stranger.

Now on his way to the O'Malley farm, he found himself wondering what he'd find there. He knew nothing about her family, except that she had a cousin named

Josh. Had her parents grown up with his mother? Did they, like Megan, think he was heartless for staying away all these years?

This lane was unfamiliar, the forests on either side thick and endless yet somehow welcoming.

Amid the sea of coarse bark and lush green leaves, splashes of vivid pink caught his eye. Phlox. The delicate flower blanketed the forest floor in this particular area, a pleasing respite from the verdant landscape. Farther on, yellow lady's slippers decorated a mossy slope. And later, white-and-pink painted trillium. The peaceful, majestic beauty reminded him of his estate outside New Orleans. Not that these mountains could compare to his beloved lowlands, but he felt the same sense of serenity here, of freedom and completeness, that he did there. Curious.

By the time he'd reached Megan's farm, his mind was blessedly clear.

Taking the worn path veering from the lane, he passed a fair-sized vegetable garden and a crude, open-air shelter fashioned from four sawed-off tree trunks topped with a slanting, wood-slat roof, under which sat a wagon. The barn, while sizable, had seen better days. Boards were warped or missing altogether. Beyond sat a corncrib and smokehouse in much better condition. Diagonal from the barn, its roof sheltered by the branches of a towering magnolia tree, sat a two-story, shingled-roof cabin with a long, narrow porch running the length of the dwelling. Stacked river rock formed the supports. Flowers spilled from crates on either side of the door, spots of color in the porch's shadow. Two rocking chairs waited, still and silent, for someone to relax and enjoy the view.

Nearing the barn, Megan's voice drifted out through the open doors, and he stopped to listen.

"Mr. Knightley," she all but crooned, "we can't go for another jaunt in the woods today. It's almost time for supper."

Lucian frowned. Who was Mr. Knightley? Another suitor? Treading silently, he edged closer to the shaded opening, craning his neck for a glimpse of her and her companion.

"How about tomorrow afternoon? If the weather co-operates, that is."

There was no response. Seeing a flash of her blond hair, he moved into the barn itself and saw that her Mr. Knightley was in fact a beautiful bay dun.

"Bonjour."

With a gasp of surprise, she pivoted his direction. Her eyes were huge and dark. "Lucian! I didn't hear you come in."

"That's a fine horse you have there." He advanced farther inside, noting the neatness and order, gardening tools and pails stacked in one corner. A dairy cow shifted in her stall as he passed. Fresh hay littered the earth floor.

When he reached her side, he placed a hand on the horse's powerful neck, inches from where hers rested. She didn't speak at first, simply stared at him as if trying to absorb the fact that he was actually here, on her property. The air around them shimmered suddenly with energy, sharpening his senses. She was so very close. Adrift in blue eyes that reminded him of the mysterious ocean deep, Lucian found his ability to speak failed him. As did his common sense.

He covered her hand with his own. Edged closer. Inhaled the faint rose scent that clung to her. Captured a wayward curl and wrapped it around his finger.

"Lucian?" Her whisper caressed his neck.

His heart thundered inside his chest. "Has anyone ever told you that your hair is like moonlight?" he murmured, his gaze freely roaming the silken mass. "So pale it practically glows luminescent?"

Her peach-hued lips curved sweetly. "Actually, you're the first."

That smile nearly felled him. His gaze homed in on her lush mouth, and he bent his head a fraction. Her breathing changed. He stilled.

What was he doing?

"I'm sorry. I—" What could he say? That he'd temporarily forgotten all the reasons he mustn't fall prey to her charms?

Uncoiling his finger, he put distance between them. Focused on the horse. Mr. Knightley. "I take it you're an admirer of Jane Austen? *Emma,* in particular?" Averting his face, he grimaced when his voice sounded more riled bear than human.

Megan didn't move. "Y-yes, I am as a matter of fact. You're familiar with her works?"

"You sound surprised." He dared a glance at her, watched her expression change from bemused to contemplative.

"Not surprised, exactly. *Pleased* would be a more apt term. Some men consider female authors inferior and, as such, unworthy of their attention."

"And here I thought you'd be surprised that I read at all."

Lifting a shoulder, she averted her gaze and stroked her horse's neck. "Charles mentioned he'd passed his love of books on to Lucinda. I surmised she taught you to do the same."

Lucian didn't respond. She was right, of course. His earliest memories were of sitting on his mother's lap, snug and warm, listening to bedtime stories. She'd read to him until he'd learned to do it for himself. Growing up, he'd passed countless afternoons hidden away in their estate's library, immersed in one adventure or another.

"I have to admit, I never did warm to Emma and her matchmaking. I prefer *Mansfield Park*."

"Indeed?"

"Megan—" they turned as one at the feminine intrusion barreling into the barn "—what's taking you so…long?"

The raven-haired beauty's momentum faltered when her wide-eyed gaze encountered him. She pressed a hand to her chest. "Oh, I didn't realize we had company."

Once Megan made the introductions, Lucian nodded in greeting, surprised that, besides their striking eyes, the sisters didn't share any other physical similarities. He instantly recognized the calculating gleam in Nicole's, having witnessed it in scores of other young ladies' gazes. What schemes was this young minx entertaining? He had a feeling she caused her poor parents a fair share of grief.

"Supper's on the table," Nicole announced brightly, smoothing her lace-and-ribbon-embellished purple skirts. "Please say you'll join us, Mr. Beaumont."

He glanced at Megan, uncertain of her feelings on the matter. He wanted to accept, not because he was particularly hungry, but because his curiosity had only increased in the time he'd been here.

Her hesitation lasted a fraction of a second before good manners kicked in, and she smiled her agreement. "Yes, please do. You can meet our younger sister, Jane,

and taste her fine cooking. It's simple fare," she has-
tened to add, "nothing like you're used to, I'm sure."

"Not all of my meals are seven-course fanfares," he
said leaning towards her, a slight smile playing about
his lips. "In fact, when I'm out hunting, I sometimes
make do with a can of cold beans and hard biscuits."

"I can scarcely believe it," she responded with mock
horror. "Lucian Beaumont, lord of the manor, eating
out of a can? What would people say if they knew? I
hope you at least had a fork and weren't forced to use
your fingers."

Lord of the manor? Was that how she saw him? As
some stuffy stick-in-the-mud?

"Well, beans aren't on the menu tonight, thank goodness!" Nicole said with relief. "Jane's fixed pot roast
and all the trimmings. Let's go eat before it gets cold."

With a shrug and a smile, Megan fell into step beside
him, explaining the whereabouts of her mother, Alice,
and sisters Juliana and Jessica. There was no mention
of a father, which meant the man had either abandoned
his family or passed on. The question would have to
wait until later.

Preceding Megan into the cabin, he stepped into a
rectangular, low-ceilinged room crammed with furniture. Oval-backed chairs surrounded one long, chocolate-
brown settee and a yellow-gold fainting couch. Two
oversize hutches monopolized the wall space opposite
him, while sewing baskets, fabrics and supplies occupied a low table in the far corner. To his left, impossibly
steep stairs disappeared into an opening in the second
floor. Beyond the living area, he glimpsed a narrow
passageway that contained the dining table laden with
dishes and, past that, the kitchen.

The rich aroma of succulent meat and fresh-baked

bread hit him. His mouth watered. Perhaps he was hungrier than he'd thought.

As he understood it, until recently, six females had shared this cabin. That number was now at five. Despite the crowded nature of the space, they did a remarkable job of keeping it clean and clutter-free.

Auburn-haired Jane, he found, did resemble Megan to a degree. While her hair and eyes were different, she had the same cheekbones, nose and chin, though that last part lacked her older sister's stubbornness. That could be due to her young age. Jane exuded the same gentle sweetness, but she lacked Megan's spark, the inner fire that drew him unwillingly to her. *Ignore it or fight it. If you don't, you could wind up getting burned.*

Beside him at the table, she was unusually quiet. She didn't have to utter a word, however, for him to be aware of her every movement. Did she resent having him here?

He should've felt awkward, outnumbered as he was by unfamiliar females. However, the delicious meal and the younger girls' eager inquiries about city life put him at ease, as did the realization that Nicole didn't have her sights set on him. In fact, the thoughtful glances she slid between he and Megan indicated she had ideas about the two of them.

Pity she was bound to be disappointed.

Tonight Jane's pot roast didn't melt on Megan's tongue. It was difficult to chew and even harder to swallow, and it was all *his* fault. Every time Lucian shifted in his seat, his shoulder brushed hers and her stomach took a dive. Once, when his knee bumped hers, she nearly toppled her lemonade. His masculine presence filled the room, robbing her lungs of air. All she could think about was that scene in the barn. He'd almost kissed her! The worst part was the acute disappointment she'd experienced when he didn't. If anything, she should be relieved.

Kissing Lucian would have disastrous consequences. One kiss from him and she'd be planning their wedding. Risking a sideways glance, she tried to imagine him in formal black wedding clothes. His unruly waves slicked back…

Lowering her gaze to her still-full plate, she swirled the potatoes through the gravy with her fork. *Have you forgotten the children? He's made it plain he seeks to circumvent Charles's will. I guarantee he won't be quite so attractive if you have to cancel story time and explain to them that their fun is over.*

Besides, his home was hundreds of miles away. If she allowed herself to get close to him, to care for him, he'd take a part of her heart with him when he left. Could she endure that? Pining hearts made for great fiction…why else would she have pored through the pages of *Pride and Prejudice* half a dozen times? She wasn't so certain she wanted to experience it in reality.

"Megan," Jane's voice intruded, "would you like a slice of pie?"

"No, thanks." She dredged up a smile, laying her fork aside when she noticed everyone had finished. "I'll help clear the dishes."

Rising, she began to stack them.

"Jane and I will clean up," Nicole protested, rising and taking the plates from her hands. "Why don't you and Mr. Beaumont have a seat on the front porch while we dish up dessert?"

Megan stared. Nicole didn't volunteer to do anything unless it suited her purposes. What was she up to?

Lucian stood, as well, and placed a hand against his flat stomach. "That was a fine meal, ladies. I enjoyed this evening very much. Thank you for your generous hospitality."

Jane flushed. They'd all noticed he'd eagerly accepted second portions. "It was our pleasure, Mr. Beaumont."

After inviting her sisters to call him by his first name, he turned that intense focus on her, waiting for her to lead the way. Where they'd be alone again. Her nerves zinged with equal parts anticipation and dismay. Would he touch her again? She hoped not. Really, she did.

Outside, darkness blanketed the land, obscuring the distant mountain peaks. Moonlight cast the yard and outbuildings in a muted glow, glancing off the treetops while the thick forest below remained cloaked in impenetrable blackness. The nearby stream's hushed journey over and around moss-covered rocks formed a backdrop to the cicadas' calls and frogs' songs. The night air was pleasant against her skin, not too warm and not too cold. Perfect.

Lucian stared into the night, one shoulder propped against a wooden support. She moved to rest her back against the one opposite, arms crossed over her chest. She studied his proud profile, wondered if he ever truly let go and allowed himself to relax. Lost the brooding tension humming along his body.

"What's the city like at night?"

He didn't answer immediately. "The air is humid, almost sticky, and sweet with the scent of magnolias and beignets. Buggies and people roam the streets at all hours, the sounds of horses and wheels clattering over bricks, laughter and jazz flooding the night. It's a vibrant place."

If it was so wonderful, then why did he sound dissatisfied? Wistful for something else?

"What are beignets?"

"Fried dough dusted with sugar."

She smiled. "Sounds delicious."

"They are, indeed, especially when accompanied by café au lait. We use chicory in our coffee, which makes it stronger, more bitter than what I've tasted here." He angled his face to study her. "I think you'd like it there, Megan, especially the waterfront. The nonstop activity. Interesting characters. The boats and the water."

"I've yet to leave these mountains. Not sure I ever will."

He shifted so that his stance mirrored hers, his back against the support. "You surprise me. I would've guessed that a young lady such as yourself yearned for adventure, hungered to see the world you read about in all those books."

"I'll admit I've often wondered what other places are like. I'm realistic enough to know, however, the opportunity will probably never arise." She shrugged. "That's all right with me. I'm content right where I am."

"The mountains are all right," he agreed offhandedly.

"Just all right?" She dropped her arms, indignation pushing upward. "How can you say that—"

"There's no need to get huffy, *mon chou*," he responded, amusement deepening his accent. "I was merely teasing. While I prefer the lowlands, I can't deny East Tennessee is lovely. In fact, it sort of reminds me of my property outside New Orleans. The landscape is vastly different, of course, but the feeling I get is the same. A feeling of freedom. Free of constraints, of expectations. I can let down my guard there."

During supper, she'd found his descriptions of his life in the Crescent City fascinating, if somewhat confining. The thought of all those strict social rules and expectations, not to mention the head-spinning whirl of parties and engagements, made her break out in a cold sweat. Made her grateful she wasn't part of a prominent, wealthy family like the Beaumonts.

No wonder he was coiled tighter than a copperhead about to strike. How much time would it take for him to let his guard down here?

"Do you go there often?"

He paused. "Not nearly as often as I'd like."

"Have you ever considered leaving the city behind?"

"I have." He heaved a sigh. "This last year, especially."

Because his mother was gone.

Lying in bed last evening, she'd prayed for him, asked God to comfort him as he sorted through the truth. His instinctive denial, his difficulty in accepting that his mother might've deceived him in this matter, revealed how deeply he'd loved her. Treasured her, even. Recalling his pained denial, outrage had bloomed inside Megan. How could Lucinda betray him that way? Deny both men a chance at a close relationship? She couldn't begin to understand the woman's reasoning or motivations.

With tears wetting her pillow, it had dawned on her that she no longer blamed Lucian for not visiting Charles. Lucinda had led him to believe his grandfather was apathetic. And perhaps worse. Her actions had inflicted deep hurt on two men. Charles, her friend and substitute grandfather. And Lucian, someone who, if the circumstances were different, she could come to care a great deal about.

But they're not. Remember that. He's not the hero you've been dreaming about your whole life.

Needing to divert her treacherous thoughts, she grasped blindly for a change in subject.

"Did your house sustain any damages last night? I trust you didn't discover any handprints on the furniture." She hoped he didn't detect the breathless strain in her voice.

"I didn't find any when I inspected the parlor in the morning light."

Oh, why did the man have to have a sense of humor beneath that brooding reserve? Where was the haughty arrogance she despised?

"No misplaced children after I left?"

"No," he said with mock sternness. "I can assure you that if I had, I would've brought them straight here for you to deal with."

"Aw, but look at how well you handled Ollie and Sarah."

"If you dare to leave me alone with that boy again, there will be dire consequences."

She couldn't hold back her laughter, the thrill his subtle teasing sent rushing through her.

"Go ahead. Laugh. You think I'm jesting when in fact I'm completely serious."

"Right." The tremor of humor belied his words. Holding her stomach, she laughed harder, recalling his look of strained patience when dealing with the boy.

When Lucian pushed away from the post and stalked towards her, black eyes burning, the laughter died in her throat. Uh-oh. Every nerve ending stood to attention. What were his intentions?

He came very close, clasped his hands behind his back even as his upper body bent towards her. A good three to four inches taller than her, his broad, muscled chest and capable shoulders blocked the moonlight. His nearness didn't trouble her in the least. She welcomed it, felt sheltered by him. She pressed her arms tighter around her middle to keep from reaching up and weaving her fingers through his brown locks, from pulling him to her. *That would be unwise. Extremely unwise.*

That didn't mean she didn't long to do so. This enigmatic man tugged at her heart, her soul, like the pull of the moon on the ocean's waves.

"Has anyone ever told you that your laugh is like a song? A merry tune brimming with unbridled enthusiasm?"

"Has anyone ever told you that you've a heart of a poet?"

Surprise flashed across his face. "No. Never. It must be your influence." His gaze roaming her face was like a physical touch. "You are so incredibly beautiful." His warm breath fanned her mouth.

Her lungs hung suspended. Was he going to kiss her?

The door opened then, and Nicole appeared, interrupting them a second time. Megan didn't know whether to be irritated or relieved.

He straightened, his eyes hooded. Unreadable. The air whooshed from her lungs. Why did she feel as if she'd just missed something special?

"Dessert's on the table," Nicole announced brightly, unaware of what she'd interrupted.

"I, ah, am sorry to have to decline, after all." Lucian backed towards the steps. "But it's later than I realized. I need to be going."

"Oh." She blinked, glanced between them. "Next time, then."

"Good evening."

"Wait!" Megan ducked inside for a kerosene lamp. Their fingers brushed as she handed it to him and an unexpected pang shot through her. There was such strength and warmth in those hands. Gentleness, too. "To light your way," she said.

His features tightened briefly. "Thanks."

Then he turned and walked away. And Megan was glad she was smart enough to know not to fall in love with the man. Something deep inside warned that it wouldn't be the happy-ever-after kind of love. More like the Romeo and Juliet, tragic kind of love. For them, there could be no happy ending.

Chapter Seven

Standing in the flower garden Monday afternoon, Lucian turned at the sound of angry footsteps.

"Cabbage?" Megan marched his direction, her pastel-pink skirts skimming the stone path and swiping the blooms unfortunate enough to be too near the edge. "*That's* what you've been calling me?"

"Good afternoon." He gestured to the clear blue skies overhead. "Nice day for a stroll, isn't it?"

Her pink blouse, with fitted bodice and flared sleeves, delineated her slender waist, while the delicate hue enhanced her pale beauty. Her skin glowed with health and vitality. She'd captured the top layers of her curls in a pink ribbon at the back of her head, while the rest cascaded down her back. A silver ribbon choker encircled her neck, a small cameo brooch in the center. She was a delicate rose of incomparable beauty, but not without a few thorns.

Reaching his side, she jammed her fists on her hips. The color in her cheeks matched the red tulips planted along the back porch. She wasn't going to let this go.

"I spoke to my cousin's wife Kate today. You know,

the one from New York? She studied French, so I asked her what *mon chou* meant." When he didn't immediately respond, she narrowed her gaze. "Well? Care to explain in what way you believe I resemble a cabbage?"

"She's right. It does mean that." She opened her mouth to speak, but he held up a hand. "It's also slang for…little pastry."

One pale brow arched in a way he was coming to adore. "That's supposed to make me feel better?"

"Actually, yes." And because he didn't trust himself not to do anything rash, like he very nearly had last night, he pivoted on his heel and began to stroll away from the house. As expected, she followed.

"Why?"

He sighed, uncertain if he was strong enough to maintain self-control. To keep things between them platonic. Businesslike would be even better, though at this point, all but impossible. No other woman had ever gotten under his skin like this one.

Waving a hand in dismissal, he drawled, "You know, your skin is like heavy cream and your eyes the hue of blueberries. Your lips—"

"I get the picture," she spoke up hastily.

Silence stretched between them, their boots striking the stones and birds twittering in the trees filling it. He was glad she was behind him, unable to see the struggle in his expression.

"How was church yesterday?"

"Good." She hesitated. "Though I'm not sure I appreciated the onslaught of questions about you."

That brought him around. His brows met in the middle. "About me?"

"Yes, you." She met his gaze openly. "This is a small

town, remember? People are curious about Lucinda's son, Charles's grandson."

He absently rubbed his chest, so accustomed to the pressure he was beginning not to notice it. "I'm sorry you were put in an uncomfortable position on account of me."

"It wasn't that bad." Concern flooded her gaze. She touched his wrist, her fingers lingering against his skin. "Are you all right? I've noticed you doing that a lot."

He lowered his hand, forcing her to drop hers. "It's a habit." Turning, he resumed walking. This time, she fell into step beside him.

"You aren't having chest pains, are you?"

"No, nothing like that. Just pressure and sometimes an uncomfortable tightness. My physician checked me out and declared me healthy. Said I needed to slow down for a while." He skimmed the flowers with his flattened palm, an ironic smile on his lips. "Stop and smell the roses."

Sensing her regard, he turned his head to meet her probing gaze.

"It appears this trip could accomplish that, if you'd let it."

"You don't understand." He stopped short to face her, throwing his hands wide. "I don't *want* to be here. I don't want that house," he confessed, jabbing a finger at the yellow structure visible in the distance. "This garden. I don't want to meet people who knew my mother, to listen to them say how sad they are that she never came back. How my grandfather regretted how he handled my parents' marriage. How he died all alone, with no one to comfort him."

He passed a shaky hand over his face. Frustration and sorrow churned inside him, and he wanted to rail at someone or something, needed to release these emotions before they consumed him. But his mother wasn't here to explain herself and neither was his grandfather.

"No one blames you," she said quietly, his grief mirrored in her face. "I'm sorry for the things I said before. I made assumptions about you, about your motivations, that I now know were wrong." Slipping her slender hand in his, she gently squeezed. "Charles wasn't alone at the end."

"What?"

Her lips trembled. "I was with him. So were Mr. and Mrs. Calhoun. He was ready to meet Jesus. He went peacefully."

"That's good to know," he scraped out. He felt raw inside.

What if everything he'd ever believed about the man was untrue, distorted by deception? All those years wasted harboring resentment. Feeling unworthy. Outraged on his mother's behalf, hurting for her. Had he been wrong about it all?

He held on to her hand like a lifeline. "Did he ever say anything about me?"

"A few times."

"I see."

"He loved you, Lucian," she said, pressing closer, "but it was a painful subject. In many ways, your grandfather was a very private man."

Nodding, he swallowed hard. He shared that particular trait.

"Lucian—"

Reaching up, he cradled her cheek with his hand, skimmed his thumb along the petal-soft skin. Battled the urge to find comfort in her arms. "I wish I knew what to believe." *Who* to believe.

Everything in him screamed Megan was trustworthy. That she was a good person. That the compassion in her eyes was real.

"I'm sorry you're struggling with this."

Inhaling, he dropped his hand and stepped back. "You truly believe he wanted us here?"

"I do."

He nodded, glanced out over the gardens, not really seeing anything.

Megan felt helpless in the face of Lucian's anguish. She would like nothing more than to hold him, but she didn't dare. *Father God, please bring the truth to light somehow. Give him clarity and closure. Help him to see how much You love him.*

"I have an idea," she ventured softly. "You haven't seen much of the town yet, have you? Why don't we take a walk? It will do you good to get your mind off things."

The questions in his eyes shouted his mistrust. "Why do you want to help me? I haven't changed my mind about the house. If my lawyer finds a way around that stipulation, I'll take it."

It hurt that he still didn't trust her motives, but she understood it wasn't about her. Not really. "I'm praying he doesn't. But if he does, I'll just have to trust God to open up another way for us to minister to the children and the community." She hadn't answered that other question. Couldn't. Not without alerting him to the fact he was fast becoming important to her.

As for the house, she couldn't find it in her to be angry. Not now that she realized everything it represented for him, the upheaval, the painful reminders. She just wished there was a way to meet everyone's needs. Perhaps, if he came to trust her fully, he might agree to leave the house in her care so that he could return to New Orleans.

Assessing her, he appeared to come to a conclusion. "At least you're honest." He held his arm aloft. "Very well—let's go exploring."

Walking arm in arm down Main Street with Gatlinburg's latest arrival caused quite a stir. Because news traveled fast here, a good majority of folks would know of Lucian's connection to the town. Some stopped whatever they were doing to stare unashamedly, speculation in their gazes. Speculation about Charles's grandson. And about the two of them.

Lucian tilted his head, speaking for her ears alone. "Do I have dirt on my face? Something on my shirt, perhaps?" He paused and ran a hand over his coat and vest, inspecting his front.

His hair fell forward, softening his features. Making him look...vulnerable. "There's nothing wrong with your appearance," she said wryly.

"Then why is everyone staring?"

She smiled. "You're big news around here. They're wondering, how long is he in town for? Is there a chance he might stay? What does he think of Gatlinburg? What's he like?"

"All that, huh?"

And more. Most likely, they were wondering what, if anything, was going on between the two of them. "Make no mistake, dinner conversations will be lively tonight."

Lucian didn't comment. The tension sparked by their earlier conversation yet lingered in the stiff set of his shoulders and the lines about his mouth, but his eyes were not as black, his expression less formidable.

"Does the attention bother you?"

He shook his head. "No. I'm accustomed to it, though not while walking down the street, I admit."

Megan experienced an unwelcome spurt of jealousy. He was referring to the balls and social engagements he attended nearly every evening. With his wealth, social standing and devastating good looks, of course he'd have scores of girls vying for his attention.

Her fingers tightened on his sleeve. This wasn't good. She mustn't start thinking of Lucian as hers. He wasn't. Never would be.

"Does it bother you?" he asked, guiding her closer to the storefronts to avoid a collision with a group of men.

"Not really." She smiled in response to their friendly greetings. "Besides, it's simple curiosity. Nothing malicious."

Pulling back on his arm, she urged him to stop. His glance was questioning.

Gesturing to the plate-glass window beside them, she said, "Recognize the name?"

"K. O'Malley Photography and J. D. O'Malley Furniture." One black brow lifted. "That's an interesting combination. Your cousin and his wife?"

"Would you like to go inside and meet them?"

"Certainly."

The shop's interior was divided into two separate areas—Kate's studio on their right and Josh's furniture on their left. Neat and organized, the place was a feast for the eyes. Landscape photographs of New York and Tennessee lined the walls, as did examples of personal portraits—couples and families and babies. In the back, an oversize black curtain hid the log walls and rough-hewn floorboards where a settee and two chairs were set up, along with her camera and equipment.

In an effort not to overcrowd the space, Josh had chosen his finest pieces to showcase his work. Customers had the option to buy the inventory or put in special orders. A gleaming cherry dining set, an intricately carved walnut hutch, a writing desk and a few other pieces were situated about the area with enough room for folks to meander and touch and inspect.

The bell above the door jangled, and Josh, who seemed to be comforting Kate, looked up.

"Megan."

His lips quirked up in a welcoming smile, but he couldn't quite hide his worry. Immediately, concern washed over her. Kate lifted her head from his shoulder and, hurriedly wiping her eyes, stepped out of the shelter of his arms. Attempted a smile.

"Megan, hi." She eyed the man at her side with interest.

"We can come back another time—" Megan began, unhappy they'd interrupted a private moment.

"No, that's all right." Clasping Josh's hand, Kate pulled him forward. "We'd like to meet your friend."

All the while making the introductions, she tried to guess what was the matter with her best friend. She hadn't noticed anything unusual about Kate's behavior, although, now that she thought about it, she *had* been quieter than normal these past few weeks. A touch withdrawn. The joy and pride that had been a constant on Josh's face ever since their wedding last fall was still there, but he seemed distracted. Concerned for his wife.

Please, Lord, don't let it be anything serious. If anyone deserved happiness, it was Kate.

Threading her arm through Kate's, she addressed her cousin. "Josh, could you show Lucian around? I'd like to speak with Kate for a few minutes."

"Sure."

She looked to Lucian for approval. "Do you mind?"

"Not at all." His mouth eased into an almost smile, his expression thoughtful.

Once inside the small storage room in back, Megan took Kate's hands in hers. "What's wrong?"

Since finding love with Josh, the petite, refined lady who'd known more than her fair share of loneliness and heartbreak had blossomed into an outgoing, confident woman with a ready smile and infectious laughter. Today, though, her wide green eyes were filled with unshed tears. She looked miserable.

Megan's heart squeezed with compassion. "Why are you so upset? Are you ill?" She held her breath, braced for bad news.

"No, nothing like that." Freeing one hand, she smoothed dark chocolate wisps away from her forehead. Her luxurious mane, normally trained into an elaborate twist, was caught back in a simple bun. "Although, I'm afraid something may be wrong with me."

"What do you mean?"

Kate's cheeks grew pink, and her lashes swept down. "I—I'm afraid I won't be able to have a baby. Josh and I have been trying since the wedding, and, well…" She trailed off, worried her lower lip.

"Oh." Relief swept through her that Kate wasn't facing a health crisis. "It's early yet. You've only been married a little over six months."

"But look at how quickly it happened for Juliana and Evan!" she protested. "What if I can't give Josh a son or daughter? For so long, I dreamed of having a family of my own, and now that I've found Josh, I want that dream to become a reality. I want a little boy with his daddy's honey-colored hair and blue eyes. And a little girl I can teach to take photographs and cook and read…" Her eyes welled up again. "What if God doesn't think I'd be a good mother?"

"Don't think that way, Kate," she admonished with a gentle smile. "You are the most nurturing, kind, loving woman I know. You'll be the best mother ever! God knows the desires of your heart. Just keep praying and waiting on Him. I'll pray, too."

She nodded slowly. "I have been. I suppose I'm impatient."

"God's timing isn't always our own," Megan agreed, thinking of her own longing for a husband. "What's Josh saying about all this?"

Her quick smile lit up her lovely features. "He's been very supportive, very patient with me. He's my voice of reason, something I desperately need right now."

"I'm not surprised. He loves you so much." Last fall, when Kate left Gatlinburg to return to New York, Megan had worried the pair would never find their happy ending. She thanked God that Josh had come to his senses and gone after her.

"I've been truly blessed." Kate paused, reflective. "Not only do I have a husband I dearly love, I have new friends and family. I need to remember my many blessings instead of focusing on what I don't have."

"There's nothing wrong with wanting things," Megan said, "but you're right—if we focus too much on what we don't have, it can affect our outlook."

Kate gave her a quick hug, then leaned back to smile at her. "Thanks for being such a dear friend, Megan. I think of you as a sister, you know. I love you."

A lump formed in her throat. "I love you, too."

Thank You, Lord, for bringing this delightful woman into my life. Kate's friendship eased the ache of Juliana's absence.

Turning speculative, Kate rested her hands on her hips. "Charles's grandson is certainly a distinguished gentleman. You failed to mention how utterly handsome he is!" Her brow furrowed. "He does seem a bit haughty, however. Is he a cold man?"

Megan rushed to his defense. "That was my first impression of him, too, but he's not at all that way. Actually, he's quite kind. Lucian's a good man—he's just... going through a rough patch right now."

"It sounds as if you've learned a lot about him in a short amount of time."

"You could say that."

Strange—she couldn't recall what life was like without him around. There was a connection between them, one she hadn't experienced with anyone else. One she must ignore, must fight against. At the very most, they could be friends. There would be risk involved, of course, but she was certain she could withstand the temptation to care for him more than was wise. He was only here temporarily, after all.

"Be careful, Megan," Kate warned. "I wouldn't want to see you hurt."

"Don't worry. I'm perfectly aware that Lucian isn't the one for me."

"Hmm." She moved to the door. "Well, I believe we've left them to their own devices long enough, don't you?"

To Megan's relief, the men were involved in a deep discussion about furniture. Josh winked at her, continuing to talk as he placed an arm about Kate's shoulders. She took it as a sign that he liked Lucian, which pleased her. Both were businessmen, so they had something in common. Lucian searched her face as if trying to ascertain if everything was all right and, apparently satisfied, returned his attention to Josh. His stance was relaxed yet focused.

Twenty minutes later, they were back on the boardwalk.

"Do you want to return home?" she asked.

"Not unless you do."

Shielding her eyes with one hand, she scanned the blue sky above. No clouds. Good. "I can show you our favorite picnic spot, if you'd like. It's a twenty-five-minute walk from here."

"I'd like that."

They were quiet as they left the town behind, each lost in their own thoughts. Walking side by side in the forest, Megan was acutely aware of his commanding presence. There was no compulsion to fill the silence with inane chatter.

Spotting one of her favorite birds, she tugged on his sleeve to stop his forward progress, pointing to a branch above their heads. "Do you see that?"

He tipped his head back to study the elegant golden-hued bird with a splash of red on its wings.

"That's a cedar waxwing," she told him, suddenly reminded of a verse she'd read the night before. "'Look at the birds of the air; they do not sow or reap or store away in barns, and yet your heavenly Father feeds them. Are you not much more valuable than they?'"

His gaze turned quizzical. "That sounds familiar. Is it from the New Testament?"

"The book of Matthew. And Luke writes, 'Are not five sparrows sold for two pennies? Yet not one of them is forgotten by God. Indeed, the very hairs of your head are all numbered. Don't be afraid; you are worth more than many sparrows.'"

"You've memorized quite a bit of Scripture."

"That's true, but you're missing the point." She spread her arms wide. "Since God took the time to create an astonishing array of creatures for His pleasure and ours, don't you think He'd care about us, who are created in His image?"

His mouth lifted in an indulgent smile. "*Oui,* it would make sense." He didn't elaborate, however, leaving her wondering if she'd gotten through to him. When he resumed walking, she had no choice but to follow. He shot her a sideways glance. "Thank you, Megan."

She stepped around a large hole in the ground, likely a gopher's. "For what?"

"For caring."

Uncertain how to respond, she merely nodded and averted her gaze. When they reached the forest's edge, she paused in order for Lucian to take in the view. A wide, sweeping green field sprinkled with clover lay before them, and in the distance, a tree-lined river meandered through the valley. On the far side of the river, green hills and pastures gave way to the mountains, rounded peaks shining in the sun.

Inhaling the fresh, sweet-smelling air, he wore a look of appreciation. "I can see why you like it here."

"Our families come here to relax. My ma, aunt and uncle normally sit and talk while the rest of us swim or fish or play games."

He held out his hand. "Want to walk to the river?"

Placing her hand in his felt like the most natural thing in the world. The sun warmed their skin and the light breeze teased their hair as they crossed the field.

"Your cousin is an astute businessman," he said after some time. "I enjoyed our discussion."

"More importantly, he's a good man. He's like a protective older brother—irritating at times but always looking out for my best interests."

"His wife seemed upset when we arrived. Is everything all right?"

Megan hesitated, not because she didn't trust him but because it was a delicate subject. How to say it? "Kate is eager to start a family."

His grip on her hand shifted so that their palms fit snugly together, his fingers firm and sure. He shot her a sideways glance. "And it's not happening as quickly as she'd like?"

Heat rushed into her cheeks. "Exactly."

"I see."

Oh, dear. In this moment, she didn't resent that phrase quite so much.

They stopped at the river's edge and stood on the low, gently sloping bank, their boots sinking slightly in the soft earth as they watched the clear water tumbling past. Thousands of tiny rocks littered the riverbed, all shapes and sizes and colors. Pond-skater bugs pushed across the surface. Fish the size of her thumb darted back and forth.

Lucian didn't release her hand. She'd hoped he wouldn't, relishing the connection although she knew she shouldn't.

He turned to her. "How many children do you want?"

"Me?" The question startled her. "Oh, I don't know. Five or ten." A laugh burst forth when his jaw dropped.

"Surely you jest!"

"I love kids. I'll take as many as the good Lord sees fit to give me."

He shook his head in wonder. "I noticed you seem to have a way with them." He asked quietly, "Is Tom the lucky man?"

"What? Tom and I? No."

His face inches away, his dark gaze pierced her. "I got the impression that the two of you are more than friends."

"I don't feel that way about him."

Was that relief in his eyes?

Breaking eye contact, they stood and gazed at the scenery. After long moments of silence, she asked, "What about you? How many do you want?"

Hitching a shoulder, he spoke matter-of-factly. "I need a son to carry on the Beaumont name. If my first-born is a son, then I'll have only the one."

His detached attitude made her feel slightly nauseous. "You make having a child sound like a duty," she accused.

His gaze sharpened, his jaw hardened into marble. "That's because it is. Unlike you, I won't marry for love or some other fickle emotion. I'll do so because I have a responsibility to my family to further the Beaumont legacy."

Snatching her hand from his, she lifted her chin. Why was she so angry? "Let me guess—only the brightest, richest, most well-connected young debutant will do?"

His eyes shuttered, he jerked a nod. "That's the way things are done in my world."

"Then I'm glad I inhabit a different one." Trembling now, she hitched a thumb over her shoulder. "We should probably be heading back."

Without a word, they retraced their path. Only this time, the silence was strained, heavy. As disheartening as it was, she'd needed this reminder of their vast differences, not only in their stations but their outlooks. While she envisioned marriage as a union of hearts, he saw it as a cold, emotionless business arrangement.

She could never live that way, and it saddened her that Lucian would choose such a life.

Rounding the base of a live oak, he nearly trampled a patch of pink heart-shaped flowers. He stopped short. "What are these?"

"Bleeding hearts." Joining him in the shade, she gently traced a petal. "There's a legend associated with them," she said offhandedly. "It involves a tale of a young man's quest to win the love of his life."

He cradled one flower against his flat palm. "Is it an interesting story?"

"I'll let you be the judge of that." Snapping one off, she removed the two pink petals and, balancing them on her hand, lifted them up for his inspection. "A young man fell deeply in love with a wealthy and beautiful maiden and, in an effort to win her love, gave her extravagant gifts. The first gift consisted of two rabbits to keep as pets."

One black brow snaked up as he eyed the petals. "I see the resemblance. Let me guess—she didn't want them?"

"Oh, yes, she did. She accepted the gift, but rejected the giver." Pulling out the white inner petals, she said, "He didn't give up, though. Next, he gave her a pair of silk slippers. The finest money could buy."

"Well, I know for certain she kept those," he drawled. "What woman would turn down a pair of shoes?"

"You're right—she did. But she still wasn't interested in him. Desperate now, he spent the last of his money on a pair of extravagant earrings." She showed him the question-mark-shaped stamens.

Lucian outlined her palm with his fingertip. "It didn't work, did it?"

His light touch and husky voice sparked shivers along

her skin. Her gaze caught in his, she shook her head. "No."

"What did he do?"

"He had no more gifts to give," she murmured, unable to maintain eye contact, "and no way to win her love, so he took his knife and plunged it into his heart." Placing the stamens side by side, she created the heart shape. The green pistil represented the knife. "They say the first bleeding-heart plant sprung up in the spot where he died."

All of a sudden, she wished she hadn't told the story. Just as there was no hope for the mythical characters, there was no hope for her and Lucian.

When she started to drop the disassembled flower onto the ground, he stopped her. "May I have that?"

"Of course." When she'd transferred the pieces to him, he placed them in a handkerchief and, folding up the sides, tucked it into his pocket. He didn't offer an explanation. And she didn't ask for one.

At the lane leading into town, she stopped to bid him goodbye. She resorted to twirling her hair, a nervous habit she'd developed as a small child and one she'd mostly abandoned. "I need to get home and help the girls with supper."

His hands at his sides, he stood tall and straight and formal. "Thank you for showing me around. I know you have responsibilities to tend to."

The solemn expression on his handsome face, the weariness in his dark eyes, called to her. How she yearned to throw her arms around him, to pull him close and smooth all the cares from his brow. She ruthlessly squelched the urge. Heartache lay down that path.

"I was happy to," she said in all honesty.

He sketched a bow. "Until Friday evening."

"Yes, I'll see you then."

She watched him go, his long, sure strides carrying him quickly in the opposite direction, his shiny Hessians winking in patches of sunlight. A solitary figure with the weight of the world on his shoulders. Megan desperately wanted to be the friend he needed. But at what price?

Chapter Eight

In Charles's study Tuesday afternoon, Lucian refolded the letter and, sliding it inside the top desk drawer, let his head fall back against the leather chair. Stared at nothing in particular. His lawyer had written not to impart news, but to reassure Lucian of his efforts to find a way around the stipulation. Upon seeing the return address on the envelope, he'd assumed it meant his stay here in Tennessee was coming to an end. Not another delay. Apparently the gentleman hadn't been able to give the matter his immediate attention as he'd been wrapping up a delicate legal matter.

He needed to leave and *soon*. He had work and responsibilities. A life to resume. With nothing pressing calling for his attention here, his mind was free to wander down paths he'd rather not explore.

He'd spent the better part of the day searching his mother's and grandfather's rooms for clues, anything that might shed light on the status of their relationship in recent years. He'd rifled through this desk, examined the bookshelves. No letters. Nothing. No way to know what, if anything, had transpired between them.

The lack of evidence was telling in and of itself. Besides a couple of photographs, Charles hadn't kept anything near him that would remind him of his estranged daughter. And there certainly wasn't anything here linked to Lucian.

Going from room to room, touching their belongings, he'd felt like an intruder.

Pushing to his feet, he crossed to the single window, taking in the sweeping view of property, the flower gardens and beyond, the forest and distant mountain peaks. He could easily picture Megan there, a vision in pink. Had it been only yesterday that she'd stormed up to him, demanding to know the reason for her nickname?

Hands curling into fists, his nails bit into his palms. Megan was the primary reason he couldn't afford to stay much longer. The alluring country miss was dangerous to his peace of mind, to his goals. Too much time in her company, and her naive dreams about love and marriage might start to make sense.

He'd purposefully shocked her yesterday, spoken plainly about his expectations all the while knowing her views were in complete contrast to his. The censure in her beautiful blue eyes had stayed with him the rest of the day and long into the night. Of course a romantic like her would find his businesslike approach to marriage difficult to swallow. A man such as he—practical-minded, cynical, uninterested in love and without a single romantic inclination—could never meet her high expectations, would only disappoint her.

His housekeeper poked her head in the door. "Mr. Lucian?"

He turned and motioned for her to enter. "Mrs. Calhoun. What can I do for you?"

Although in her mid-sixties, the woman had boundless energy and could accomplish more than ten men put together. A hard worker, she was pleasant without being intrusive. He appreciated that.

Her shoes squeaking on the polished floorboards, she held her folded apron in her hands. "I'm off to the mercantile. Is there anything in particular you need?"

"Not that I can think of."

"All right, then." She made to leave.

"Uh, Mrs. Calhoun? If you give me a list, I'll go for you," he blurted, unable to shake the restlessness plaguing him. Needing *something* to do, he was even willing to do her shopping for her. If she didn't accept his offer, he was going to go find Fred and help him weed the gardens.

"Well…I do have a new recipe for buttermilk pie I'd like to try out. I could do that while you went to town. Are you sure you don't mind?"

"Not at all." Moving around the desk, he pointed out, "I'm not used to having this much time on my hands."

"Rest isn't always such a bad thing, you know. I suspect you don't get much of it back home."

Shrugging, he brushed aside her words. "I prefer to keep myself busy." So he didn't have to face his problems. To think about this past year and all its disappointments and losses. The glaring mistakes. *Coward,* a taunting voice accused.

Shaking her head in motherly concern, she sighed, turned and led the way to the kitchen where she handed him a slip of paper.

"Is this everything?" He scanned the ten items.

Retying the apron around her ample hips, she instructed, "Give the list to Emmett or his wife. They'll gather everything for you. Don't be surprised if you have to wait a little while. They fall behind sometimes, depending on how many orders they have to fill. Besides, I'm in no hurry." She thumped a bag of flour on the work surface, alongside a bowl. "And if this here recipe of Juanita's is any good, you can have a slice of pie when you get back."

Smiling, he rubbed his stomach. "I don't see how Fred has managed to stay fit after all these years eating your cooking. Our chef could learn a thing or two from you."

Though she waved away his compliment, she fairly beamed. "He works it off doing all that yard work."

"Ah, I see." He glanced out the window to where Fred was trimming bushes with a wicked-looking pair of shears, sunlight bouncing off his sweat-slicked bald head. "If I'm here much longer, I'll have to join him if I don't want to go home stouter than I arrived."

"It's been a pleasure having you here." She held a spoon aloft, gazing at him with disconcerting nostalgia. "It's almost like having Charles here again." Then she turned her attention back to her recipe.

He didn't know what to say to that. He supposed it would be strange for the elderly couple to work here with no one around. They'd been here for most of their lives, were here while his grandmother, Beatrice, was still alive, and his mother was small.

Slipping the paper in his pocket, he asked as casually as he could manage, "Were they a happy family? Charles and Beatrice and my mother?"

Lifting her head, she gave him a surprised smile. "They were very happy."

"Good." Bittersweet relief curled through his body. At least they'd had a taste of happiness before...well, before his grandmother died and his father came and ruined it all. "I'm glad."

He left then, before he peppered her with more questions. Waving to Fred, he went to the barn to hitch up the wagon. His valet was there mucking out stalls.

Lucian stopped short. Laughed at the sight of the normally fastidious gentleman sweaty, his hair mussed and bits of hay clinging to his pant legs. "You must be as in need of a diversion as I am."

Smith didn't stop what he was doing. "You would be correct, sir."

Still smiling, Lucian went about his business, glad to be doing something as simple as hitching horses to a wagon. He had to admit, it beat sitting in the stuffy shipping offices pushing papers across his desk and having his father assess his every decision as if he hadn't a clue what he was doing.

It didn't take long to reach Main Street. Pulling up in front of Clawson's Mercantile, he glimpsed a flash of blond hair through the window. Megan? Setting the brake, he jumped down to the dusty ground and stepped up on the weathered boardwalk. Who else could it be? No one else in this town had hair the color of moonlight.

Anticipation humming along his veins, he opened the door. The bell clanged above his head and she looked up, full lips parting. The eager welcome surging in her wide eyes buoyed his spirits. Apparently she'd set aside her irritation.

"Lucian?"

"Good afternoon, Megan." Sweeping off his black hat, he tucked it beneath his arm and, shoving his unruly hair out of his eyes, approached the wooden shelves lined with personal items such as combs, mirrors and shaving supplies.

Refreshingly lovely as always, her simple, unadorned dress would have been deemed boring were it not a pleasing aquamarine, its exact hue putting him in mind of the sea he loved but couldn't handle. Dratted seasickness.

"What are you doing here?" Her quizzical gaze slid to the wagon outside.

"I'm running errands for Mrs. Calhoun." He lifted a finger to touch the porcelain doll she clutched to her chest. "I didn't realize you still played with baby dolls," he teased, arching a mocking brow.

The witty retort he expected didn't surface. Instead, regret pulled at her mouth as she replaced the frilly-dressed doll on the shelf. "I'm on my way to Owen Livingston's to deliver food. I'd like to purchase this for Sarah, but it will have to wait."

He finally noticed the cloth-lined crate at her feet. "Are they ill?"

"No, but it's hard for him to manage the farm chores and still find time to cook. From what I understand, he's not an experienced cook, anyway. Ever since Meredith died, the ladies of our church have taken turns taking food to them twice a week."

"How long ago did she die?"

"Six months."

So the loss was still fresh. What a nightmare for Livingston and his small daughter. To have lost not one, but two cherished loved ones at the same time. A wife and mother. An innocent baby.

Sympathy clogged his throat. "It appears your townsfolk take care of their own."

"You're right about that." She lifted her chin a notch. "Like any other small town, we have our not-so-great moments, but I have to say I'm proud to be a part of this community."

He could tell she meant it. Unlike Nicole, who'd made

it clear she found small-town life confining, often declaring her intention of leaving it behind, Megan loved her life. She didn't care about fashion or fancy houses or money. She cared about people. That much was plain in how she chose to spend her time…whether it was entertaining little children or preparing and delivering food.

How could he have ever doubted her integrity?

Heart beating out a warning, he forced his attention away from her. It wasn't easy. Not now that he'd come to his senses and could see her as she truly was…compassionate, sensitive to others' needs, a heart full of love.

He picked up the doll. "How about I purchase this for Sarah?"

"I can't ask you to do that."

"You didn't." He guessed she didn't have enough money for such a splurge. How to put this to her without hurting her pride? "I think a little girl who's missing her mommy might be cheered by a gift such as this. You're right to want to give it to her."

"But it won't be from me if you pay for it."

Leaning closer, he suggested softly, "Why can't it be from the both of us?"

"You have a soft spot for her," she stated with sudden clarity. "Don't try to deny it."

"If I do have one—and I'm not saying I do—it's because she reminds me of a certain sassy storyteller," he said, gently tapping her nose.

The bell clanged as another patron, a skinny, awkward girl who looked to be in her teens, entered the mercantile. Straightening, Lucian dipped his head in greeting as Megan offered her a quiet hello. The girl smiled shyly before darting to the fabrics' section.

Get a hold of yourself, Beaumont. Have you forgotten your surroundings? No wonder the girl acted em-

*barrassed...you were too near Megan, touching her in
a familiar manner right here for all the world to see.*

Megan was looking far too pleased with herself, like
a cat with a big bowl of cream.

"What?"

"I thought you said you didn't like children."

Wagging a finger, he passed the doll to her and lifted
the crate. "No...I recall saying I have no experience
with them."

Walking beside the shelves towards the long counter
where the Moores measured out goods and calculated
totals, Megan fell into step with him, a huge smile on
her face. Her eyes sparkled with friendly challenge.
"If it's to be from both of us, that means you'll need to
come with me to give it to her. I'm heading over there
now."

"We can take my wagon," he agreed smoothly, sliding the crate onto the counter so that he could retrieve
the paper from his pocket. "Let me give them Mrs.
Calhoun's list and have them wrap up Sarah's doll, and
then we can go."

"Fine with me."

Ruthanne Moore exclaimed over the doll, chattering
endlessly as she wrapped it in crisp white paper. At long
last, they escaped outside, the humid heat that made it
difficult to breathe preferable to the stuffy confines of
the mercantile and the speculative glances of the pro-
prietress. He stowed their belongings in the back. Ran
a finger beneath his stiff cravat where it stuck to his
damp throat.

"Today seems hotter than usual."

Megan huffed a laugh as he assisted her up onto
the wooden seat. "This is nothing. Wait until July. You

won't want to go outside after eight o'clock in the morning."

He wouldn't be here come July, he wanted to remind her. But that would only chase away her smile, and what was the point in that?

At the turnoff leading to the Livingstons' homestead, the front wagon wheels hit a dip that jostled Megan. Pitching sideways, she very nearly landed in Lucian's lap. Without a moment's hesitation, he put an arm around her. Anchored her to his side.

"You all right?" His warm gaze assessed her, strong hand settling heavily on her waist.

Licking suddenly dry lips, she nodded. He was looking at her as if seeing her for the first time…the same look he'd given her in the mercantile. There'd been a flare of *something* in those shrewd black eyes. Insight maybe? Whatever it had been gave her hope. Was he finally coming to realize she wasn't out to gain possession of his house or anything else that belonged to him?

She would have gladly remained this way for the rest of the afternoon. Tucked in the shelter of his arm, inches away from his firm jaw shadowed by a hint of a beard and his generous mouth, infused her with tingling delight. His nearness was more exciting than any adventure she'd ever read, more thrilling than any romance put down on paper. This was real. *He* was real. Better than any hero her imagination could've constructed.

You mustn't think that way, Megan. It isn't wise. While Lucian was certainly hero material in the minds of New Orleans socialites, he wasn't *her* idea of a hero. Her hero would marry for love instead of duty. Her hero would want children to love and cherish, not simply to carry on a family name. She couldn't afford to forget that.

As the cabin came into view, she pulled away, the heat of his hand lingering long after he'd removed it. Sarah emerged from the darkened doorway dragging a bucket behind her. A black dog trotted beside her, pink tongue lolling. Lucian frowned at the little girl's untidy braid and smudges of dirt on her cheeks.

Sarah stopped and stared. Her mouth formed a little O. "Miss Megan! Mr. Lucian!"

Megan climbed down without bothering to wait for Lucian's assistance. "Hi, Sarah." Bent with her hands perched on her knees, she pasted on a smile for the little girl's benefit. The sight of the two crude grave markers beyond the barn had sucked the joy from the day. "Where's your pa?"

"Fixin' a fence."

Her blue eyes were large in her thin face as she watched Lucian pat the dog's head. Lips pursed, his sharp gaze swept their surroundings. The farm was showing signs of neglect. Weeds threatened to choke out the vegetable plants in the small patch of garden beside the cabin. Dirt streaked the window panes. Without Meredith to help him, it appeared Owen was falling steadily behind.

Megan held out her hand. "Why don't you take us to him so we can let him know we're here?"

Dropping the bucket, Sarah placed her tiny hand in hers. So solemn. Megan wished there was something more she could do to help the devastated family.

"Are you coming, Mr. Lucian?" Sarah held out her other hand.

A startled look, quickly masked, flashed across his face as he took her hand. The trio bypassed the barn and passed through the wide field to where Owen was struggling to do a chore better suited to two men. Shrugging quickly out of his coat and looping it over the fence, Lucian rushed to assist him, grabbing hold of the other end of the heavy post.

Surprised, Owen's puzzled gaze shot between Lucian and Megan. The men had met at story time but hadn't spoken at length. From his reaction, he plainly hadn't expected the smartly dressed gentleman to willingly assist in menial labor.

"You looked as if you could use some help," Lucian grunted by way of greeting. "Just tell me where you want this."

Owen barked instructions. Together, they worked to repair the fence. Nonplussed, Megan stood there and watched. If one were to discount Lucian's green paisley vest, tailored shirt and extravagantly tied cravat, which were more suited to a well-appointed drawing room than an isolated mountain farm, one would have no trouble believing he was accustomed to getting down in the dirt and working with his hands. His back and shoulder muscles rippled beneath the taut cotton; his biceps strained the material. This was no idle aristocrat.

Realizing she was gawking, Megan suggested to Sarah that they return to the cabin so she could bring the food inside out of the direct sun. The one-room dwelling wasn't filthy, exactly, but it needed attention. And, since Lucian was occupied, Megan immediately set to work, sweeping the floors while waiting for the water to heat, which she'd use to clean the work surfaces and stack of dirty dishes in the basin. She settled Sarah at the table with a slice of buttered bread and a glass of milk. The little girl didn't chatter like most five-year-olds. Instead, she sat silently observing Megan, her gaze occasionally lighting on the wrapped package. Megan bit back a smile, anticipating Sarah's reaction to Lucian's gift.

Beneath his aloof demeanor beat a compassionate heart.

By the time the men returned, the kitchen fairly sparkled and not a speck of dirt lingered on the floors. When Owen's gaze settled on Sarah, nestled in Megan's lap with a book, her face scrubbed clean and hair brushed and rebraided, embarrassment, guilt and gratitude marched across his rugged features. The ever-present sorrow lurked in his eyes.

"You didn't have to do this, Megan," he said gruffly.

"I didn't mind."

He worried the hat in his hands. "Appreciate it." Nodded to Lucian, who was standing slightly behind him. "You too, Beaumont. I was about ready to give up when you arrived. Thanks."

Lucian's smile eased the austerity of his features. "I ought to be thanking you. You saved me from yet another tedious day of staring at the walls. I'll be back tomorrow, if you don't mind."

Both men's clothing were dirt-stained, but they'd washed up at the outside well. Their faces and hands were clean, their hair wet and slicked back from their foreheads. Lucian's cravat was now stuffed into his pocket.

Owen's mouth turned down. "I can't afford to pay you."

"I don't want your money." He held up a palm. "Trust me, I'd be doing it as much for myself as for you. I need the distraction."

"I don't know."

Lucian appealed to Megan. "I thought you said this community helps each other out."

"We do." To Owen, she said gently, "You know you'd do the same if the situation were reversed. You should let him help you."

Kneading the back of his neck, he jerked a nod. "Okay. If you change your mind…"

Lucian stuck out his hand. "I won't."

Shaking hands, Owen remarked lazily, "You won't be wearing clothing like that tomorrow, will you? I'd hate to feel responsible for ruining those fancy duds."

Lucian chuckled. "I think I can find something more appropriate to wear."

Megan urged Sarah off her lap and stood up. "Before we go, Lucian and I have something we'd like to give Sarah."

Looking wary, Owen slipped his hands in his pockets as she waved Lucian over to the table and gave him the package. "You give it to her."

"Why don't you?" he whispered, brows raised.

"Are you afraid of a five-year-old girl?" she whispered back.

"Of course not. That's ridiculous." Taking it, he pivoted and, walking slowly to where Sarah stood with wide-eyed anticipation, crouched to her level and held it out. "For you."

Gingerly, her tiny fingers peeled back the paper. Her gasp of wonder made all three adults smile. "A dolly!" Carefully, she touched the blond ringlets and the silky blue dress.

"Look, Papa!" Dashing to his side, she lifted it for him to inspect.

He cleared his throat. Smiled and smoothed a tender hand along his daughter's hair. "She's beautiful. What will you name her?"

Sarah bit her lip, staring intently at her new gift. "Megan."

Pushing to his feet, Lucian arched a brow at Megan. Owen looked surprised. "Well, I suppose that's a fitting name, seeing as how she brought it to you."

"She looks like her."

"Oh. Yes, I suppose she does. What do you say, Sarah?"

Hugging the doll to her chest, she looked at Megan and Lucian. "Thank you."

"You're welcome."

"We should get going." Lucian looked to Megan. "I have that order to pick up for Mrs. Calhoun."

As they made to leave, Sarah rushed over to give them each a hug. Although clearly discomfited, something like affection shone in Lucian's gaze.

Once again perched high on the wagon seat, she gazed at his profile. "That was a nice thing you did back there."

He shrugged. "What about you? From Owen's reaction when we walked through the door, that cabin must've been in dire need of a cleaning."

"Yes, well…I know him. You, on the other hand, are a visitor. Once you leave Gatlinburg, you'll probably never see him again."

He gave her a sideways glance. "So that means what? I should only help people I know?"

"No, of course not." She spread her hands wide. "I just— It was unexpected, is all."

"I was being honest back there. I'll go mad if I don't find something to fill the hours."

He could remedy that if he'd only entrust the house to her and go home. But she didn't say that out loud.

The thought of him leaving, of never seeing him again, troubled her.

"You seemed to know exactly what to do. Have you fixed a fence before?" Doubt rang in her voice.

"More times than I can count. I have the estate, remember?"

"Don't you have hired men to do that?"

"I do. However, I like fixing things. Working with my hands. I never aspired to manage our family's shipping empire. I wanted to be a ship captain, toiling on the open sea, not cooped up in an office all day. Physical labor gives me a sense of accomplishment that signing a contract or reviewing ship inventory lists doesn't."

"Why didn't you become a ship captain?"

"Seasickness. As a teenager, I spent a lot of time down at the docks and on the ships my father owns. My father didn't approve of my wish to captain my own ship, but I was determined. Shortly after my fourteenth birthday, I snuck aboard a ship departing for New York. One long, agonizing day and night later, I realized the futility of my dream. I couldn't move without getting violently ill."

Megan stared at his profile, absorbed in this glimpse into his past. She could imagine him as a young teen, determined and intense even then, coming to grips with the loss of his dreams. "Was your father angry?"

His laugh was harsh. "Angry? He thought the whole thing quite amusing. Said I got my just deserts for defying him."

"So now you oversee things from a distance."

"Yes."

"I'm sorry it didn't work out for you."

He lifted a careless shoulder. "It wasn't meant to be."

"What about when you're in the city? Do you fix things there, too?"

"Oh, no. My father would have a fit of apoplexy. I spend a large part of my free time at my gentleman's club boxing. Or fencing."

Megan could only stare. "Boxing? Isn't that a brutal sport?" No wonder he was in top physical condition.

"It can be. Lucky for me, I've only ever suffered the occasional black eye and busted lip." He ran a finger down the length of his straight nose. "No broken nose. Yet."

His rakish grin transformed his features. Irresistible.

Forcing her gaze straight ahead, Megan retreated into silence. Attempted to make sense of these new revelations. There was certainly more to Lucian Beaumont than she'd given him credit for. And that made it even more difficult not to care for him.

Chapter Nine

Since Megan had insisted on taking a bundle of Owen's and Sarah's clothing to her aunt for mending, Lucian convinced her to let him take her there in his wagon. No point in her toting it across town. She waited patiently while he retrieved the supplies from Clawson's and delivered them to the house. Mrs. Calhoun came outside and invited her in for a slice of pie, but as it was nearing supper time, she declined. Having encountered the sweet aroma permeating the kitchen, Lucian promised he'd eat a slice upon his return. All that hard work had stirred his appetite.

His clothes might be dirty and his body weary, but he felt terrific. The best since his arrival, actually. This was a good kind of tired. Plus, he'd come away knowing he'd helped a man in need. Recalling Sarah's reaction to the doll, his chest squeezed. Maybe because of her resemblance to Megan or maybe because—like him—she'd recently lost her mother, the little girl had somehow wormed her way into his heart. He hoped the gift would bring her a measure of happiness.

Megan sat quietly as he guided the team along the

shaded lane. It was cooler here, the profuse, overhead canopy a barrier against the sun. They'd crossed the wooden bridge spanning the Little Pigeon River a quarter of a mile back, so they'd be coming upon the turnoff to Sam and Mary O'Malley's place shortly. He'd passed it before on his way to Megan's. Apparently the two properties were adjoining but Sam and Mary's cabin was situated closer to town.

"There it is." She pointed to a break in the trees.

The first thing Lucian noticed when they emerged into the clearing was the picturesque view, quaint cabins and outbuildings nestled in a verdant valley and framed by sprawling mountains. The main cabin was a two-story structure with a porch running its length and a massive stone chimney scaling one end wall. Blue-and-white gingham curtains hung in the sparkling windows. On the opposite side of the clearing, tucked beneath the trees, sat a one-room dwelling also with a porch. A large barn dominated the space between the two structures, along with a corncrib, chicken house and smokehouse. Neat rows of vegetables comprised a good-sized garden.

"Who lives there?" He indicated the small cabin.

"Nathan. Josh built it for himself and his intended bride—Kate's sister, Francesca. When Kate arrived in her stead, Josh moved back in with his parents so that she could have the cabin. When they got engaged, Josh decided to build a larger one. He doesn't like to admit to being sentimental, but I think he did it to spare Kate's feelings. He wouldn't want to live with her in a home originally intended for himself and her sister," she said with a knowing grin. "Their home is located behind my aunt and uncle's house, beyond the apple orchard."

"Wait." He was having trouble reconciling this revelation with the obviously head-over-heels-in-love couple he met the other day. "Josh was supposed to marry Kate's *sister?*"

Her expression took on a dreamy quality. "Yep. It's a rather complicated story. Here's the short version—Francesca married another man and Kate came here to deliver the news. Josh eventually came to realize that Kate had all the qualities he'd been searching for in a wife, and they fell in love."

"Just like that, huh?"

She rolled her eyes. "I told you, it's complicated. Theirs was not an easy road to happiness."

"I'm sure you enjoyed observing it firsthand."

"It wasn't as enjoyable as you might think," she remarked, swaying in the seat as he guided the team to a stop beside the porch. "There were times I questioned if they would end up together. It was all quite stressful, let me tell you." Squinting, she jerked her chin. "Look, there's Nathan."

As usual, she didn't wait for him to assist her down. As his boots touched the ground, he reminded himself she wasn't the helpless type. Nor was she the type to manipulate the situation to her advantage, pretending to be helpless so that he'd be forced to help her at every turn.

The tall, dark-headed young man striding across the yard resembled Josh in height and build. Similar facial features, too. Only this man was clean-shaven, unlike Josh, who sported a mustache and goatee, and his eyes were an odd silver instead of blue. He smiled broadly at Megan, yet his eyes were assessing when his gaze met Lucian's.

"Nathan, this is Charles's grandson, Lucian Beaumont. Lucian, Nathan is the middle son. Don't let his quiet nature fool you. He's as stubborn as the rest of us." She elbowed her cousin in the ribs.

His response was to tuck her against his side. He stuck out his free hand. "Nice to meet you."

The two men shook. "Ma's got supper on the table. Why don't you join us?"

The way Nathan said it made it sound almost like a challenge.

"I wouldn't want to intrude. Besides, I'm not exactly dressed for dinner." He indicated his wrinkled shirt and grass-stained pants. He wasn't even wearing a cravat, for goodness' sake. And who knew what his hair looked like. As usual, it was hanging in his eyes.

Megan laughed. "Trust me, you'll fit in. You don't look any different than Nathan here. Uncle Sam, too, I'm sure."

"She's right," Nathan agreed.

While Megan was looking at him expectantly, her cousin retained his watchful air. Did Nathan regard all strangers with a dose of suspicion, or was Lucian's association with Megan the cause? She'd mentioned the O'Malley cousins had grown up together and were practically like brothers and sisters. Lucian wouldn't blame the man for being protective.

He had two choices. Eat with the O'Malleys and spend a little more time in Megan's presence. Or eat at the house. Alone.

"All right, then, I accept."

Reaching in the wagon bed, he retrieved the sack of clothes and followed them inside.

The cabin was roomier than Megan's. On their right was a wide staircase made up of smooth, white pine boards, same as the floorboards. An oversize stone fireplace dominated the living area, family portraits lining the mantel. Kate's work, perhaps?

Tossing her bonnet on the side table, Megan motioned for him to follow her. Windows lined the dining area, providing a sweeping view of the front lawn. The succulent smells emanating from the kitchen filled his nostrils. His stomach rumbled. Lunch seemed ages ago.

Megan introduced him to Mary O'Malley, who welcomed him like a long-lost relative. The type of lady who immediately put a person at ease. Sam, Josh and Kate entered through the kitchen door just as he and Megan were handed platters to carry to the dining table. Like his wife, Sam was friendly, with a bespectacled gaze that seemed to miss nothing.

Lucian didn't have a chance to feel self-conscious. The lively bunch swept him along to the table, seating him beside Megan and around the corner from Sam. Mary and Nathan sat opposite. Josh occupied the opposite end from his father, with Kate on Megan's other side.

"Is Caleb joining us tonight?" Kate asked, indicating the one empty chair.

"I don't think so," Sam said in a subdued voice. Mary's mouth pinched with worry.

Megan placed a hand on Lucian's sleeve and leaned in close, her shoulder bumping his. "Caleb is the youngest brother. You'll meet him later. I hope."

He nodded, wondering what she meant. What Caleb's absence meant. Family trouble?

As soon as the blessing had been said, conversation surged as platters passed around the table. Chicken and dumplings. Pickled beets. Green beans. Fried potato cakes. The food melted in his mouth. He could quickly grow accustomed to this.

He liked Megan's family. Like Josh, Sam was well-spoken and intelligent. A solid, practical man. Humble, too. A quality Lucian didn't encounter often in his world. Nathan didn't offer much to the conversation, but when he did, there was quiet wisdom laced with humor. Lucian intercepted his probing gaze more than once. What did he see between himself and Megan that bothered him? Lucian had made a conscious effort not to touch her. Or lean too close. Or whisper in her ear.

When the women began to clear the table, Nathan offered to show him around. Lucian accepted. He was interested in seeing the farm. Curious, too, if the other man would confront him with whatever was bothering him. A half an hour later, he had his answer.

Lounging against a barn stall, Nathan tossed a hay sliver to the ground and turned his enigmatic silver gaze on Lucian. "There's something you should know. Megan is family, and I make it my business to watch out for family. I've noticed the way she looks at you." His gaze narrowed. "And the way you look at her. Seems to me you're more than friends, which doesn't make a whole lot of sense seeing as how you're not sticking around here."

Lucian didn't speak for a moment. Exactly *how* did Megan look at him? *Focus, Beaumont.* "You're right— we are friends. But that's the extent of our relationship." He could not allow it to develop further. "I like your cousin. I respect her. The last thing I'd want to do is cause her harm."

Nathan pushed upright, crossed his arms. Set his jaw. "You *like* her? Correct me if I'm wrong, but I was under the impression that you suspected her of selfish motives where Charles and that house are concerned. Accused her of things she's incapable of doing."

"I can't deny that I misjudged her." He held Nathan's gaze. "I was wrong."

"Have you told her that?"

"No, not yet." He sighed and lowered his gaze to his boots. She deserved an apology. "But that's something I plan to remedy."

Nathan considered that a long moment. Relaxing his stance, he jerked a nod. "Good. Oh, and Beaumont?"

"Yes?"

"Megan is a one-of-a-kind girl. Folks around here wouldn't look too kindly if you were to hurt her in any way."

"I understand."

No use telling Nathan his warning wasn't necessary. Any punishment the townspeople might mete out wouldn't compare to Lucian's own guilt and self-recrimination were he to cause her pain.

Megan was ensconced in the rocking chair, exhausted from the day's chores and enjoying a moment's rest when Lucian and Nathan emerged from the barn. Keeping the chair in motion with the toe of her boot, she observed the two men as they headed her direction. They weren't speaking, and the waning light made it impossible to read their expressions. She'd noticed the looks Nathan had sent Lucian, looks that troubled her. Sometimes Nathan took his role as protector a bit too seriously.

Her gaze naturally strayed to Lucian. Slightly taller than her cousin, Lucian's posture, the way he carried himself, commanded respect. Restrained strength combined with rakish good looks equaled devastating appeal. He was so incredibly handsome. And far, far out of her reach.

Climbing the porch steps, Nathan asked, "Where is everybody?"

Megan stood and smoothed her water-stained skirt. There was nothing she could do about the dirt clinging to her hem. "Josh and Kate went home, your ma is already mending Owen's and Sarah's clothing and Uncle Sam is reading his Bible."

Lucian paused on the top step, one hand resting on the handrail. "I'll give you a ride home, if you'd like."

"Thanks." She gave Nathan a hug. "Good night."

"Take care."

Lucian was quiet during the short ride to her place. When he halted the team, his warm fingertips grazed her knuckles. "Allow me to help you down."

Puzzled, Megan waited as he came around to her side and lifted his hands. Setting her hands on his shoulders, he gripped her waist and swung her down. His fingers tightened when she would've pulled away. Pulse jumping, she searched his features, barely visible in the low light cast by the kerosene lamp.

"Lucian?"

"Please, I have something to say." His voice was gruff, apologetic, as his hands dropped to his sides. He didn't move to put space between them, however. His heat and closeness were reassuring. "When I first arrived in town, I accused you of a lot of things, none of them good, and now that I've gotten to know you…well, I realize you aren't the type of person who would take advantage of an old man. Or anyone else, for that matter. I know what a conniving, manipulative woman is like and, frankly, you're not it. I'm sorry, Megan. Will you forgive me for my utterly absurd error in judgment?"

Megan couldn't think to respond. He was apologizing? Admitting he'd been wrong about her?

"Aren't you going to say something?" he said at last.

"I, uh, wasn't expecting this. Of course I forgive you."

"I mean it. I shouldn't have rushed to judgment like that."

"I made assumptions of my own, remember? It happens. But I'm glad we're past all that now."

"Me, too." He sounded as relieved as she felt. Glancing at the cabin, he said, "I should get going. It's been a long day. I have a feeling I'm going to fall asleep the second my head hits the pillow."

When he made to move past her, she snagged his hand. "That comment about manipulative women… what did you mean by that?"

"Only what I said. You have a good heart. Nathan was right," he responded as he squeezed her hand. "You're a one-of-a-kind."

"Whoa. You and Nathan talked about me?" She wiggled her hand free. "Did he put you up to this?" If the apology wasn't his idea, it meant nothing.

"I didn't need Nathan or anyone else pointing out what I had already figured out myself," he said with a hint of asperity. "Yes, your name came up in the course of conversation. He cares about you, you know."

"I know." Still…

"That apology was mine alone. My thoughts, my words." His tone brooked no argument. And honestly, was he really the type of man who'd do something purely because someone else suggested it?

"All right. I believe you."

With a speaking look, he circled around the horses and climbed up onto the seat. *"Bonne nuit, mon chou."*

"Bonne nuit."

A tentative happiness settled in around her heart.

Lucian's trust in her was responsible for that. Only his mention of manipulative women hampered it. Why had he refused to offer an explanation? She wasn't naive. A man like him wouldn't lack for female attention. So who had tried to hurt him? And why did she suddenly want to strangle the unknown perpetrators?

Chapter Ten

"I'm off for the day." Mrs. Calhoun poked her head in the study door late Thursday. "Your supper is warming on the stove. Don't leave it there too long," she said with a smile, "else the potatoes will get soggy and the creamed corn will cease being creamy."

Lucian turned from the window. "I'll remember. Thank you."

"Is there anything else you need before I leave?"

"Actually, I was wondering if you could answer a few questions for me." These past few days with Owen and Sarah had kept his own family in the forefront of his mind.

Her wrinkles became more pronounced. "I'll do my best."

Coming around the desk, he leaned his weight against the edge so as not to tower over her. Embarrassed to be involving her in private family matters, but determined to find answers, he forged ahead. "Did my grandfather ever mention wanting my mother and I to come and visit?"

Resting a hand on the back of a chair for support,

Mrs. Calhoun regarded him with regret-filled eyes. The subject obviously troubled her. "After your mother left, Charles became a different man. He spent much of his time closeted in here or in the library, preferring to be alone. I'm sorry, I wish I could help you, but he didn't speak with me or Fred about what happened. We wanted to help. And although we made it clear we were available if he needed a listening ear or a shoulder to cry on, he chose not to come to us."

Disappointment gripped him. "He apparently didn't have a problem opening up to Megan."

Her face smoothed, brightened. "Her friendship brought a bit of joy back into his life. I'll always be grateful."

"You didn't think it strange?" he felt compelled to ask. "A young woman spending time with an elderly man when she could be out doing a hundred other more exciting things?"

"Megan is a helper by nature, a nurturer. The type of girl that, when she sees someone in need, drops what she's doing and rushes to their aid. In Charles, she saw a hurting, lonely old man."

"So she befriended him."

"Yes."

Lost in thought, he trod back to the window and leaned against the frame.

Perhaps he *should* leave the house in her hands. Even if he did find a way around the stipulation and put it up for sale, who knew how long it would take for a buyer to materialize? He could be tied to this place indefinitely. A shiver of alarm worked its way up his spine. No, he couldn't have that.

"Mr. Lucian?"

He jerked around, having forgotten the other woman's presence.

"You seem to be a fine man. I'm certain Charles would've been proud." A warning worked its way into her eyes. "But you'll be returning to New Orleans soon, and I'd hate to see Megan hurt. She's a very special young lady. The townsfolk wouldn't look kindly on anyone who took advantage of her kindness."

Lucian stared. She thought he was like his father? Capable of sweeping an innocent girl off her feet and wresting her from the only home she'd ever known, only to revile her the rest of her days? Once settled into married life, Gerard had come to resent Lucinda's lack of social connections, of town polish and upper-class education.

He spoke stiffly. "You have no need to worry on that score, *madame*. I have no intention of engaging in a passing indulgence and absolutely no designs on Megan O'Malley."

Oh, didn't he? Hadn't he nearly kissed her twice already? Did he not think of her practically every moment?

Shoving the hair off his forehead, he softened his stance. "Your concern is understandable. The last thing I want to do is cause problems for her."

Lips pursed, she studied him, gave a brisk nod. "Well, now that I've said my piece, I'd better get home. Fred will be wanting his supper."

Preoccupied, he bade her good evening. Before he could change his mind, he sat down at the desk and, locating a sheet of blank paper, began to write. His lawyer probably wouldn't understand his instruction to cease and desist, but it made all the sense in the world to him. Leaving Megan in charge meant he could go home and put this unhappy chapter behind him. His mother and grandfather were gone, their secrets buried with them.

What's done was done.

Running again? an accusing voice prompted. *When are you going to face your problems head-on? The grief will follow you wherever you go, you know. You can't avoid it forever.*

"There are no answers here," he grumbled aloud. No way to discover if his mother had, in fact, deceived him. And, coward that he was, wasn't he glad of that? Relieved?

No, this was the best way for all involved. The house would stay in the family, which meant the next Beaumont generation could come and visit one day. Learn about their ancestors. Perhaps even take up residence here.

Lucian would not return. But he'd never forget this place…or Megan.

By the time Friday afternoon rolled around, Lucian was certain he'd made the right decision. Owen had told him not to come today because he had errands to tend to, so he'd meandered aimlessly about the house. All this free time was making him antsy. And fanciful. He'd caught himself entertaining thoughts of Megan, wondering what it might be like if she were mistress of this house, picturing the two of them together sharing breakfast in the garden or playing a game of chess in the parlor. Holding hands in the moonlight, stealing kisses beneath the stars…

The doorbell rang. He blinked, threaded fingers through his hair. He really needed to get back to New Orleans. Perhaps even begin his search for a wife. There were a number of young ladies who'd made their eagerness to fill the position clear and who'd meet his qualifications perfectly. They wouldn't marry him expecting anything other than financial security and his good name. Easy enough expectations to meet.

Steeling himself to face Megan, to resist the pull she had on him, he left the study and made his way to the front of the house. Wall sconces threw soft light against the floral papered walls. His boots striking the hardwood echoed throughout the cavernous Victorian. Lucian couldn't wait to see her reaction when she learned he was giving her charge of it.

But when he swung open the door, it wasn't her waiting on the porch. A silver-haired man dressed in an inexpensive brown sack suit and a woman whose jet-black hair belied her age stood smiling at him.

"Mr. Beaumont?" The man, who topped Lucian by about three inches, stuck out his hand. "I'm Reverend Monroe and this is my wife, Carol."

"How do you do?" His nod encompassed them both. Spying the cake in her hands, he stepped back. "Would you like to come in?"

In the entry hall, Mrs. Monroe lifted the plate. "Would you mind if I take this to the kitchen? I know the way."

"Certainly. *Merci beaucoup.*"

The reverend accompanied him into the parlor. Lucian offered him a seat, but he declined, regarding him with wise eyes that seemed to have the ability to pierce a man's facade. Lucian forced himself to meet the man's gaze without flinching.

"I'd intended to come much earlier to welcome you to town, but Carol's sister and her family have been visiting. How are you settling in?"

"The truth is I'm not here for much longer. This was to be a short business trip. Due to unforeseen circumstances, I've stayed longer than I'd originally planned. But I'll be leaving next week." He pursed his lips together. Why was he blathering on like this? He had nothing to hide.

Except, this was a man of God. Could he somehow sense Lucian had fallen away? That he hadn't darkened the door of a church in more than a year? And that he kept his mother's Bible close but never opened it?

The reverend's expression revealed sincere regret. "I'm sorry to hear that. I was looking forward to getting acquainted. Your grandfather was a faithful member of our congregation. A fixture on the front row in all my years of preaching in this town. Every Sunday on his way out the door, he'd shake my hand and tell me he was praying for me."

Emotion clogged his throat. Hearing that his grandfather was a praying man made the emptiness inside yawn wider, a cavern that refused to be filled. A yearning for something he couldn't pin down.

Mrs. Monroe joined them then, saving him from having to reply. "I left your cake with Mrs. Calhoun. The children will be arriving soon for story time, won't they?" She nudged her husband. "We should get going."

"I'd actually like to stay."

At his unspoken question, Lucian said, "Please do. A few of the parents stick around and help serve the refreshments."

Mrs. Monroe beamed her approval. "I think it's wonderful how you've allowed the town to continue using this place. You're a generous man, Mr. Beaumont."

If they only knew… He realized suddenly that Megan could've easily spread the word of his original intentions, turning the tide of the town's opinion against him. It would've been a strategic move, a way of putting pressure on him. But she hadn't done it. Further proof of her selflessness, her kind and humble spirit.

He glanced at the mantel clock. She was late, which wasn't like her. Had something happened? Was she ill? Crossing to the window, relief spread through him at the sight of her coming up the lane. He squinted. What on earth was she wearing?

Anticipation she shouldn't be feeling danced along her nerve endings, hammered her heart against her rib cage and lengthened her stride. In the past few days, she'd thought of little else besides Lucian and the many reasons she mustn't care for him. Since she was a daydreamer by nature, often preoccupied with her thoughts, her sisters hadn't noticed anything out of the ordinary.

Her life was good—like a rich chocolate cake. Plain. Unexceptional. But good. Lucian's presence in her life was like sweet, decadent icing on that cake. His presence added depth and excitement and meaning. Paired together, the two created a delicious concoction.

Well, you'd better get used to cake without icing, because Lucian isn't sticking around. He has a life to get back to. A perfect, beautiful, spoiled young debutant to choose.

That put a damper on her anticipation.

Climbing the steps, a scowl twisted her mouth. She really was a foolish, naive girl. Her wayward heart had actually entertained the notion that he could come to care for her. *Her.* A simple mountain girl who would stick out like a sore thumb in his glittering world. She didn't know the waltz. Or which fork to use. When she laughed, it wasn't a polite twitter but a full laugh that would no doubt shock polite society.

Josh was right. She read too much. This was real life, not fiction.

The door opened before she could press the bell. Instead of admitting her, Lucian crossed the threshold and pulled the door closed behind him.

The humor warming his black eyes to melted chocolate robbed her lungs of breath. He was always so serious and somber that this unexpected lightheartedness made him seem like an entirely different man.

Folding his arms across his strong chest, straining the shoulders of his gray, pin-striped coat, he looked her up and down. "Who are you supposed to be? Or should I say what are you?"

She smoothed the furry pelt covering her hair, the one Nicole had fashioned into a sort of headdress for her. It was hot and itchy and tended to pitch forward into her eyes, but the kids would love it. "Tonight's story is *Little Red Riding Hood.* Can't you guess who I am?"

Eyes twinkling now, his head fell back and he laughed, a rumbling, husky sound that tickled her ears. The unrestrained curve of his generous lips, the flash of white teeth, the glimpse of happiness in his otherwise stern face, evoked an intense yearning deep within her. A yearning to see this man happy more often. To see his smile. To hear his laughter.

Oh, wow, she was in way too deep. She couldn't start caring about his happiness!

"Ah, *mon chou,* you are something else." Grinning, he shook his head. "I've never met anyone quite like you."

She didn't have a response to that. So she simply gazed at him, soaking in this new Lucian to remember later, after he'd gone. Gradually, the humor faded and was replaced with his customary intensity. Her disappointment was sharp.

"I need to talk to you about something." His gaze shifted past her shoulder to the lane. "Ollie and a few others are here. Later, all right?"

"Yes, okay."

What could he possibly want to talk about? Her stomach dipped. What if he'd heard from his lawyer? What if he'd found a way to circumvent Charles's wishes?

Her nerves were stretched taut throughout the evening. She rushed through the story and afterward had trouble making small talk with the parents. Distracted, that's what she was. Just when she thought they'd bidden good-night to the last of the guests, Tom showed up. She hadn't seen him since the previous Friday night, the night of their confrontation. As impatient as she was to learn Lucian's purpose, she couldn't bring herself to dash the cautious optimism on her good friend's face.

Tom may not be cake icing, but he meant a lot to her. *He* wasn't going anywhere.

Asking him to wait in the entryway while she gathered her things, she hurried to the parlor where Lucian was finishing the cleanup.

Picking up her reticule from the settee, she slipped her hand through the ribbon loop. "I'm sorry. Our conversation will have to wait. Tom's waiting to walk me home."

An empty pitcher in his hands, his gaze shot to the door and back. He didn't look pleased. "Do you have free time tomorrow?"

"Once I finish my morning chores. Do you want me to come here?"

He considered the matter for a moment. "Would you mind showing me some more of the area? I can ask Mrs.

Calhoun to prepare a picnic lunch. My horse is in need of exercise," he tacked on.

An entire day with Lucian all to herself? The prospect eclipsed any dread of what he might tell her.

A smile bloomed across her face. "I'd like that."

"Magnifique." His answering smile, slow and easy, heated her inside and out. She would never, ever take that smile for granted. "Shall I meet you at your place, say, around ten o'clock?" he asked.

"I'll see you then." *Please let this night pass quickly!*

When he waved away her offer to help with the chairs, she rejoined Tom, ignoring the questions in his eyes. On the walk home, they talked of inane things— his customers, his ailing mother, Megan's impatience for news from Cades Cove. Nothing too personal, thank goodness. True to his word, Tom didn't press her or even mention their earlier conversation. But it was there nonetheless…a strange tension between them that hadn't been there before. One day soon, she was going to have to muster her courage and admit she wasn't interested in pursuing a romance with him.

Please, Lord, grant me wisdom and courage. Prepare his heart to hear what I have to say. I hate to think of what this will do to our friendship, but the longer I remain silent the harder it will be on the both of us.

She couldn't do it tonight. Not with her blood still humming from the effects of Lucian's smile. Her body singing with excitement in expectation of their outing. Her words would tumble out a tangled mess, and she'd end up hurting him more than was necessary. Better to wait, to prepare. Frame her thoughts in the best way possible.

When he invited her to go fishing with him the following morning, she declined without telling him of her plans. Trying to cover his disappointment, he smiled and bade her good-night, waiting until she was safely inside the cabin before he left.

That night, she dreamed that Lucian, herself and Tom were seated around their dining table, a humongous chocolate cake in the middle. It all started out normally. They each ate their slice of cake while engaging in polite conversation. The next thing she knew, they were fighting over what was left of it, a fight that quickly turned into a full-fledged tug-of-war!

She awoke just as Tom smashed a gob of cake into Lucian's face.

What a strange, unsettling dream. One thing was certain—she would never look at chocolate cake the same way again.

"C'est magnifique." Sitting astride his most trusted and favored mount, Lucian rested his hands on his thighs, enjoying the view while waiting for Megan's Mr. Knightley to crest the hill. To their left, rounded peaks dense with trees reached for the blue sky, the undulating ridges stretching into the distance. On their right, the fertile valley dotted with cabins and other structures lay far below, a verdant oasis sheltered by the mountains.

Pulling astride, Megan patted her horse's neck and smiled over at him. She wore a sturdy, navy blue riding dress that made her eyes seem that much bluer and a stiff-brimmed bonnet in the same hue that hid her curls. He did not care for that bonnet, he decided.

"Your father is French, right? Is he the one who taught you to speak the language?"

"No, but it was important to him that I learn to speak it fluently, so he hired a native French tutor for me.

Now my father and I converse strictly in French." His mother had attempted to learn but couldn't quite master it. He knew she'd felt left out whenever he and his father spoke together.

"That's why you slip so easily into it."

"*Oui, mon chou,* that's why."

A becoming pink stole along her cheekbones. "It's a beautiful language. I could sit and listen to you speak it for hours, even though I wouldn't have a clue what you were saying."

Pleasure spread through him at the revealing statement. "Is that so?"

Her blush deepened, spreading to her slender throat, and she turned her head, the bonnet's brim shielding her. He forced his gaze to the impressive scenery. This was to be their final day together. After lunch, he would tell her of his decision and his plans to leave in two days' time. The pleasure he'd experienced seconds ago twisted into something painful, and he realized with some shock that he'd grown attached to this young woman.

Better a quick break now than a slow, tortuous parting later.

He would enjoy this one day with her. Tuck the memory away for safekeeping.

"You didn't tell me what your horse's name was," she ventured, taking in his mount's sleek, muscled frame.

"D'Artagnan." He waited to see if she recognized Alexandre Dumas's character.

"*The Three Musketeers* is a favorite of yours?"

He smiled, not surprised she had. "I've lost count how many times I've read it. I could probably even quote parts of it."

Guiding their horses away from the main trail and into the woods, they discussed books they liked and ones they didn't. It was a lively, stimulating conversation, one he couldn't imagine having with any debutant in his circle. Megan's intelligence and observations impressed him.

"Why don't you try your hand reading to the children sometime? I'm certain they'd enjoy a change of pace—having a man read to them."

"I can't do that, Megan. I—" He stopped at the sight of her frown. "What is it?"

Pointing ahead, she said unhappily, "The meadow I wanted to take you to is beyond that stream, but it's too swollen to cross. I'd hoped to have our picnic there."

As they neared, Lucian gauged the width and depth. "It doesn't appear to be that deep. Our horses won't have a problem crossing."

Her gloved fingers gripped the reins. "It's the swiftness of the current that has me worried. I wouldn't mind walking across on those larger rocks, but on the back of a horse…" She shuddered. "I've seen too many men swept downstream when their horses lost their footing." Twisting in the saddle to study the land behind them, she said, "We can have our lunch here somewhere, and hopefully go to the meadow another day when the water level's lower."

But there wouldn't be another chance. Dismounting, he walked around to her side and held out his hand. "Don't worry, *mon petite,* I will get you to your meadow."

"I don't know—"

"Trust me."

With a quizzical smile, she placed her hand in his and allowed him to help her down.

"Wait here."

Vaulting into Mr. Knightley's saddle, he leaned down

and, gathering D'Artagnan's reins, guided them both across the stream. As he'd suspected, it wasn't deep. They made it to the other side without a single misstep.

Megan waited for him on the opposite bank, white teeth worrying her bottom lip. Standing in a patch of buttery sunlight, she was a vision in blue, a burst of color amid the vast green landscape. He wished then for a camera or a canvas and paints, any way to capture this image to keep for all time.

Splashing through the cool water to reach her, he lifted her into his arms without a word of warning.

"Lucian!" she exclaimed, fingers clutching at his coat lapels. "What are you doing?"

"What does it look like I'm doing?" He grinned, re-entering the water. "Hold on tight."

Encircling his neck, she pressed into his chest. Hid her face in the hollow between his neck and shoulder. "Please don't drop me."

He tightened his hold about her waist, delighting in her soft, warm weight. Her delicate scent. "I'll do my best."

Her response was to snuggle closer. Up on the bank, water sluicing from his boots, he was loath to put her down. But he did, slowly lowering her, steadying her. The undisguised yearning in her wide blue eyes did him in.

"This bonnet has to go." The unsteadiness in his voice took him by surprise.

Her brow puckered. "I realize it isn't fashionable or new, but it's durable."

"It wouldn't matter if it was fresh from the store or twenty years old, I still wouldn't like it."

Tugging on the bow beneath her chin, he undid the loops. When no words of protest followed her audible breath, he carefully lifted it from her head, stepping away only long enough to hook it on the saddle horn. Her white-blond mane shimmered in the sun's rays. Still not satisfied, he reached around and untied the blue ribbon at her nape. Curls cascaded down past her shoulders.

"Much better," he murmured.

Their gazes locked, she didn't move or speak, but her wishes were written there for him to see. Cradling her face, he skimmed a thumb across her mouth. "Has anyone ever told you that your lips are the color of ripe peaches?"

"A-actually no," she whispered, her hands coming up to grip his forearms. "You're the first."

"They haunt my dreams," he ground out, dipping his head and capturing them with his own. He slid his fingers into her glorious hair, cool, liquid silk whispering across his skin.

Ah, yes, she was as sweet as he'd imagined. So much so that his chest ached with the knowledge that she would never be his. A whirlpool of need, accompanied by emotion he couldn't identify, spiraled through him, and he deepened the kiss. Megan's arms looped around his waist to hug him close. Her mouth was soft and inviting, clinging with a tenderness that made him want to weep.

Chapter Eleven

In the haven of Lucian's arms, Megan felt protected. Cherished. And blissfully happy. Knowing it couldn't last, she savored every second, memorizing the feel of his broad chest, the leashed strength in his powerful arms, the delightful sensation of his fingers threading through her hair. His kiss was warm, insistent yet tender.

She'd been right about the effects. Already she was picturing herself in a beaded gown and flowers in her hair, pledging herself to this man. She was mentally sliding the ring on his finger when he literally jerked away as if burned.

Startled, she gripped the sides of his coat to stop his retreat. "Lucian?"

His hands resting heavily on her shoulders, he struggled to regain his composure. There was a vulnerability in his dark eyes that hadn't been there before. Regret pulled his mouth into a grimace. "I'm leaving Monday morning."

It took a moment for his words to sink in. "What? Why?"

"I'm leaving the house in your care. You may do with it what you wish, except sell it. I prefer for it to remain in my family."

When his hands fell away, she relinquished her hold. He moved downstream, leaving her to process the news. Denial ripped through her. She'd known this day would come, of course—she just hadn't expected it so soon.

"What about the lawyer?"

Head bent, his dark layers slid forward and concealed his eyes. Near his jawline, a muscle twitched. "I've written him to call off his search. It's clear you cared a great deal for my grandfather, and I have faith you'll take care of the house just as you've done in the months since his death."

Speechless, she scuffed the grass with her boot. The elation she should be feeling didn't come. Wasn't this what she wanted? Hadn't she prayed that he'd change his mind and let her use the house?

"I shouldn't have kissed you. Not when I have no plans to court you."

His blunt words chilled her to the bone, his cool reserve chasing away the warm and fuzzy feelings of a moment ago. Hugging her arms about her waist, she looked away. Couldn't risk him seeing how much this hurt.

"Look, I don't want this to ruin our last day together. I've enjoyed spending time with you, Megan." His voice deepened as he spoke. "I'd like to carry good memories back home with me."

Tomorrow he'd be preparing for his trip while she was attending church and having lunch with her family. They'd both be too busy to do much more than say goodbye. After tomorrow, she would likely never see Lucian again. Sadness leached the color from her surroundings, muting the grass and rushing water and sky above. Even the birds' songs seemed to take on a hollow, mournful quality.

"If you'd rather return home," he continued into the lingering silence, "I'll accompany you. No hard feelings."

"I suppose we shouldn't let all that food go to waste." She waved a hand towards D'Artagnan's bulging saddlebags. "Not after all the trouble Mrs. Calhoun went to. And then there's the matter of your boots. You would've ruined them for nothing."

Water streaks marred the mirrorlike surfaces and bits of mud clung to the heels. She knew how their condition must irk him.

"You didn't ask me to carry you across. I did that all on my own." He shrugged. "It's nothing a little spit and polish won't fix."

"All right, then." Snatching her bonnet, she crossed to her horse and thrust her boot in the stirrup. "We have another quarter of a mile to go."

They rode the rest of the way in silence, giving her time to regain her composure, to marshal her emotions. Time enough to deal with them later. Like Lucian, she wanted things to be peaceful between them. If memories were all she would have, she wanted them to be good ones.

A break in the trees, a wide swath of sunlight streaming through the overhead canopy shone down on her favorite meadow. A thick carpet of grass intermingled with purple-and-blue wildflowers. Butterflies flitted above blooms. She soaked in the sight, remembered all the fond memories associated with this spot.

"How did you find this place?" Lucian unlatched the saddlebag containing their lunch.

Taking the quilt he held out to her, her gaze tracked the massive tree trunks up to their leafy branches far above. "My father and I discovered it long ago on one of our bird-watching hikes. We came here often. Sometimes Juliana would tag along, but for the most part, it was just he and I. He'd sit and play his harmonica while I read or made friends with the butterflies."

He straightened, a square, lidded basket in his arms. "Where is your father?"

"He passed away when I was young. Heart attack." Even after all these years, she still missed him. "Sometimes a man will walk past me on the street, and I'll get a whiff of the cologne Father used to wear. In that moment, the grief resurfaces and I long to tuck my hand in his again. See his smile once more. He had a great, booming laugh that shook the walls."

Lucian winced. Too late, she understood the wounds her words were likely to inflict on someone whose loss was still fresh.

He wore a grim expression. "Does it ever get easier?"

"Time helps. And lots of prayer." Making her way through the grass, she chose a good spot and, shaking out the quilt, bent to smooth it. He set the basket aside to assist her. "My father's passing was unexpected. One minute he was sitting on the porch, rocking and playing his harmonica, and the next he was gone. We didn't even have a chance to say goodbye. The shock would've devastated us were it not for God's comforting hand. 'Blessed are those who mourn, for they will be comforted.'"

The quilt smoothed, Lucian settled the basket in the middle and waited for her to sit before lowering himself to the ground. Long legs stretched out so that his boots rested on the grass, he watched silently as she unpacked first the dishes and silverware, then the jar of tea and the food.

"I haven't found any measure of comfort in my mother's death."

Megan's hands stilled. His bitter grief hung in the air between them. Beneath the black coat that molded to his athletic build like a second skin, his back and shoulders were rigid. Anguish swirled in his eyes like an out-of-control tempest.

"You haven't allowed yourself to grieve, have you?"

"I'm not sure I know how. I have to be honest—I'm… angry at God for taking her. She was too young. And vibrant. If He cared about me like you say He does, then how could He take away my one true friend?"

"Oh, Lucian, I can't answer that." Heart heavy for his loss and his loneliness, she covered his hand with her own. "No one can fathom God's intentions or reasons. Why did my father have to die when he did? Why are precious babies taken from their mothers before they even have a chance to live? No one travels through life untouched by heartache, but God is there to help us. He promises to never leave us."

Flipping his hand beneath hers, he threaded his fingers through hers. "I carry her Bible with me everywhere I go. When I'm out riding, it's in the saddlebags. When I'm at home, it's on my bedside table. She cherished that Bible. Keeping it nearby helps me feel close to her."

"But you don't read it, do you?" When he shook his head, she suggested, "Maybe it's time you started. We keep Father's on the living room mantel so that we all have access to it. He wrote sermon notes in the margins and underlined important passages. It's a glimpse into what he was thinking, the things the Lord was teaching him. Perhaps Lucinda did the same."

His gaze flicked to his horse, standing in the shade with Mr. Knightley and nibbling on grass. "Perhaps you're right."

Disengaging her hand before she did something foolish, like pulling him into a hug, Megan focused on dishing out the fried chicken and potato salad. Lucian poured tea into the glasses.

"You know, I hadn't intended for this outing to become so somber. You're probably wishing you'd stayed home."

She handed him a filled plate and cloth napkin. "On the contrary. I'd much rather speak plainly than ignore the deeper issues. What would be the point in that?"

Funny. She hadn't felt that way the night before. With Tom, she craved the exact opposite. Had been relieved to speak of nothing of import, to avoid the one subject they needed to address.

Accustomed to giving thanks before meals, Megan said a silent prayer before picking up her fork. She wasn't as hungry as she should've been. In a hurry to finish her morning chores, she'd settled for a single biscuit slathered with blackberry jam.

When they'd eaten their fill and cleared away the dishes, Lucian asked if she'd mind reading to him. A little self-consciously, she agreed. He lay back, tanned hands folded on top of his chest, and closed his eyes. Before long, he was sound asleep.

Megan lowered the book to her lap. The harsh set of his features relaxed in sleep, he looked ten years younger. And at peace. Watching the even rise and fall of his chest, her throat closed as unshed tears sprang up. Lifted trembling fingers to her lips. *Oh, Lord, I'm going to miss this man so.*

He was leaving, and there was nothing she could do to stop him. She felt helpless and a bit frantic. Desperate. Was this…love? Surely not. Surely it wouldn't hurt this much. Surely she wouldn't have been so foolish!

Jumping up, the book slipping from her lap, she strode across the meadow and into the forest's cool shelter, not stopping until she was certain she wouldn't cry. Lucian would see the evidence and seek to discover the reason. Better to wait until he was gone.

She'd have the rest of her life to cry over him.

Lucian stirred from his slumber, disoriented at first. Then he remembered. He'd drifted to sleep to the soothing sound of Megan's voice. Propping himself up on one arm, he scanned the meadow. Where was she? The book she'd been reading lay facedown on the quilt, some of the pages bent. Frowning, he righted it and got to his feet, turning in a circle to search the surrounding woods for a sign of her.

"Megan?"

"I'm here," she answered, as she ducked from behind his horse. "I've got most of the supplies packed away. We should probably be heading back."

Lucian rested his hands on his hips. Something was wrong. Beneath her bonnet's brim, her face was pale, without expression, and she was avoiding his gaze. Was she angry he'd fallen asleep? Suffice it to say, he wasn't exactly thrilled he'd wasted precious time with her.

"I didn't mean to fall asleep like that. I'm sorry."

She faltered and her lips softened. "I don't mind. You needed the rest." Then she passed by him without another glance. Turning, he followed and helped gather the rest of their things.

When they were about to mount up, he stopped her with a hand on her arm.

"Are you all right?"

The smile lifting her lips didn't quite reach her eyes. "I'm fine."

While he didn't believe her, he refused to argue. "Thank you for bringing me up here. For sharing your special place with me. I don't know when I've enjoyed myself more." It was the best he could give her without admitting how much she'd come to mean to him. She was a once-in-a-lifetime woman. *Yet you're going to turn your back on her.*

Her blue eyes grew luminous. "I'm glad. I—I enjoyed our time together."

Shaking off his hand, she climbed into her saddle and signaled her horse to head out. Lucian caught up to her, and they rode side by side, lost in thought. At the stream, he halted his horse but didn't dismount. Absorbed the magnificent view one last time.

Megan seemed as reluctant to move as him. Was she thinking about the kiss they'd shared? He longed to take her in his arms again. Glancing back at her, he was disappointed to find her face hidden from view. Dreadful bonnet.

"Lucian."

Staring at the ground, she held herself very still.

"Lucian, don't move."

He started to scan the ground. "What—"

Tension screaming from her body, she hissed, "There's a copperhead close to D'Artagnan's rear leg, and he's poised to strike."

Heart pounding, teeth clenched, his fingers tight-

ened on the reins even as he forced his muscles not
to react. Sweat popped out on his brow. The rushing
water masked the sound of the snake's warning hiss.
If his horse was struck, Lucian would be forced to put
him down. He couldn't let that happen. Not to this loyal
friend.

Megan was inching her hand towards her boot.
"What are you doing?" he demanded softly.

She didn't answer, and he didn't shift in the saddle
to look for the reptile. He was afraid that if he moved
even an inch, D'Artagnan might sidestep. When she
scooted up her skirts, Lucian averted his gaze. What
on earth was she doing?

"Hold on," she ordered.

He did look then, shock reverberating through his
body at what he saw. A gun. She was holding a gun.
A mean, dangerous-looking weapon more suited to a
lawman than a young lady like herself.

The sudden blast spooked the horses. D'Artagnan
reared. Lucian felt himself slipping backward. In his
haze of disbelief, he'd let go of the reins. Too late. He felt
nothing but air as the hard earth rushed up to meet him.
The sound of bones cracking as he landed echoed in his
ears an instant before he registered mind-numbing pain.

Chapter Twelve

"Lucian!"

Megan watched in horror as he hit the ground, face contorting as he cradled his right arm against his body. Sheathing her weapon in her leg holster, she worked to calm her horse. When he'd settled, she scrambled down and, sidestepping the dead snake, sprinted to where Lucian lay on his side.

"I'm so sorry," she stammered, reaching out a hand to touch him only to snatch it back when he grimaced, burst forth with a slew of French. Pale beneath his tan, breathing fast, he held his injured arm tight against his midsection.

"The snake?" he pushed out through clenched teeth.

"Dead. But I'm afraid D'Artagnan bolted."

He closed his eyes. Muttered in French again.

Sick with worry, she went to her knees beside him, looking for evidence of other injuries. "Does anything else besides your arm hurt?"

He grunted a negative response.

"You didn't hit your head?"

"Non."

She skimmed shaky fingers over his scalp to be sure, then turned her attention to his arm. "We need to get that coat off so I can take a look at it. Check if the bone pierced the skin."

She prayed it hadn't. That would mean surgery and the potential for complications, as well as risk of infection. *Oh, God, please...*

"I don't feel any blood soaking through," he panted, wincing as she helped him into a sitting position.

"That's good. Is it the upper or lower part?"

"Forearm."

His hair hung in his eyes and bits of grass and dirt clung to his clothes. First she removed the sleeve of his good arm, then she moved around to the other side, sliding the material down as carefully as she could to avoid aggravating the injury. When he flinched and sucked in a harsh breath, she clamped down on her lip to keep from crying.

This was all her fault. She was the reason he was in such agony. *Berate yourself later. Right now you have to focus on helping him.*

There was no sign of blood, thank the Lord. But when she rolled up his sleeve, she noticed the swelling right away. And the beginnings of an angry bruise.

"I'll need to splint this."

The muscles in his jaw working, he nodded. His dark eyes bored into hers. "I know what you're thinking, and you can stop it right now."

Swallowing hard, she pulled her hands away. "If I hadn't shot at such close range—"

"My horse would be dead."

"Your horse is gone." And with him, Lucinda's Bible. His most treasured possession.

He looked away. "At least he's alive. Maybe..."

"As soon as we get to Doc Owens, I'll send for my cousins. They'll search for him."

"You did warn me. I just—" Perplexed, he shook his head. "Why didn't I know you were carrying a gun? And where did you learn to shoot like that?"

"I'll explain later. We need to get that splint on you and get you back to town as quickly as possible." Brushing the hair away from his face, she peered closely at him. "Are you dizzy? Nauseous? I've read the body can go into shock after an injury like this."

"I'm okay."

Of course he would say that. Strong and stubborn man that he was, he wouldn't be quick to let on how much he was hurting.

"Well, if you do experience any symptoms, tell me. I'm going to go find a stick."

It took her five minutes to find one the thickness and length she desired, another five to rip her petticoat into strips. He didn't utter a single sound as she wound the strips about his wrist and the area below his elbow, securing the stick. She used an extra-long length of cloth to fashion a sling.

When she'd helped him to his feet, he stepped over and toed the lifeless reptile with his boot. "Good shot."

Scooping his coat off the ground, she quickly folded and stowed it in the saddlebag. Leading Mr. Knightley over to him, she took in the pitiful picture he made, his right side all wrapped in her shredded undergarments. "How are we going to do this? You can't lead him, but if I sit in front, I'm afraid I'll accidentally bump your arm. The last thing I want to do is cause you additional pain."

A fine sheen of sweat was visible on his forehead. "We'll just have to take that chance. I'll try to shield it with my good arm."

With one boot in the stirrup and a hand on the saddle horn, Lucian hauled himself up behind Megan. A wave of dizziness washed over him. His body went first hot, then cold, his arm one throbbing mass of pain.

Dear God, Megan insists You care about what happens to me. Well, I'm in a bit of a bind here. Not really sure I can make it to town without sliding off the back of this horse in a dead faint. She's already feeling guilty about this whole thing, so I can't exactly tell her how bad off I am. Can You help me stay upright? Please? For Megan's sake?

He didn't get a response. No inner voice acknowledging his request. No giddy feelings. Still, it felt good. And right. He hadn't prayed like that since he was a young boy, when he and his mother would pray together every night before she tucked him into bed. She was the one who'd taught him about God and about His son Jesus, had read the Scriptures to him. As he'd grown older, he'd lost interest in those rituals he'd considered childish.

Now he wasn't so sure he wasn't missing out on something vitally important.

Oh, and God, could You please bring my horse back to me? He and I go way back, and, well, I'd hate to lose him. And my mother's Bible. I'd like to have that back, too. I promise I'll read it this time.

The trek down the mountain dragged on interminably. Due to the slope of the land, he had to fight gravity, lean backward at a slight angle so as not to fall forward into Megan's back. The shade was both a blessing and a curse, depending on whether he was sweating or shivering. His body couldn't seem to make up its mind.

Megan had asked him only once if he thought he could make it. After that, she'd concentrated all her attention on guiding her horse so as not to jar his arm. Now, though, he needed a distraction. Something to focus on besides his screaming wound and occasional dizzy spell.

"Talk to me, Megan," he murmured. "Tell me about the gun."

Her backward glance gave him a glimpse of her eyes, huge and dark with worry, at odds with the determined set of her chin. Beneath her feminine softness and delicate beauty lay a brave soul, strong and courageous. He counted himself fortunate to be in her capable hands. Many other young ladies in her position would've fainted or indulged in a fit of hysterics.

"It was a present from Josh. After our father passed, he thought we needed to learn how to protect ourselves and our property should trouble arise. He taught all of us girls how to shoot. Except for my mother. She refused to learn."

"Why don't you wear a holster about your waist? Where did you have it hidden? In your boot?"

"Josh fashioned a leg holster for me." She hitched a shoulder. "I don't wear it around the cabin or in town. Just when I'm out exploring. You never know who might be passing through."

"Or what wild animals you might have to defend yourself against."

The horse stepped into a dip. Lucian's hand shot out and cupped her waist as a way to brace himself. She rested hers atop his, pressing hard.

"Are you all right?"

"Yeah." He wanted to curl his arm about her and pull her snug against him, but his busted arm prevented him. He settled for this small connection.

"Have you ever broken anything before?" She tilted to the left to avoid hitting a low-slung branch face-first.

He mimicked her action. The forest had thickened, the trees growing closer together here. She concentrated on navigating around gnarled roots jutting out of the ground.

"No, I haven't."

"So, thanks to me, you've just suffered your first broken bone." Her sigh was rife with self-disgust. "Great. Just great."

He gripped her waist a fraction tighter. "Stop blaming yourself. I saw the gun. I knew what you were planning. I should never have let go of the reins. This injury is a result of my own stupidity, Megan."

"You do know what this means, don't you?" Her voice was low and strained.

Of course he did. He opted for a lighter note. "That I won't be penning any poems for a while?"

"Lucian—"

"Stop the horse and look at me."

Easing back on the reins, she waited until they had stopped to half turn in the saddle.

He cupped her chin, forced her to look him square in the eyes. He spoke clearly and with conviction, determined to make her see reason. "What you did back there took guts and skill. I'll always be thankful you saved D'Artagnan's life. I'd rather him be roaming these mountains without me than lying dead from my bullet because of a snakebite." He jerked his chin towards his arm. "This is a temporary setback. So I'll have to postpone my return. So what? Trust me, New Orleans will survive just fine without me."

He refused to think about what a prolonged visit might lead to. More than anything, he was petrified he wouldn't be able to stay away from her, that he'd wind up hurting her. Megan was a true innocent, her pure heart untouched by the cynicism with which he viewed the world. He would not be the man to tarnish that well-spring of optimism or dash her dreams of a marriage based on mutual trust and love.

But when her lower lip quivered and tears welled in her great big eyes, his heart went butter-soft.

"Please don't cry over me," he pleaded on a ragged whisper, unable to resist pressing his lips to hers, if only to stop their trembling. *Sweet. And vulnerable.* He broke contact, reluctantly, and brushed away a tear that had escaped. "I'm not worth it, *mon bien-aime.* Surely you know that."

"Oh, yes. Yes, you are." Her fierce expression dared him to argue the point. In that instant, Lucian understood how precariously close he was to tumbling into love with this woman. Him. A man who'd sworn off love and all the complications that went along with it.

He grimaced, aching physically and emotionally. "How much longer until we reach town?"

"Another half an hour. Can you make it? Do you need to dismount and rest for a bit?"

The concern and caring in her gaze made him feel reckless. He gritted his teeth, willing himself to think of all that was at stake. His sanity, for one. And her heart—well, he couldn't very well risk that, could he? "I can make it."

Thankfully, she turned and nudged Mr. Knightley into motion once more. By the time they halted outside the doctor's home, Lucian was light-headed and weak from holding himself rigid in the saddle. Somehow he managed to dismount without landing on his rear in the dirt. Wouldn't that make a nice impression on the upstanding folks of Gatlinburg? Lucian Beaumont sprawled in the middle of Main Street trussed up in a lady's undergarments?

As Megan assisted him inside the neatly furnished parlor, he swayed. Sat down hard in the nearest chair and fought the unpleasant queasiness in his middle.

"I'll go get Doc," Megan assured him, rushing from the room.

All he could do was sit there and hope he wasn't about to embarrass himself by getting sick right there in the doc's parlor.

"I'd advise you not to travel for at least a month," the doctor announced as he washed his hands in the basin. "You need to give that arm plenty of time to heal. If you injure it further before then, there's no telling what kind of permanent damage you might sustain."

Lucian's eyes were closed. "I understand."

Perched in a chair beside the bed, Megan worried the material of her skirt. Having refused chloroform and put off the laudanum until he got home, he'd endured the doctor's examination and the wrapping of his lower arm in plaster of Paris without pain reliever. She'd remained at his side throughout the entire process, had felt each wince and grimace clear down to her toes. He was holding back on account of her. And it had cost him.

Tension bracketed his mouth, his clean-shaven jaw like carved stone. His brown hair was damp with sweat.

Wearing his usual stern expression, the doctor came and rested a hand on her shoulder while addressing his patient. "Count yourself fortunate to have had this one along. She did everything right, from the splint and sling to getting you here in a timely manner."

Lucian's lids lifted a fraction. "She was amazing out there, sir."

Megan dipped her head. Wasn't he forgetting something? Like how he wouldn't be in this predicament if it weren't for her? Guilt weighed heavily. She'd desperately wanted Lucian to stay, but not like this.

To Megan, he instructed, "Make sure he takes the laudanum as soon as you get him home. He's going to need lots of rest."

"Yes, sir." Rising, she briefly touched Lucian's hand. "Josh is waiting out front with the wagon. I'll go tell him you're ready to go. He can help get you settled."

"I'm not an invalid." Nostrils flaring, he swung his legs over the side of the bed and pushed himself into a sitting position with the use of his good arm. "I can make it on my own steam."

"There's nothing wrong with accepting a little help now and then, young man," the doctor chided.

Lucian dragged a hand down his face, then looked at Megan. "I didn't mean to sound ungrateful."

"I know that." He was in pain and trying desperately to hide it. The sooner he was tucked in bed, the better. "Ready?"

He stood, pausing for a minute to get his bearings. Ignoring her instinct to hover, she preceded him out of the room and down the hall, his footsteps heavy behind her. As they emerged on to the porch, Josh looked up from the book he'd been reading and snapped it closed. Pushing out of the rocking chair, he approached with concern marring his brow.

He gave Lucian a once-over. "Everything all right?"

"It could've been worse," Lucian admitted. "It wasn't bad enough to require surgery, thank goodness."

"Just the one bone was broken," Megan added.

"That's something to be thankful for." Eyeing the sling, he nodded and rubbed his goatee. "Nathan and Caleb are out searching for your horse. I'll join them as soon as we have you settled."

"I appreciate the help." Gratitude laced his voice.

Lucian rode in the back of the wagon, while Megan joined Josh on the bench seat. She couldn't help glancing back every few minutes to check on him.

"He's going to be just fine, you know." Her cousin shot her a knowing grin.

Frowning, she explained in a low voice about Lucian's plans to leave. How she was the reason he'd been forced to postpone his plans.

"Does he blame you?" Josh managed to look incredulous and irritated at the same time.

"No, of course not." She rushed to defend Lucian. "He's adamant that he's glad I did what I did and thankful his horse is still alive."

"Good." The tension left his shoulders. "For a minute there, I thought I was going to have a little chat with our friend."

Megan sighed and rolled her eyes. Who needed big brothers when she had Josh to defend her honor? And Nathan and Caleb? "You wouldn't dare."

"Um, yeah, I would." His blue eyes narrowed. "Any man who dares to treat you or the girls in an ungentlemanly fashion will have to answer to me."

"Wasn't it you who taught us to stick up for ourselves?"

"I'm not implying you can't do that. I'm just saying that I won't ignore such behavior. With your pa gone…" He trailed off, shrugging.

She laid a hand on his arm. "I know you have our

best interests at heart. You're more than a mere relative, you know. You're a true friend."

The tips of his ears turned red and his smile had an awkward tilt, but his eyes were warm as he curled an arm about her shoulders and hugged her close. "Are you trying to make a grown man cry, Goldilocks?"

"I would never do such an underhanded thing," she protested with a smile, adding on a more serious note, "Kate and I talked the other day. I'm praying for you both."

The amusement faded from his face. "Thank you."

"If you need someone to talk to, I'm here."

He only nodded, clearly troubled but not willing to discuss the subject. She knew him well enough not to push. When and if he wanted to talk, he'd let her know. Until then, she would continue to pray.

Josh didn't come inside the house, preferring to leave right away and join the others in their search. Mrs. Calhoun didn't fuss over Lucian as Megan had feared she might. Although clearly concerned, she seemed to sense, like Megan, that he wouldn't welcome being coddled. He turned on the bottom step, his good hand propped on the wall for balance.

"Go home, Megan," he said gently. "It's long past supper time, and I'm certain your sisters are growing anxious. You need rest, as well. My valet will help me rid myself of these atrocious clothes and boots."

Her cheeks heated. Of course her helping him into bed was out of the question. Still, she would've liked to hang around until he was settled, to make sure he was comfortable. "I'm not that tired. I can wait down here—"

He ran his knuckles lightly down her cheek. "You're swaying in your boots. Go home and eat something. I'll still be here tomorrow if you want to check up on me," he said wryly, one black brow arched.

"All right, I'll go, but only if you promise to be a good patient and take the laudanum. You won't be able to truly rest if you're in pain."

His generous mouth curved, softening the aristocratic features. "I give you my word, Nurse Megan."

"I'm praying for you, Lucian." At his arrested expression, she ventured softly, "What? Has no one prayed for you before?"

"Only my mother," he admitted, his dark eyes swirling with emotion.

"Well, I know for a fact that as news of your accident travels through town, the number of people praying for you will grow."

"I should tell you something." He hesitated. "I prayed today like I haven't done since I was a young boy. A real prayer—not like grace before a meal or a quick plea for help. I really talked to God. Not sure if He heard me or if He even cares, but I did it. And it felt…good."

"Oh, Lucian, that's wonderful." She smiled tremulously. "He does care. I have that on authority of His Word."

He gazed at her without speaking, mulling over her words. "Yes, well, I just wanted you to know."

"I'm glad you told me. Good night, Lucian."

"Bonne nuit, mon chou."

With his whispered farewell lingering in her ears, she let herself out. Walking home, she pondered their conversation, her burden of guilt sitting a little lighter on her shoulders. If this delay accomplished only one thing—deepening Lucian's faith—then it was worth her guilt and even his momentary suffering.

God worked in mysterious ways. He had His reasons

for allowing the accident to happen, reasons they may never understand. All she knew was that Lucian wasn't leaving as planned, which meant she wouldn't have to say goodbye right away. Had been granted a reprieve. What that meant for her heart she was afraid to find out.

Chapter Thirteen

Descending the church steps after the morning service, Megan felt a hand on her arm and glanced up into Tom's smiling face.

"Hey, pretty lady, can I have a moment?"

She smiled back. "Of course."

At the bottom, she stepped off to the side to avoid the stream of churchgoers heading to their wagons. He motioned for Jane and Nicole to join them.

"What are your lunch plans?" His eager gaze touched each of theirs.

"Leftovers," Nicole said with a sigh, her displeasure marring her perfect features. Wearing her smart green ensemble, a feathered hat perched atop her shiny black mane, she looked like an angry china doll.

"Why do you ask?" At nearly sixteen, Jane exhibited more maturity than her older sister. Her serene expression couldn't mask the telltale loneliness in her eyes. Megan wondered how Jessica was handling this separation, the twins' first. The more outgoing of the two, Jessica wasn't as sensitive as Jane.

Lifting his hat to fluff his hair, he hooked a thumb towards his wagon. "I took a chance and ordered a picnic lunch from Plum's in the hopes you three ladies would agree to join me. I thought about heading over to the river." He mentioned their family's favored picnic spot.

She'd planned to pay Lucian a visit immediately after lunch, but Tom had already purchased the food, and the look Jane shot her was hope-filled. Besides, a tiny part of her dreaded seeing Lucian. He had an awful lot of time on his hands. Time to think, to replay yesterday's events and the consequences. What if he'd finally come to the conclusion that she'd caused nothing but trouble for him since the day he'd first arrived? What if he was angry? What if—

"So what's it going to be, Megan?" Tom stood with his hands on his hips, waiting expectantly.

She took a deep breath. "We'd love to join you."

"Great." White teeth flashed in a wide grin that had no effect on her whatsoever. Nothing like Lucian's potent smiles.

She surreptitiously studied her friend, trying to study him objectively as a girl new to town would do. Dressed like the locals in pants, band-collared shirt and suspenders and boots, he was tall and lean and sturdy-looking. He was a tidy man, both in appearance and practice. He kept his barbershop spotless. His home, too. Attractive in an understated way, his green eyes were his only intriguing feature. Tom may not be the kind of man that would stand out in a crowd, but he was nice-looking in his own quiet way.

Why, oh why, wasn't she drawn to *him?* A local with no plans to leave. A man who knew where he stood with God, who lived to honor Him. A man who *wanted* to court her, who wanted a wife and children.

Why couldn't she be practical-minded? At times like

this, she despised her romantic nature, her idealistic dreams of how her life should be.

Tamping down her frustration, and a childish desire to stamp her foot, Megan refocused on the conversation.

Jane was smiling shyly up at Tom. "It was very thoughtful of you to plan this outing, Tom."

His wink caused a blush to spread along Jane's cheeks. "I must admit to selfish motives, Janie-girl. It's not every day a man is blessed with the company of three lovely ladies."

"Don't you mean three of the loveliest ladies in Gatlinburg?" Nicole smirked.

"Tom," Megan interjected to save him from having to reply, "will you mind stopping at the cabin long enough for us to change?"

Amusement dancing in his eyes, he nodded, and, taking her hand, he placed it in the crook of his arm. On the drive out to her place, he made casual mention of Lucian's accident. Even if he hadn't heard it through the town grapevine, he would've learned about it in church this morning as Reverend Monroe had spoken of it from the pulpit, asking the congregation to pray. She skirted the issue in an effort to deflect personal questions. No way did she want to discuss her and Lucian's relationship—or lack thereof—with Tom.

Kind man that he was, he allowed her to steer the conversation into safer waters. He waited patiently in the wagon while the girls changed out of their Sunday best and into everyday dresses. Nicole, in particular, was happy to have a reprieve from kitchen duties. The only chore she enjoyed was sewing clothes, and she excelled at it. Everything else that needed to be done around the farm she considered beneath her. One would think she believed herself royalty rather than a simple mountain girl. Megan loved her sister, but sometimes she didn't understand her.

They weren't the only ones at the river. When they arrived, they discovered a handful of families scattered along the riverbank, enjoying the fine spring weather before it turned hot and humid and far too uncomfortable to lounge about in the noonday sun. Waving to familiar faces, they selected a spot in the flower-strewn field and set out their quilts and the mouthwatering food Mrs. Greene, the Plum Café's owner, had prepared for them. Ravenous now, their prayer of thanks was a brief one. Companionable silence reigned as they ate.

Children's delighted shrieks carried on the wind, punctuated by adult laughter. The meandering river trickled over rocks and occasional fallen logs, birds chirped and whistled. One family in particular caught Megan's eye—a sharply dressed man and his wife and their small toddler, a boy with a shock of dark hair the same hue as Lucian's.

Her heart constricted. Longing for the impossible sliced through her, left her bleeding and sore. She and Lucian didn't have a future together. They would never be that family—a loving husband and wife and children filling their lives with laughter and joy.

Despite this delay, Lucian would eventually return home. He would choose a suitable bride, perfect in every way, one who would dutifully provide him with his sole heir. Irrational jealousy gripped her, soured her stomach. She set aside her plate, sipping her lemonade in the hopes it would wash away the bitter taste in her mouth. It would serve him right if his future wife gave him a passel of daughters. How many until he gave up hope for a son? Six? Nine?

"I'm going for a walk," she abruptly announced,

heartsick at the image of him and his ice queen surrounded by rosy-cheeked girls with black eyes.

Tom's forehead bunched in concern. Eyes crinkled at the corners as he squinted against the sun. "You haven't finished your lunch."

"I wasn't as hungry as I thought. I'll finish it later." She covered her plate with a cloth and placed it back in the basket, safe from flies and ants, then strolled down to the river's edge.

Watching the water flow past, she trailed a line in the damp earth with her boot.

Tom joined her after five minutes. "Want to tell me what's on your mind?"

She shrugged. "Nothing interesting."

He took both her hands in his. "We're friends, remember? No matter what happens between us, we'll always be friends first. I can tell something's bothering you. You haven't been yourself lately, and frankly, I'm a bit worried."

While his words indicated one thing, in his eyes she saw the hope for something more. "I'm just concerned about the girls. Jane mopes about the house missing Jessica, and Nicole…well, you know how she can be. Multiply that by ten. It's a big responsibility Ma placed in my lap, and she hasn't yet sent word what's happening with Juliana. We don't know if she's had the baby yet and if so, how they're both faring."

All of that *was* weighing on her mind. And it was all she was willing to share with him.

"I'm sure your sister and the baby are just fine. I don't know much about females, but I'll help with your sisters in any way I can."

"That means a lot to me." She lightly squeezed his hands before pulling free.

A loud splash, followed by a woman's alarmed cry, startled them both. Tom whirled around. Lunged for the little boy who'd landed on his rear in the water. The one who'd reminded her of Lucian.

Noticing the tears welling in his eyes and the curl of his bottom lip, Tom picked him up and, heedless of the water dripping everywhere, hugged him against his body. "Hey there, little buddy. What's your name?"

Before he could get a word out, his mother rushed up. "Lenny! Are you all right?"

He wiggled to get down. Tom lowered the tyke to the ground so he could toddle over to his mother.

"Thank you," she said, taking hold of the boy's hand. "Stay close to Mama from now on, Lenny. Let's go dry you off." She led him back to their quilt.

"Cute little guy," Tom said with a grin, seemingly oblivious to his damp clothing.

"How many kids do you want?" Megan blurted, her gaze still trained on mother and son.

His brows lifted. "I think four is a good goal. What about you?"

"Ten."

"I can see that." He smiled and slowly nodded. "You're good with kids. You'll be a wonderful mother someday."

She didn't comment and, after moments of silence, he ventured, "Why do you ask, Megan? Are you...? Have you thought more about my courting you?"

Her gaze shot to his face alight with anticipation. Oh, no. What had she done? Thoughtless girl.

"Oh, Tom, no, I—I was simply curious. A friend and I were discussing the matter the other day, and Lenny reminded me of the conversation. I didn't intend to imply that I'd made a decision." Seeing his crestfallen expression, she decided she couldn't leave him hanging any longer. Not only was it unfair, it was cruel. "Actually, Tom, I don't need to make a decision. I—"

"Wait." He stepped closer. "I can see you're upset and worried about hurting my feelings. Let's not rush things. Like you said, you have a lot on your mind right now. I think it would be best if we waited until things have calmed down a bit to discuss this."

"But—"

"No buts." Smiling gently, he jerked his head towards the field where Jane and Nicole waited. "Let's rejoin your sisters. I promised them an entertaining afternoon, and I aim to deliver."

Megan woke before dawn Monday morning. Padding to the window in her bare feet, she pushed the curtain aside and peered into the silent darkness. *Where are you, D'Artagnan?* Josh and Nathan had stopped by after supper last night with unhappy news—two days of searching had gotten them nowhere. Lucian's horse was still missing, and it fell to her to tell him.

Her cousins couldn't take any more time away from their work to search, which meant D'Artagnan—and Lucinda's Bible—might never be found. *Lord, this is important to Lucian. Please lead his horse back safe and sound.*

Wide-awake and restless, she tackled her chores and even made a simple breakfast of ham, eggs and toast, a task that usually fell to Jane. Then, unable to wait a moment longer, she set out for Lucian's house.

Mrs. Calhoun came to the door, wiping her hands on her apron. "He's in the garden parlor. Go on back and say hello. I'm in the middle of fixing breakfast."

"Sorry to interrupt you." Megan paused in the entrance hall to remove her bonnet and straighten her apricot skirts. "I know it's early, but I was eager to check on him." Only half-past eight. Not exactly proper visiting hours.

"No need to apologize, dear. Company will do him good. Fred and I hung around yesterday to see to his needs, but I caught him watching the door off and on. Probably hoping for a visit from you." Turning, she preceded Megan down the hall, stopping in the doorway leading to the dining room and, beyond, the kitchen. "I'll be along shortly with breakfast. Will you be joining him?"

"No, thank you. I already ate."

"A cup of coffee, then?"

"That would be wonderful, Mrs. Calhoun. Thanks."

When the older lady bustled off, Megan went in the opposite direction. Situated along the back of the house, the garden parlor was a long, rectangular room with high ceilings and a row of windows overlooking the rear porch and gardens. Done primarily in hues of cream, gold and sage, with occasional bursts of poppy-red and apricot, it possessed an airy, open feel that Megan found inviting. Botanical prints dotted the papered walls, and potted ferns flanked the windows thrown open to catch the floral-scented breeze. Gauzy drapes fluttered softly.

Advancing into the room, her steps muted by the sage-and-cream-swirled rug, she spotted Lucian stretched out on the sofa sound asleep. She rounded the carved mahogany coffee table. Edged closer. He was dressed more casually than she'd ever seen him. No boots, of course. His stocking feet peeked out from beneath chocolate-brown pants and beneath his sling, he wore a loose cream shirt open at the neck, giving her a peek of his smooth, tanned throat. A day's worth of stubble darkened his jaw, his brown hair mussed.

Had he slept here the whole night through? From the looks of him, he must've. Was Mrs. Calhoun right? Had he been expecting her yesterday?

Bending at the waist, she carefully smoothed a lock of hair that had fallen on to his forehead. When he didn't stir, she gave in to the temptation to repeat the action, trailing her fingertips lightly through the silky waves. He sighed. Nestled his head deeper into the feather pillow, a small smile on his lips. Lips that had touched hers, sparking dreams of a future.

Leaning down, she kissed his cheek, smiling when his whiskers tickled her chin. She straightened, gasped when her gaze encountered his confused one.

"Megan?" he said, voice raspy from sleep. "Am I dreaming?"

Embarrassed, she acted as if he hadn't just caught her kissing him. "*Bonjour,* Lucian. Did you sleep well?"

"*Bonjour,*" he responded slowly, his brow wrinkling. "You speak French now?"

Twisting her hands behind her back, she said, "Kate told me how to say that. Although, I can't pronounce it quite like you do."

He struggled to sit up. Needing to distance herself from his irresistible male presence, she backed away, plopping clumsily into a nearby chair when her legs bumped against it. Lucian slouched against the sofa cushions, legs planted wide, one hand resting in his lap.

This rumpled version of him, unrestrained and a touch untamed, had a devastating effect on her equilibrium. Her heart jerked about in her chest in an uneven rhythm.

"Are you here because you're feeling sorry for me?" Raking her from head to toe, his gaze challenged her.

"Or because your misplaced guilt became too much to bear?"

She hadn't expected an assault. "Why do you do that?" she demanded, chin lifting. "Why do you suspect everyone around you of ulterior motives? Couldn't I have come simply because I wanted to see you? To find out how you're feeling?"

"You didn't come yesterday." The slip in his customary confidence dispelled her ire.

"I wanted to, believe me, I—"

He held up a hand. "That was out of line. Forgive me. There's no need for you to explain." Lowering it, he appeared both stern and thoughtful, saying, "I suppose it stems from a lifetime of people befriending me on account of my last name, the wealth and power associated with my family."

Leaning forward, she studied the shadows of past pain in his eyes. "There's more to it, isn't there?"

Frowning, his gaze drifted to the floor. "There was a woman, Dominique. We traveled in the same circles, she and I, and crossed each other's paths quite regularly. Shortly before my mother's death, we were seated together at a friend's musical and, throughout the course of the evening, found we had similar interests. We... became close."

Megan sat stock-still, hands locked together in her lap, insides withering. To hear Lucian speak of another woman in this manner was like walking barefoot across burning coals. *Dominique.* With a name like that, she must be lovely and soft-spoken and well dressed, not a single hair out of place.

He had courted Dominique. Yet, he'd made it clear he wouldn't court Megan. She wasn't quite good enough, was she? Didn't fulfill the lofty standards required of the wife of Lucian Beaumont.

"I thought she was different from the rest. I believed the extras didn't matter, that she was interested in *me*. After all, she came from old money and was in possession of a pedigree even more stellar than mine." His scowl was directed more at himself than anyone else, as if *he* was to blame for the betrayal. "I misjudged her. About a month after my mother's death, Dominique came to the conclusion that she would be better served if she aligned herself with my father. He's the one who wields the reins, so to speak. The head of the family and the shipping empire."

Megan's stomach dropped to her toes. This woman, this Dominique, had betrayed him in the worst possible way. And at the worst possible time. What kind of woman would do such an underhanded thing, especially when he was mourning the loss of his mother?

"I had to wonder if she'd been using me the entire time to get to him."

Suddenly the pieces fit together like a well-written horror story. His accusations and suspicions, his inability at first to believe her motives were pure. Why discovering that Lucinda, the mother he'd adored, might possibly have hidden the truth from him was so hard to accept.

"I'm so sorry, Lucian." Her jealousy and self-pity seemed very pathetic in this moment. She ached for this lonely, stoic man. "Did your father— What I mean is, did he—"

"Did he court Dominique?" he snorted. "No. And not due to any loyalty to me. No, he'd only recently rid himself of my mother. He wasn't about to tie himself to another desperate female."

"Is she the reason you don't want to marry for love?"

"The truth is, I'd rather not marry at all. Dominique made me forget, for a little while, a decision I made many years ago—that if I must marry, it would be a marriage based on social compatibility and companionship. *Not* emotions as changeable as the sea, as unstable as shifting sand beneath your feet. Dominique's betrayal turned out to be a blessing, really. Brought my goals back into focus."

He passed fingers over his injured arm beneath the sling and winced. "My parents' marriage was a disaster. Enamored of my mother's beauty and innocence, my father rushed them both into it without taking into account their differences. They had vastly different upbringings, as you know, which resulted in wholly different mind-sets. The physical attraction that had brought them together didn't last, at least not for my father. When he realized my mother wouldn't fit in his world, he made no attempts to hide his disdain. But no matter how ruthless he was, she never stopped loving him. Never stopped hoping they could recapture what they'd lost. She did everything in her power to change, to fit his idea of the ideal wife.... In the end, she only ended up losing herself." His expression grew fierce and his eyes blazed molten fire. "I refuse to live that way, to hurt a woman like my father hurt my mother. That's why when I marry, I'll make certain there are no attachments on either side. No feelings of any sort beyond common respect. That way, neither one of us will suffer."

Neither will he experience the joy of true love, she thought morosely, the satisfaction of shared dreams. The beauty of hearts in tune, woven together by God's sure hand. She wanted to argue with him. To plead with him to give love a chance. Just because Gerard and Lucinda's marriage was a failure didn't mean Lucian's would be. But he was a stubborn man, and she could tell by looking at him that he wouldn't be swayed on this. He was convinced that to marry for anything other than duty would be a grave mistake.

They made quite a pair, didn't they? The cynic and the dreamer. Lucian would not allow himself to love, and she…well, she would never stop yearning for it.

"I can see how a romantic-minded young lady such as yourself would have a tough time digesting all of this," he said with quiet intensity. "However, if you'd lived my childhood perhaps you would have an easier time understanding my point of view."

"I was blessed with two parents who loved each other." Her broken voice mirrored the state of her heart. Lucian's determination to live without love deeply saddened her. "So much so that my mother refuses to marry again."

Steps heralded the arrival of Mrs. Calhoun. "Breakfast is served." Sliding the tray onto the coffee table, she eyed Lucian. "I've prepared another dose of laudanum for you."

"Thank you." His gaze remained on Megan, and she knew without asking that he wasn't planning on taking it.

"Oh, it was no trouble. If you don't need anything else, I'll leave you two to your conversation." At his nod, she left them.

"How bad is the pain?"

He shifted beneath her scrutiny, unable to hide a sudden grimace. "Nothing I can't handle."

"Why won't you take the medicine?"

"I did take it that first night, as promised. However, I

don't particularly enjoy the way my head feels as if it's going to topple from my body and as if I've swallowed a ball of yarn. I'd much rather deal with the discomfort."

"It would help you rest," she persisted.

"I'm not a man who needs a lot of rest," he muttered with a frown, even as he absently massaged the spot above his heart.

She was reminded of his doctor's recommendation to slow down. Lucian may not wish to take it easy, but this forced inactivity could turn out to be the best thing for him. He couldn't run from grief indefinitely. At some point, he was going to have to deal with his loss. And come to terms with Dominique's deception.

"I'm afraid my cousins weren't able to locate D'Artagnan."

He nodded. "I wasn't hopeful. Still, I'm grateful they were willing to try."

"There's still a chance he'll find his way back."

"I suppose. If he doesn't, I'm okay with that. I just hope he finds himself a new owner soon. There're dangers out there."

Scooting to the edge of the cushions, he awkwardly lifted the coffee cup to his lips.

She pointed to the stack of johnnycakes drizzled with molasses. "Would you like my help with that?"

One black brow arched. He lowered the cup a fraction. "Are you offering to feed me?"

"It can't be easy feeding yourself with your left hand," she retorted, cheeks heating at the lights dancing in his eyes.

"I *have* nearly stabbed myself half a dozen times. And Mrs. Calhoun has had to sweep beneath my chair after every meal because the food doesn't seem to want to stick on my fork."

"Poor Lucian," she teased.

"As much as I'd like to take you up on your offer, I think I'd better get used to doing things a bit differently. I can't expect to have you with me for every meal, now can I?"

"I'll leave you to it, then." Standing, she slipped her reticule over her wrist. "I have to go."

"So soon?"

"My sisters and I are picking strawberries this morning to make into jam. Without Ma and Jessica here to help, canning it all will take longer than usual. Nicole and I aren't as handy in the kitchen as the rest of our family. We'll slow Jane down, I'm sure. Depending on how much we get done today, I may come back this evening and bring Jane. Would that be all right?"

"Only if you aren't too tired," he cautioned. "And bring both your sisters. We'll play chess or charades or something."

"How are you supposed to play charades?"

One side of his mouth lifted. "I'll be the guesser."

Tucking an errant curl behind her ear, she gave him a small wave. "Enjoy your breakfast, Lucian."

Leaving him there, she wished she didn't have to go, wished she could indeed share every meal with him. They were the foolish wishes of a careless heart. A heart that was falling for a man who wanted nothing to do with love.

Chapter Fourteen

Friday evening, Lucian found himself in a precarious position. Apparently he hadn't given adequate consideration to which chair he occupied for story time, for the moment he lowered himself into this one—set apart from the rest near the fireplace—the children had descended.

Sarah, the sweetheart, had climbed into his lap without a single word and snuggled against his uninjured side, her head a barely perceptible weight against his shoulder. Ollie had plopped down on the rug at Lucian's feet and was now pressed against his leg. Others whose names he couldn't recall had joined Ollie, crowding in so that Lucian was afraid to move for fear of crushing their little hands beneath his boots.

Megan, the little minx, was thoroughly enjoying his plight. Her attempts to curb her smile had failed, and of course, there was no masking the delicious glee in her beautiful blue eyes.

Sarah shifted, her fine hair tickling his chin. Small and warm, she smelled like sunshine and lemonade. His protective instincts kicked in, and he found himself wishing he could take away her pain. He knew the anguish of losing a mother. How much worse must it be for a young child?

Would he feel this way about his own child? He'd only ever considered having a son. Sweet Sarah spawned thoughts of a girl. One who looked an awful lot like Megan. It was a dangerous path to wander down...imagining what it might be like if he and Megan were to marry and have children of their own. She was a natural with kids. Nurturing and kind. Patient. Wise. There wasn't a single doubt in his mind that she would make an exceptional mother.

For some other man's children, not yours. A local man. Someone like Tom Leighton.

Why did that prospect hit him with the force of a direct blow to the gut?

If he shifted his head slightly to the left, he could see the man in question leaning against the wall, watching Megan with undisguised admiration and longing. Tom made no effort to hide his feelings. Did he comprehend what a treasure he had in her? If he succeeded in winning her, would he truly appreciate her?

Megan deserved to have her happy-ever-after. Lucian wanted that for her. Even if he couldn't be the one to give it to her, even if it wounded him to imagine her setting up house with another man.

Lucian couldn't afford to make the same mistakes his father had. He would not rip an innocent girl from the only home she'd ever known, separate her from family and friends and then subject her to a world that was oftentimes cruel and cold. Megan was a small-town girl through and through. She belonged here in East Tennessee with her mountains and the people she'd known her whole life and the children who adored her.

Besides, he wasn't exactly levelheaded when it came to her. With her around, his determination to remain detached, to hold his heart apart, disintegrated like parchment in flames into a pile of smoldering ashes. If he married her, duty would have nothing to do with it. And that would prove disastrous for them both.

"The end." Closing the book, Megan's warm gaze connected with his and her slow smile made him wish for the impossible.

The kids at his feet surged as one and descended on the dessert table. Sarah scooted off his lap and joined them at a more sedate pace.

Muscles stiff, he pushed himself upright. He'd learned to live with the persistent throbbing in his forearm, and, as much as he wanted rid of the sling, he knew it kept him from further discomfort. The one night he'd attempted to sleep without it, he'd flipped on to his side, pinning his arm beneath him. He'd awoken in agony. Worried he might have done further damage, he'd summoned the doctor the following morning, who'd examined him and declared him a fortunate man. He'd also urged him to take the laudanum before bed. Lucian had agreed to think about it.

Megan appeared before him, familiar concern lurking at the back of her eyes as her gaze touched on his sling. Nothing he said to try to ease her guilt seemed to make a difference.

"No costume tonight?" he asked, appreciating how her peach blouse enhanced her peaches-and-cream complexion. Her flawless skin glowed, her mass of moonlight curls skimming her shoulders and caressing her nape with every movement of her head.

Surely noting his approval, she blushed becomingly and locked her gaze on his cravat. "There wasn't time.

We finished our last jars of strawberry jam about an hour before I was to leave to come here."

She'd brought him a jar, bless her. Chewing on her lip, she'd been a bit unsure of his reaction. As she'd pointed out, he could purchase the finest-quality jam from anywhere in the world. Touched by her humble offering, he'd assured her he would take it home and enjoy it on Cook's delicate croissants when he breakfasted in the estate gardens. It would remind him of her and her sisters, of the good times they'd shared. The trio had gifted him with their presence nearly every evening this past week, chasing away his boredom with laughter and good-natured teasing.

At that last bit, her smile had been tinged with sadness, a sadness that echoed in his own soul every time he thought of never seeing her again.

"If you don't have any objections, I'd like to stay for a little while after everyone leaves." She appeared pleased about something. Eager. "I have news to share."

He placed a hand on his chest. "*Moi?* Objections to your company? Never."

Her blue eyes shone with pleasure. "Good."

Tom approached with a glass of tea in each hand, expression pensive as he observed their interaction. "Evening, Lucian. How's the arm?"

"Not bad."

He passed a glass to Megan, who murmured her thanks. She didn't appear entirely comfortable in his presence. Why was that?

"I hope it heals quickly so you can return to New Orleans." Sipping his drink, he smirked.

"Honestly, Tom." Megan's brows lowered in rebuke.

"What? I'm sure the man has commitments to tend

to. People eager to welcome him home. Don't you, Lucian?"

Lucian stiffened. How dare he disregard Megan's feelings on this issue? Didn't he know she blamed herself? Assuming his most imperious expression, he inserted frost into his response. "You're right, I do. However, I can't complain. I find I'm rather enjoying my prolonged visit. Megan and her sisters have proven to be delightful company, a most pleasant diversion from my plight."

Lowering the glass to his side, he scowled. "Is that so?"

His eyes narrowed in silent challenge. "Indeed."

"Well, that's…swell." He curled an arm about her shoulders, retaliating with a challenging gaze of his own. "Mind if I steal my girl away for a few minutes?"

"That's entirely up to her."

With an apologetic glance at Lucian, she said, "We'll talk later." Then she allowed him to lead her out of the parlor.

Lucian stalked in the opposite direction, seeking sanctuary in Charles's office before he gave in to impulse and punched something.

"I've never known you to be rude." Arms crossed, Megan waited impatiently for an explanation.

Tom walked to the porch railing and turned to face her without a trace of apology. He whacked his hat against his thigh. "What's going on between you and Lucian Beaumont?"

"We're friends."

He scoffed at that. "If you could see the way he looks at you…"

"And just how does he look at me?" she retorted.

"*Not* like a friend," he stated flatly. Pushing away from the railing, he shoved his hat on his head and stopped in front of her, settled his hands on her shoulders. "He's not the man for you, Megan. He's going home as soon as his arm mends. Do you really want to hang your hopes on a man who would willingly leave you behind?"

Megan didn't speak. He wasn't telling her anything she didn't already know. Still, to hear it spoken aloud gave it more weight. Made it more real.

He dipped his head to meet her gaze directly. "I would never leave you. You know that, right?"

"Tom, I—"

The door swung open, and Ollie and his parents appeared in the doorway. Tom dropped his hands. When they'd exchanged farewells and the trio had descended the steps and were making their way across the grass, he turned to her, more somber than she ever recalled seeing him.

"Will you allow me to walk you home?"

"Not tonight. I'd like to stay and help clean up."

Nodding, he attempted a smile. "All right. Good night, then."

"Good night, Tom."

More people streamed through the door, bidding her good-night. With one last glance at Tom's retreating figure, Megan slipped inside and went in search of Lucian. She found him in the office, staring out the window at the gardens awash in fading pink-tinted light.

"I'm sorry about that." She stopped beside the desk and stared at his broad back, defined muscles stretching the soft cotton shirt. Because of the sling, he couldn't manage a vest or coat. Without them, he was less formidable. More approachable and yet, still elegant.

When he turned, there was speculation in his black eyes but he didn't mention Tom. "Are you all right?"

"I'm fine." It was an automatic response, not necessarily an apt description of her mental state. How could she *possibly* be fine? Her life was a mess. Her friend was hurting on account of her, and she'd yet to find a way to tell him how she truly felt. Even worse, she wasn't listening to her voice of reason where Lucian was concerned. She should steer clear of him. Instead, she seized every chance to be near him.

As was his habit now, he rested a protective hand over his injured arm. "Has everyone left? My curiosity about your news has reached tortuous heights."

The ever-so-slight curve of his generous lips lifted her spirits. His smiles were rare gifts, their effect on her unmistakable. Perhaps, it wasn't such a bad thing to focus on the here and now. To disregard the future. For now, Lucian was here with her. She should savor this time, for memories were all she'd soon have.

"You must be patient awhile longer. There were still a few people lingering about the dessert table."

He looked regretful. "It's the cream puffs. They're hard to resist."

She laughed. "You're right about that. If we start straightening up, they may get the hint and leave."

His expression brightened. "Let's go."

Placing his hand at the small of her back, he guided her through the house. The heat of his fingers burned through her dress, his touch protective and possessive at the same time. She liked it very much. *Too* much.

In the parlor, she moved away with a warning. "Your job is purely supervisory. I can handle the chairs on my own." Like she had before he came. And would after he was gone.

He didn't like that. "I'm not accustomed to standing by while a lady does all the work."

"Too bad."

Mrs. Calhoun and another man pitched in to help her rearrange the furniture. Out of the corner of her eye, she noticed Lucian piling dirty dishes on top of each other. He was determined to help one way or another, it seemed. By the time they'd righted the parlor, the last guest had left.

Lucian appeared at her side, his good arm aloft and eyes alight with anticipation. "Care to take a stroll about the gardens with me, my lady?"

Alone at last. A thrill pulsed through her as she curved her fingers around his biceps. "I'd like nothing better."

They exited through the rear door that led out to the porch. The humidity from earlier in the day had eased somewhat and the air, heavy with the scent of earth and grass and blossoms, was pleasant against her skin. Cicadas hummed. In the distance, a dog barked. Another splendid spring day was coming to a close.

Lucian led her along the stone path at a sedate pace, content to soak in the colors and textures of the plants and trees on either side. In this moment, he appeared completely at ease, his customary tension conspicuously absent. He seemed almost…happy.

"Have you ever considered leaving the city? Settling somewhere else?" she blurted. *Like here?*

He halted, looking down at her in question. "Not seriously. I've toyed with the notion of relocating to the estate, but there's no one out there but a handful of staff. It's a rambling old mansion, too large for a single person."

Slipping her hand free, she went to sit on a wooden

bench beneath the rose arbor, arranging her skirts about her. He came and sat close beside her, his leg brushing hers.

His face was inches away, his dark gaze a caress. "Tell me your news."

"We finally received a letter today." Her joy overflowed into a huge smile. "Juliana had her baby—a healthy boy with a shock of black hair like his pa's. They named him James, after his late uncle. They're both doing great. Evan is over-the-moon excited. Ma wrote he hasn't stopped smiling."

Lucian's smile was curiously wistful. "Congratulations—you're an aunt now. Auntie Megan."

"I like the sound of that. I hope to go and meet him later on this summer, perhaps in August. Jane is anxious to go, as well."

"Not Nicole?"

"Nicole isn't what you'd call sentimental. And she doesn't get excited about babies."

"That may change. She's young yet."

"The twins are younger than her, yet they're more mature. I'm not sure if she'll ever grow out of her selfishness."

"Everyone matures at a different rate. Give her time."

"I hope you're right."

"Thank you for sharing your news with me." His low drawl wrapped her in cozy warmth.

He was close enough to kiss. Memories of that other kiss by the stream, of how it felt to be held in his arms, rushed in. Her fingers gripped his sleeve. She leaned closer, tilted her face up a fraction. Lost herself in his molten gaze. Waited for him to lower his mouth to hers in tender possession. Waited in vain.

His expression darkened. Frowning, he disengaged

her arm and, surging to his feet, strode purposefully away from her.

Megan ducked her head. Hot color infused her face. How could she have been so bold? He'd made it clear he thought kissing her was a mistake. That other kiss on the horse had been an impulse, an attempt to comfort her and assuage her guilty conscience.

"It's getting late," he said without looking at her, his shoulders rigid. "You should go. I don't like the idea of you walking home in the dark."

Humiliated and hurt, she shot to her feet. "I can take care of myself, you know."

He turned, one brow arched. "Yes, I know. Humor me."

So, he wasn't really concerned for her welfare. It was an excuse to get her to leave.

"Fine. I won't stay where I'm not wanted."

As she passed by him, his hand snaked out and snagged her wrist. "Don't ever think you're not wanted, *mon bien-aime,*" he forced out. There was a battle going on inside him, emotions warring on his face. "I'm trying very hard to protect you."

Slowly, he bent his head and brushed a light-as-air kiss on her cheek. Megan's heart kicked. Longing engulfed her.

"Lucian—"

He released her wrist and stepped back, his gaze once again hooded. "Go get some rest, Megan. You've been working hard all week, and the poetry recital is tomorrow night."

"Right. Good night, then."

"Bonsoir."

He did not accompany her inside. Unsettled, she hurried down the hall, her steps echoing through the silent, empty house. *This is what it will be like once he leaves,* she thought glumly. Strange and lifeless, as it had after Charles's death.

Tears pricked her eyes. Lucian's presence had assuaged somewhat her grief, lessened the impact of Charles's absence. All too soon, he would leave her, too.

What was she supposed to do then? Especially now that she knew she loved him?

Chapter Fifteen

Lucian relented and took the laudanum that night. His body needed the rest, as did his mind. The medicine would knock him out cold, granting him a reprieve from these persistent thoughts about Megan. Resisting her had drained him of every last drop of strength he possessed. If he expected to be in her presence tomorrow night without crossing the line of friendship, he had to get some sleep.

And perspective. Perspective was good. Remembering their differences was good, too.

Sliding beneath the cool sheets, he fell asleep listing them all.

When he awoke Saturday morning, it was much later than usual. After nine. Where was his valet? Smith should've woken him. The house was silent, so the reserved gentleman was either still abed, which was not his custom, or he'd gone to the stables. Mrs. Calhoun was off duty on the weekends, but she'd be coming in at some point today to help ready the house for tonight's event.

He awkwardly pushed himself up. As expected, his

head felt too heavy for his neck, his brain a bit foggy. Hopefully a large cup of coffee would fix that. Dressing took some doing on his part, despite the fact his injury dictated he wear less clothing. Unfortunately, Smith wasn't around to assist with the buttons, so he pulled the sides of his shirt closed as best he could and slipped the sling back over his head. The windows in this guest room overlooked the back of the property, and he looked out in search of his valet. No sign of him.

Exiting his room, his gaze strayed to his mother's old one directly across the hall. He had avoided it since that first week when he'd snooped through her and Charles's things searching for answers. He hesitated. *What did you do, Maman?* He hated the suspicions rifling through his mind, tainting his memories. He'd been ready to leave here without the answers he sought, but he had time on his hands now. Perhaps he should resume the search.

He strode to the door and pushed it open, paused on the threshold. White lace curtains hung at the windows and a pink ruffled bedspread adorned the bed where two dolls—one porcelain and one handmade—lay waiting. There was a small writing desk and chair and an oversize oak wardrobe. A small stack of fancy stationery and envelopes lay untouched on the desktop, and two paintings hung above the headboard. His mother's work? She hadn't painted at home. Something else she'd given up in an effort to please his father?

He walked to the wardrobe and opened the doors, fingering the dresses hanging inside. Good material, pretty yet simple in style, fitting for life in this quaint mountain town. Similar to Megan's and her sisters' clothes, in fact. He certainly hadn't seen his mother wear anything like this. She'd dressed the part of the ship baron's wife in gowns crafted by the most fashionable designers around, ears and neck dripping with jewels and hair styled just-so. Father must've brought someone in shortly after their wedding to transform the humble mountain girl into an acceptable lady of society.

Had she missed her old life at all? He wished now that he'd thought to ask her.

He couldn't picture Megan in his world. Found it nearly impossible to picture her amid the splendor and opulence of his family's mansion in the city. What a shame it would be to try to tame her natural beauty, to mold her into an unoriginal socialite with pretty manners and shallow conversation. No. Megan didn't need extravagant clothes or flashy jewels. She was perfect just the way she was—delicate and feminine in her softly flowing dresses, her white-blond curls tamed by a single ribbon. In his eyes, she was more beautiful than any other woman in the world.

With a heavy sigh, he pushed the doors back into place, thinking he should do something with the dresses. Perhaps donate them? He would seek Megan's advice. As Charles's close friend, she might have an idea what would've pleased him.

His grandfather must've left this room exactly as Lucinda had left it. Why? Had he ever entered it again? Or had it been too painful a reminder of all he'd lost?

Dear God, I'm so confused. Help me, please, to find the answers I'm looking for. And if there aren't any to find, help me to accept that. To find peace.

He hoped Megan was right. Hoped God was listening and that He cared.

Through the window, Lucian heard someone whistling a merry tune. From the sound of it, that someone was advancing up the lane. He pushed the curtain aside with a quiet swish and stared out. His jaw dropped. His horse! Squinting, forehead pressed against the cool glass, he studied the large, sleek animal. No question about it…D'Artagnan was home.

Hurrying down the winding staircase, his hand skimming the banister for balance, questions zipped through his brain suddenly cleared of all fog. Could it be true?

Out on the porch, he held on to the post and waited for the seedy-looking character leading his horse to reach him. When the man spotted Lucian, he tipped his battered hat up and studied him. "Howdy do. Would you be Lucian Beaumont?"

"Yes, sir." He descended the steps, stopping at the bottom, his gaze sweeping D'Artagnan in search of possible injuries. Relief expanded his chest when he didn't notice any. Dirt-coated, his mane knotted with debris, all he appeared to need was a good meal and thorough brushing down.

Impatient to greet his old friend, he moved closer and, skimming a palm along his neck, murmured in French. Snickering, D'Artagnan turned his head and nudged Lucian. Transferring his gaze to the wizened old man who, by the looks of him, was a down-on-his-luck drifter, he said, "I'm sorry, what did you say your name was?"

"I didn't." He grinned, shocking Lucian with his rows of straight white teeth, made brilliant against his sun-browned skin. "The name's Cyril Hawk."

"Mr. Hawk, where did you find him? And how did you know to bring him to me?"

Shrugging, he released the reins. "He wandered on to my property last evenin'. I went through the bags and found a Bible. Can't read, so I brought him into town early this morning and showed it to Sheriff Timmons. Belonged to your ma, did it?"

Lucian nodded, gratefulness clogging his throat. Opening the bag, he clasped the large black tome and, lifting it with his good hand, held it against his chest. *Thank You, God.*

Cyril just stood watching him, wise understanding in his eyes.

"Do you live nearby?" he asked, voice gravelly.

He motioned over his shoulder. "About five miles south of town."

"Five miles?" He hadn't brought a wagon or second horse with him.

Noticing Lucian's confusion, he offered another grin. "I like to walk. Well, now that I've done my good deed for the day, I gotta be headin' back." He tipped his hat. "Nice to meet ya, Beaumont. You have yourself a good day."

"Wait."

Cyril paused midturn, bushy brows raised in question.

"I'd like to repay you for your kindness. Give me a moment, and I'll get you some money—"

He held up a hand. "No need for that. I was happy to do it. Golden rule and all that."

"I insist. You've returned something very valuable to me."

"Horses can be replaced."

Lucian gripped the Bible tighter. "This one can't."

Approval showing in his expression, Cyril said gruffly, "Your gratitude is payment enough, young man." Then he turned resolutely and headed back down the lane, whistling a vaguely familiar tune.

He watched until the stranger disappeared from

sight. *I don't know if this was Your doing or not, God, but thank You.*

Because both hands were indisposed, he buried his face in his horse's neck. "Welcome home, buddy. Wait until Megan hears this."

Stationed in the parlor entrance, Megan was able to see the guests mingling inside and those just arriving. The house was abuzz with anticipation, chatter and the clinking of glasses echoing off the walls. Nervous excitement bubbled in her tummy. The turnout so far exceeded that of any previous poetry recital, and there were still fifteen minutes before time to begin.

Her gaze was drawn once again to the fireplace, to where Lucian stood sandwiched between the Moores and the Jenkinses, his air of command making him seem a foot taller than those around him. Wearing a black vest and evening coat beneath the sling, his rich brown hair somewhat tamed away from his face, he was easily the most handsome man in the room. His austere mask didn't fool her. She was well acquainted with the sensitive, hurting heart hiding behind it.

When she realized his attention was not on his companions but on *her,* his black-as-midnight gaze intent with undisguised admiration, her breathing quickened. Sparkling awareness danced along her nerve endings. Since the moment of her arrival, she'd sensed his perusal move with her about the room.

Wanting to look her best this evening, she'd borrowed one of Nicole's dresses. Crafted from exquisite ivory silk that brushed against her heated skin like cool water, bands of seed pearls enhanced the scooped neck and fitted waist and edged the short puffed sleeves. An intricate lace overlay adorned the full skirt, and along the hem, Nicole had stitched delicate gold-and-silver flowers. Kate had secured the top section of her hair with sparkly diamond pins—family heirlooms, she'd called them—allowing the remainder of her curls to tumble down her back. Judging from Lucian's reaction, the effort had been well worth it.

Megan shoved aside the inner warning that she was playing a dangerous game.

"Megan? Hello?"

With a start, she tore her gaze from Lucian and looked up into her cousin's amused face. "Nathan!"

Surprise spurred her to hug him. Low laughter rumbled in his chest, and she eased back, smiling. "What are you doing here? This isn't your cup of tea, so to speak."

"Would you believe I just happened to have free time on my hands?" He touched his still-damp brown hair.

"You? Free time? No, sorry. Not buying it." Nathan and Caleb stayed busy around the farm, neither one much inclined for social events such as this.

"I didn't think so." He sighed with mock defeat, his gaze straying to the crowd behind her and then back. "Josh and Kate were all set to come, but then she had a dizzy spell. She insisted it was nothing, but Josh urged her to stay home and rest. She's been awfully busy lately with people wanting their photographs taken, which is good for business but you know how Josh worries. Anyway, he asked me to come in their place. Wanted someone here to support you."

He shrugged, clearly perplexed. Nathan was a good man, caring and protective of his family, if a bit too serious and introspective at times. But he'd never been in love. Seemed uninterested in finding himself a wife and utterly oblivious to the single girls' attempts to snag his attention. Of course he wouldn't understand Josh's need to take care of his wife.

"I was with her earlier today. Now that you mention it, she did seem a bit more subdued than usual." Had she been feeling unwell and hadn't wanted to let on? Or was it her longing for a baby weighing on her mind?

Nathan squeezed her shoulder. "Don't worry, the bloom was back in her cheeks when I left. Josh was plying her with tea and cookies."

"If she's not at church in the morning, I'll pay her a visit afterward."

"I'm certain she'll be there." Searching the crowd once again, his gaze intercepted Lucian's and he tipped his head in silent greeting. "How much longer do you think he'll be here?"

Megan shrugged, tried to appear nonchalant. "A couple of weeks."

His voice deepened in concern. "Are you going to be all right?"

"Of course. Why wouldn't I be?"

"Don't try and pretend he doesn't matter to you. When I walked up, the two of you were locked in your own little world. You didn't even hear me greet you the first time."

Megan's cheeks burned. Were her feelings that obvious? Was Lucian aware?

She had to be more careful. He'd made it plain there was no room in his life for love. He would not be pleased to learn she had disregarded his wishes. Had foolishly allowed her heart to love him.

"Look, I didn't mean to upset you," Nathan said into the silence hanging between them. "I'm worried, that's all."

Twisting her hands together, she forced a bright smile

to her face. She had the entire evening to get through. "You didn't." Glancing at the clock, she said, "You should go and find a seat. I—I remember something I need from the library."

His brow furrowed. "Megan—"

"I really can't talk right now."

Not daring to look in Lucian's direction, she hurried down the hall and into the blessedly empty library. The night was dark behind the curtains, and with only one lamp lit, the room was wreathed in shadows. She moved into them, taking refuge in the far corner against the bookshelves. She needed to clear her head. To regain control over her emotions.

Suddenly she wondered how she was supposed to stand up in front of everyone, Lucian in particular, and recite words of love without the truth shining through? Why, oh why, hadn't she picked something humorous? Or lighthearted?

One thing she knew—she must not look at him. Not even once. He'd see her heart's yearning and if he did... She shook her head. At best, he'd be disappointed. At worst, horrified. Repulsed.

The skin of her nape tingled then, the fine hairs on her arms standing to attention.

She whirled. "Lucian?"

He came towards her, concern pulling at his mouth. "You looked upset, so I followed you." He came very close, his expression difficult to read in the relative darkness. His broad shoulders blocked out what little light there was. "Are you all right?"

"Just a little nervous." *And going a little bit crazy worrying over you.*

"You're a natural storyteller. I'm confident you'll have them all mesmerized by your talent and grace.

That is, *if* they can focus on your words." He gently tugged on a curl and watched it spring back into place. "You look absolutely breathtaking tonight, Megan."

She couldn't think straight with him standing so near. No matter what, she wouldn't repeat last night's mistake. Sidestepping him, she moved in the direction of the door.

Anger tinged with despair thrummed through her. He wasn't playing fair! Complimenting her in that smooth-as-velvet voice, touching her when he'd rebuffed her less than twenty-four hours ago.

"Can I get you a glass of water or something?" he asked, subdued. As if she'd given voice to her rebuff.

"No, I'm fine."

Closing her eyes, she recalled the expression on his face as he'd insisted he was trying to protect her. He'd been torn, conflicted. It hit her then. He was as drawn to her as she was to him. Oh, she was under no illusion that he loved her. He wouldn't be that reckless, not when he'd clearly outlined his goals and the way he expected his life to go. For him, the attraction was merely physical. The fact that she was different from the young socialites he was accustomed to made her interesting. A passing fancy.

Anguish wrapped its tentacles about her heart and squeezed, the pressure almost too much to bear.

He came up behind her but made no move to touch her. "Megan?" A thousand questions in one word.

Opening her eyes, she lifted her chin, determined he not discover her true feelings. Ever.

Turning, she shot him a smile that hopefully appeared genuine. "It's time to start the recital. Are you coming?"

His gaze narrowed. "I—"

"I don't mean to be rude, Lucian, but I don't want to keep everyone waiting."

She left him there, not stopping to see if he followed. It would be amazing if she made it through this night.

Chapter Sixteen

Lucian followed several steps behind, slipping into a vacant seat in the back row as Megan made her way to the front to welcome everyone and introduce the first speaker. He studied her as he'd done since the moment she'd arrived, captivated by her beauty and her innate sweetness. Her smile was fragile, the customary sparkle in her blue eyes conspicuously absent. Was she always this nervous before an event? He hadn't noticed her this way with the children, but adults were a different audience. Or was it something else entirely? They hadn't exactly parted on good terms the night before. He'd planned to speak with her before the recital, to share with her the good news of D'Artagnan's return, but there hadn't been time.

The matter plagued him as one by one, the people stood up and recited their selections. He tried to listen, really he did, but his gaze kept straying to Megan seated in the first row in between Nathan and a young lady he hadn't met before. Candlelight glistened in her curls, diamonds sparkling with every tilt of her head, the intricate beading on her bodice gleaming in the golden light. Her skin, he knew, was as soft as the silk dress she wore. He wished he was sitting there beside her, wished he had the right to cradle her small hand in his and reassure her fears.

At long last, it was her turn. The final speaker of the night. Standing there looking like a woodland princess in that gauzy, flower-embellished creation, her chin tilted in unspoken defiance of he knew not what, she cleared her throat and began to speak. Speaking quietly at first, her voice gained strength as she quoted Shakespeare's "Sonnet." He was familiar with the poem, of course, but hearing the words of love spoken in her lyrical voice affected him deeply. Made him wish love like that truly existed, love that didn't try to alter the other person, love that was unbending, unmovable, never shaken no matter what storms may come. She spoke with conviction and emotion, holding the room in silent thrall.

She didn't look at him. Not once.

He knew then that *he* was the cause of her discomfiture. He'd made her unhappy. How was he supposed to handle that?

When she'd finished, the audience burst into applause. With a strained smile, she thanked everyone for coming and invited them to help themselves to the refreshments laid out in the dining room. Lucian longed to go to her, to apologize for hurting her feelings, but he held back. How could he explain that, while he liked and respected her, he found it difficult to be near her? Megan made him forget lessons learned from childhood about love and the heartache that inevitably followed.

He clenched his right hand, gritting his teeth as razor-sharp pain radiated up his as-yet-unhealed forearm. This delay was going to cost him. The longer he stayed here, the less appeal his old life held for him. A dangerous thing. He needed to go home and begin his search for a suitable wife. Once he was married, he would banish all thoughts of Megan. Bury his memories of her. Erase Gatlinburg, Tennessee, from his consciousness.

As it turned out, he didn't get a chance to share his good news. Or apologize. She made certain they weren't alone and bade him good-night with Nathan by her side.

"Thank you for everything, Lucian," she told him with her arm linked through her cousin's. "The flowers were a nice touch." Her appreciative gaze wandered about the room, lighting on the freshly cut bouquets he'd asked Fred to assemble.

"I would call the evening a success, wouldn't you?"

Her eyes touched his only briefly. "Yes, I would." She addressed Nathan. "What did you think?"

"It wasn't a bad way to spend the evening." He winked at her.

"Good night, Lucian," Megan said softly, finally allowing her blue gaze to linger on his face. But he couldn't read her expression, and it bothered him not to know what she was thinking or feeling.

"Good night." *Mon bien-aime. My beloved.*

But he mustn't say that or even allow himself to entertain such a thought.

He shut the door behind them, leaning back against the polished wood and stained glass. After such a lively evening, the stillness of the house seemed magnified. Despite his reservations, he hadn't minded having a houseful of strangers. The townspeople had accepted him into their fold without question, most of them friendly.

As the silence settled over him like a heavy blanket, he felt his aloneness acutely. More than anything, he wished Megan could've stayed a little longer and discussed the night. He enjoyed their conversations, was intrigued by her intelligence and insight and wit.

Her leaving with Nathan was probably for the best, however. Might as well get used to not having her around.

This time, the heaviness in his chest had nothing to do with not getting enough rest and everything to do with the prospect of leaving her.

At the conclusion of Reverend Monroe's prayer, Megan turned to exit her pew and was stunned to see Lucian's familiar form slipping out the door. He hadn't indicated he would be here today. Surely this was a good sign.

Outside in the sunshine, she spotted him in the hillside cemetery, a solitary figure outlined against the blue sky studded with clouds. The stout breeze ruffled his hair and tugged at his coattails.

Nicole stopped beside her, pulling wayward raven strands away from her face put there by the wind. "Are you going to talk to him?"

"No, I don't think so." Although she wanted to. Badly.

Hadn't she made enough of a fool of herself around him lately?

Jane rushed up, breathless, gray skirts swirling about her boots. "The Nortons invited me to lunch with them. Do you mind?"

Jane, Jessica and Tori Norton were close friends. "Sure. What time do you expect to be home?"

"Tanner offered to bring me home later this evening."

Megan had long suspected Jane was nursing a crush on Tori's older brother. He was a nice young man, but at twenty a bit too old for her fifteen-year-old sister. Jane had a good head on her shoulders, but Megan worried she might get hurt.

"Fine, just be home before dark."

"Thanks, Megan." Jane bussed her cheek and dashed off in the direction of the other family's wagon. The Nortons waved to her. She waved back, then turned to Nicole.

"Well, I suppose it's just you and me."

"We could always invite Lucian to join us."

Risking another glance at the cemetery, she saw that he hadn't moved from his spot. What was he thinking? What did he think of the sermon?

"Not today."

Thankful Nicole didn't question her further, they walked in silence the rest of the way home. They spent a restful afternoon reading and playing chess. Lucian was never far from her thoughts, however. While she'd managed not to look at him while standing in front of the audience, the words she'd spoken had been all for him. Her love for him was like that poem. Unshakable. Accepting of their differences. A love that time could not erase.

That's why she hadn't wanted to risk being alone with him last night, why she hadn't approached him after church today. She was afraid he'd be able to see it in her eyes, this all-encompassing love. A love he would reject in a heartbeat.

She stayed away all that week.

And, although she had every intention of leading story time Friday night, she was stricken with a terrible headache shortly after lunch that afternoon. Nicole begrudgingly agreed to go in her place, not because she liked the kids but because she liked Lucian and his fancy house. She planned to live in an even grander house than that one day, she'd declared. When she returned later that night, she told Megan that Lucian had been even more reserved than usual. Downcast, even.

Guilt and worry immediately assailed her. Was Nicole exaggerating? Questions pummeled her mind. Was he getting enough rest? Was his arm healing properly? What must he think of her absence this week? Was she right to avoid him?

Saturday morning, his valet delivered a bouquet of delicate pink roses and a note. With trembling fingers, she opened it and read his fine script.

> *Dearest Megan,*
> *While the children and I were grateful for Nicole's presence last evening, we missed you.*
> *I hope this morning finds you much improved. If you have need of anything, please do not hesitate to call on me.*
> *Your humble servant,*
> *Lucian*

By the time Sunday morning rolled around, she was desperate to see him.

Like the previous week, he occupied the last pew, slipping out at the final amen. Megan impatiently wound her way through the crowd and down the steps, relieved when she spotted him in the cemetery. She told her sisters not to wait. Walking up the hill with her skirts lifted off the ground, her pulse quickened in anticipation.

His back to her, he stood before two headstones, dark head bent.

"Lucian?"

He pivoted, the soles of his boots squeaking against the grass. "Megan." His obsidian eyes raked her from head to toe, searching for…something. His face creased in concern. "Are you well?"

Warmed by his gaze, she smiled. "I am." Lowering her skirts, she took an involuntary step closer. "I didn't have a lot of extra time this week. We stayed busy working in the vegetable garden."

"I see."

The line between his brows indicated he didn't. Was trying to work out if she'd stayed away for another reason altogether.

Before he could pursue the subject, she pointed to where he cradled his arm against his stomach. "How is your arm?"

"It's healing. More slowly than I'd like. On doctor's orders, I've been taking off the sling a couple of times each day and exercising my shoulder and biceps. He warned me I'd get stiff if I didn't."

His fawn suit coat hugged his athletic build to perfection, the pale hue lending his sun-bronzed skin a healthy glow. The noonday sun picked out highlights in his hair.

"Does it pain you?"

"Only if I make an unexpected movement or forget and clench my fingers."

Hating that *she* had put him in that cast, she only nodded. Gazed at Charles's headstone and that of his wife, Beatrice, who'd died years before Lucinda left Gatlinburg. Megan came here sometimes to place flowers at his grave, to read to him and imagine him listening from his eternal home above.

Lucian followed her gaze. "When I was very young, I often wondered what they were like. Like Mother, my father was an only child and his parents died before their marriage. Charles was my only other living relative, and I was quite curious about him. My friends all had these wonderful tales of fun-loving grandfathers who took them fishing and hunting and grandmothers who plied them with chocolates and pulled them onto their laps for hugs and stories. As I grew older, I became more persistent in questioning my mother about him. I wanted to know why he never came to visit. Why we didn't visit him.

"When she told me Charles didn't want to meet me, I couldn't believe it. Why wouldn't a grandfather want to know his grandson? I thought something was wrong with me."

Hurting for the little boy that he had been, Megan slipped her hand into his larger one. His lean fingers closed around hers, mouth twisting in regret.

"On occasion, she'd relent and tell me about this place." He gazed out over the valley, the forested mountains seemingly close enough to touch. "I think…it's entirely plausible that my mother refused Charles's requests. It makes sense. She wouldn't have wanted to upset my father by coming back. Because of her feelings for him, she would've denied herself the chance to see her home again, to mend her relationship with Charles. If that meant lying to me— She would've done anything, anything at all, to make my father love her." Bitterness crept into his voice. "Love. Pointless, futile emotion! It got her nothing but misery."

Pulling his hand free, he shoved his fingers through his hair. Frustration hummed along his rigid muscles, so intense he almost shook from it. *This* was why he spurned love. He'd only ever witnessed its destructive power.

"It doesn't have to be like that, you know," she said

urgently, curling a restraining hand about his upper arm. "Love doesn't hurt when it's right...when God is the foundation."

"What does God have to do with it?" His gaze probed hers, sincerely conflicted.

"Why, everything! God *is* love. Apart from Him, people are basically selfish, concerned only about our own interests. But with God's help, we can put others' needs and interests above our own. We can love sacrificially."

He studied her for the longest time, warring emotions marching across his face. Then he smiled such a sad smile it rent her heart in two. "My sweet dreamer, I wish I could believe in the kind of love you do. But I'm afraid I've seen too much, endured too much. I'm jaded and cynical and much too hard for the likes of you."

"No." Her grip on his arm tightened. "No, Lucian, you just haven't had the right kind of examples in your life. I know true love exists because I've seen it with my own eyes. My parents had that kind of love. Aunt Mary and Uncle Sam, too. Now Evan and Juliana. Josh and Kate. Their relationships aren't perfect, of course, because none of us are perfect. But they share a genuine love and commitment to each other. It does exist," she repeated, determined he see the truth.

"I'm sorry. You won't succeed in convincing me."

Megan bit her lip. It wasn't enough to tell him so. He had to see the evidence with his own eyes. Spend time around couples who were committed to each other.

"Hey," he murmured, tipping up her chin, "you don't have to look so sad."

"Come to my aunt and uncle's with me."

His black brows winged up.

"Please," she added with a beseeching gaze. "Have lunch with my family."

"I am rather tired of my own company," he said ruefully.

"It will be crowded and noisy like last time. Nothing formal or fancy."

"Crowded and noisy sounds perfect." Lowering his voice to a whisper, he confided, "And to be completely honest, I'm not all that fond of formal or fancy." Covering her hand, he said, "Shall we?"

Happy he'd agreed, Megan smiled and allowed him to guide her down the hill and along a nearly deserted Main Street. As they passed Tom's darkened barbershop, she sensed Lucian's perusal. If he'd noticed Tom's absence this morning, he made no mention of it.

They walked in amiable silence, nature's springtime music a well-orchestrated symphony. Beneath the wooden bridge, the Little Pigeon River churned and crashed over mossy boulders, the hum of rushing water trailing them onto the tree-lined lane that led to her aunt and uncle's farm and, a mile and a half farther down, her own home. The dense forest on either side popped and cracked, branches swaying in the breeze. Somewhere a woodpecker pecked. Thrushes and warblers whistled and cooed.

Sneaking a glance at Lucian, she wondered what he was thinking. Wondered if he would ever change his mind about love. About marriage. Would he ever learn to trust again?

And could *she* be the one to teach him how?

Chapter Seventeen

Rocking on the porch, Sam lifted his head at their arrival and gestured to an empty chair beside him. "Sit and rest a spell, Lucian. The gals will let us know when the meal is ready."

Grasping the door handle, Megan smiled her agreement. "It shouldn't take long."

As she disappeared inside, Sam commented, "Hope you brought your appetite. They tend to go overboard for Sunday dinner."

Smiling, Lucian lowered himself in the rocking chair. "Since I overslept and had to skip breakfast this morning, I'd say that suits me just fine."

"How's the arm?"

His fingers grazed the sling. "It's coming along. Doc wants me to wait two to three more weeks to travel home."

Sam gazed at him. "It's awfully generous of you to leave the house in Megan's care. Folks around here will be mighty grateful."

Lucian studied the older man, judged him to be about the same age as his mother. "How well did you know my grandfather?"

"Charles? I knew him to be a fair man. Well liked. A responsible member of the community." He nudged his spectacles farther up his nose. "You probably heard that in recent years he didn't go out much. He came to church but didn't attend any functions. Why do you ask?"

"Megan said that Charles wrote my mother in an attempt to mend the rift between them. That he wanted to meet me. My mother didn't mention any letters. She… led me to believe Charles was indifferent. I'd like to know the truth. So far, I haven't found anything in the house that can shed light on their relationship. Or lack thereof. I plan to look through her things when I get back to New Orleans. Maybe I'll have better luck there."

"I'm afraid I can't help you with that. I *can* tell you this," he said as he waved his finger. "Family was extremely important to Charles. He adored Beatrice and Lucinda. Bea's death devastated him, but at least he still had your mother. They were very close. After she left…" He shook his head in regret. "It makes sense he would try to make amends. There's no question in my mind that he would've wanted to meet you."

Lucian trusted Sam's judgment. And Megan's. Granted, Charles could've said those things simply to gain her sympathy…but he didn't think so. As difficult as it was to admit, even to himself, it appeared his mother had misrepresented the situation. And, while he understood her reasoning, it hurt to know she'd deceived him. Her only son. Cheated him and Charles out of a relationship. It hurt bad.

"Kinda tough to be angry at someone who's not around to defend themselves," Sam observed offhandedly.

He stood and crossed to the rail, stared out across the yard. "Yes, well, she did it to make my father happy.

Too bad it was all for nothing. She cheated not only herself, but Charles and me, as well." Bitterness encased his heart, dripped from his words. Didn't he have the right to be angry? Deceived by someone he'd trusted completely? This lie of hers…it had far-reaching effects.

"I'm sorry."

"Me, too," he murmured, turning as the door creaked open.

Megan's questioning gaze volleyed between her uncle and him. "Dinner's on the table."

"It's about time." Sam winked at her, pushed to his feet.

She looked at Lucian. Her gaze caught by something behind him, her face brightened. "Caleb!"

She swept past him. Turning, he spotted the youngest O'Malley loping towards the house, serious and drawn. When Megan threw herself into his arms, his head dipped, hat brim blocking his expression. He gave her an awkward pat on the back. "Hey, Meg."

Lucian shot a glance at Sam standing stiffly by the door, watching the exchange with pronounced lines about his eyes.

"I haven't seen you in weeks," she chided gently, stepping away to look full in his face. She tugged on his arm. "Come on—there's someone I'd like you to meet."

Lucian straightened from the rail, moved to the top step to intercept them. While the younger man matched him in height, he was bulkier than Lucian. His dark gaze flicked to Sam for an instant. Clearly happy to see her cousin, Megan made the introductions. Caleb angled his face to the side, but not before Lucian glimpsed a jagged scar near his eye. Hmm.

"Nice to meet you," Lucian said evenly as they shook hands.

"Likewise," he bit out. It was apparently a struggle for him to be civil. What was behind his absences? Didn't he help Nathan and Sam around the farm? Josh did what he could, but the majority of his time was spent building furniture and managing the store.

Sweeping off his hat, Caleb paused in front of his father. "Pa."

"You're just in time for dinner, son," Sam said with a strained smile as he held the door open.

Twirling a stray curl about her finger, Megan shot Lucian a meaningful look as they followed the men inside. This would no doubt prove to be an interesting meal. Everyone greeted Caleb with warmth. Warmth he had trouble accepting.

When everyone was seated and grace offered up, conversation progressed in fits and starts, the edge of tension palpable. The youngest O'Malley sat with his head bent, looking as if he wished he was invisible. Gradually, though, the mood eased.

With Megan at his side, Lucian savored the meal of roast chicken and mashed potatoes, assorted vegetables and fresh sourdough bread slathered with butter. The O'Malleys were a lively bunch. There was a lot of good-natured teasing going on. Hearing Megan's laughter, seeing her happy and relaxed, he finally understood her desire for a large family.

Perhaps if he'd grown up in such a setting, he'd want that for himself.

All through the meal, he surreptitiously studied Josh and Kate, who were seated directly across from him. Josh was affectionate with his delicate, dark-haired wife, constantly touching her hair, her cheek, whispering in her ear. Still in the newlywed phase, obviously. For some couples the phase lasted longer than others, he supposed. Watching them exchange secretive smiles, Lucian resented the fact he couldn't be so free with Megan.

Once, she'd caught him staring at the couple, and her smile had faltered, tremulous, fierce longing blazing in her expressive blue eyes…searing him with its heat, making him crazy to hold her. To lay claim to her. And then the panic had set in. He was close, dangerously close, to giving in to these forbidden feelings. To throwing caution to the wind and going down on his knees right here in front of everyone and begging her to stay with him forever.

Somehow, he garnered the strength to break eye contact. Did she notice the tiny beads of sweat forming on his brow? His uneven breathing?

All he had to do was think of his parents and know what a monumental mistake that would be. He told himself this was an infatuation. What man wouldn't be enamored of her natural beauty, her strength of character? Her compassion and wit?

What he felt for Megan was not love. Not even close.

He was so confident of this fact that he thought nothing of asking her to accompany him back to his house later that afternoon. He had yet to tell her of D'Artagnan's return, and he decided it would be more fun to show her.

At the entrance to the barn, he put a hand out to stop her. "Close your eyes."

"What?" She laughed up at him, charming curls framing her face. "Why?"

"Just do as you're told, young lady," he admonished with a grin, too content to be properly wary. With an arched brow, she complied and he took her hand and led her deep into the barn's interior. "Keep them closed," he warned.

"I'm not sure I like surprises," she said smartly, her boots scuffing the dirt as she took halting steps, her free hand outstretched to catch herself if she stumbled. Of course he wouldn't let that happen.

"I guarantee you'll like this one."

When they reached his horse's stall, D'Artagnan came close and extended his head their direction. "All right. You may open your eyes now."

Lids fluttering open, she gasped. "What? He's here?" Her incredulous gaze volleyed between him and his horse. Stepping closer, she rubbed a hand down D'Artagnan's face. "Oh, Lucian, I can hardly believe my eyes! How did you find him?"

Enjoying her reaction, he stood still and watched her. "I didn't. A man by the name of Cyril Hawk found him on his property and brought him back to me. Do you know him?"

Her brows met in the middle. "No, I'm afraid I don't."

"He must not come into town very often, then. He wouldn't accept payment."

Megan paused in bestowing affection on the big animal, brow furrowing. "And your things? Were they in the bags?"

"Yes, everything." He nodded. "Including my mother's Bible." And he'd been reading it every day since, just as he'd told God he would. "You were right about the notes. I've found lots of underlined verses and words jotted in the margins."

"You've been reading it?"

"Since it's been a while, I decided to start in Psalms. I find them…comforting. Uplifting."

"This is a positive answer to prayer, Lucian. You see that, don't you?"

"I do."

"I'm so happy you got it back. And D'Artagnan, too."

Eyes shining, Megan threw her arms about his neck, burying her face beneath his chin. Stunned, he didn't move. He'd taken his sling off as soon as they'd arrived, so his injured arm hung awkwardly at his side. Her silky hair tickled his throat. He curled his good arm around her waist in a kind of half hug, anchoring her more firmly against his chest. His eyes drifted shut, and he inhaled her rose scent. Megan here, in his arms, felt right. Natural. Meant to be.

With a tiny, reluctant sigh, she lifted her head. Touched his every feature with her hungry gaze. He couldn't *not* kiss her. Unlike the kiss at the stream, this one was tentative. Gentle. Their lips clinging in tender reverence, his heart shifted, strained towards her as if it recognized its lifelong companion...its soul mate.

He lifted his injured arm and carefully sank his fingers in her curls, luxuriating in the weight and feel of it. What was a little pain if it meant he got to touch her crowning glory? Her fingers kneaded his nape and tangled in his hair. His heart felt as if it might burst from his chest.

With bone-deep regret, he lifted his head. If only he had forever to kiss her.

She unwound her arms, sliding them lower so that her palms rested on his chest. "I should go." Her eyes were a turbulent blue storm.

His fingers flexed on her slim waist. "Are you certain? We could go inside and play a game of chess. Or read." He liked that idea, the two of them together in the cozy library, sharing funny or interesting bits of the books they were reading.

"I can't." Extracting herself from his arms, she gave D'Artagnan a final pat. "Good night, Lucian."

He stopped her exit with a hand on her shoulder. "We should talk."

"There's nothing to talk about." She was avoiding his gaze, and it gave him a panicky feeling.

Dropping his hand to his side, he demanded, "Are you planning on avoiding me again this week?"

When she shot him a helpless look, he went on beseechingly, "My time here is growing short, *mon chou*. I'd like to spend it with you."

"I'd like that, too." But the pucker between her brows revealed her disquiet.

"Why don't you and the girls come for dinner tomorrow night?"

A weak smile was his reward. "What time do you want us here?"

"Six o'clock?"

"Okay."

Standing in the barn entrance, he watched her walk away. Watched until she'd rounded the bend and disappeared from sight, a yawning emptiness in his chest.

Odd…this didn't feel like a harmless infatuation.

Megan and her sisters dined with him every night that week. Nicole's and Jane's presence acted as a buffer, making it easier to maintain his perspective and eliminate any chances of acting rashly. For just a little while, the sprawling house would transform into something resembling a true home with laughter and conversation and the glow of friendship…far removed from the stiff formality he'd known at home.

For Lucian, the hours between breakfast and dinner stretched endlessly, and he found himself prowling about the property, counting the minutes until she arrived, her smile the only antidote to his lonely, restless state. Late Thursday evening, after they'd gone and the rooms once again stood silent and brooding, he wandered into the study to where his mother's Bible lay open on the desk. He sank into the chair. Scanned the pages of John.

Peace I leave with you; my peace I give you. I do not give to you as the world gives. Do not let your hearts be troubled and do not be afraid.

Troubled? That summed up his entire year. *God, I don't have this peace. Not about my mother and Charles. And definitely not about Megan.*

Resting his head against the soft leather, his eyes drifted shut. He was exhausted. A bone-deep, soul-weary exhaustion that stemmed from frustration. No matter where he turned, the answers he sought eluded him. And the situation with Megan…it was impossible.

With a sigh, he opened his eyes and stared at the polished copper ceiling tiles, his gaze falling naturally on the shelves opposite. There, wedged between the ceiling and the shelves, sat a wooden box. Lucian's lungs hung suspended. What was that? Standing, he crossed to that side of the room and cast about for something to stand on. His palms were sweating. Heart hammering. He had a funny feeling about that box.

Shrugging out of his sling, he dragged a chair over, and, stepping onto it, he balanced himself with a hand on the shelves. It was a stretch, but he managed to scoot it close enough to get a good hold and lower it without losing his balance. Anticipation zipping along his nerves, he carried it over to the desk and placed it in the center. Stared at it.

Don't get yourself all worked up. For all you know, Charles could've stored expensive cigars in there. Or photographs.

"Only one way to find out," he murmured, lifting the lid.

At the sight of the stack of letters all tied up with a black ribbon, Lucian sank into the chair. That was his mother's handwriting. Megan was right. Charles had been telling the truth.

His mother and Charles *had* been in contact.

It took a while for him to work up the courage to lift out the stack, untie the ribbon and pull out that first letter. Then he began to read.

Strolling arm in arm towards their cabin, Jane was the first to spot Tom in the gathering dusk. At her nudge, Megan looked up. His lean body propped against a support, hat dangling from his fingertips, he was listening patiently to Nicole chatter as she rocked back and forth. Then she saw them and put her boot down to stop the motion.

"How was dinner? Did Lucian miss me?" To Tom, she declared, "We've dined at his house every night this week. One day I'm going to live in a house like that. Grander, even, in a big, bustling city where exciting things happen all the time."

Jane sighed long-sufferingly. This was nothing they hadn't heard before. "Of course, Lucian sent his regards. He's the consummate gentleman."

A shadow passed over Tom's face. Megan met his green gaze with a tentative smile. "Hello, Tom."

Leaping to the ground in one smooth move, he met

them halfway up the path. "Hello, ladies." His smile held a nervous edge. "Care to walk with me for a bit?" His gaze slid reluctantly to her sister. "You're welcome to come along, Janie-girl."

Jane's lashes swished down, and, flipping her auburn ponytail behind her shoulder, she tipped her chin up in a signature O'Malley move. "Thanks for the invitation but I'm tired. I'm going inside."

As she and Nicole disappeared inside the cabin, Tom waited for her reply. She was tired, too, but wouldn't turn him away. He obviously had something on his mind.

Falling into step, they ambled past the cabin and, entering the woods, headed without speaking to the stream. Pink-washed light penetrated the trees. Darkness would descend soon, but they weren't going far and they knew this path by heart. It was where they came to fish or visit or simply sit and daydream.

Megan despised the uneasiness she felt around him now. Would it always be this way? Would things ever go back to normal?

Once there, he didn't lounge on a rock along the grassy bank or lean against a tree and toss rocks into the meandering water as he usually did. Instead, he paced like a caged panther.

"Tom, is something bothering you?"

"Yes." He stopped short, grimaced. Shook his head. "No." Coming towards her, he stopped a breath away. "Actually, I have something I'd like to ask you."

His demeanor told her this wasn't a casual question. Her heart thumped a dull beat in her chest. Surely he wasn't about to—

Sliding his hand in his pants' pocket, he withdrew a ruby ring and held it between his thumb and forefinger.

He took hold of her hand. Cleared his throat. "Megan, it's no secret how I feel about you. I've tried to give you the space you said you needed, but I think that was a mistake. It feels as though you're slipping away."

Her gaze was riveted to that ring, glinting red sparks in the waning light. "Tom—"

"Please, let me finish."

Pressing her lips together, she nodded, wishing they could retrace their steps, wishing she'd gone inside with her sisters instead of coming here with him. She was going to hurt him, this kind, loyal man. And she hated herself for it.

"I love you," he murmured softly, his green gaze urgent. Pleading. "I want you to be my wife. I want to spend the rest of my life with you, raise a family together. What do you say, Megan? Will you give us a chance?"

Megan squeezed her eyes tight, desperately searching for the right words, the kindest way to tell him how she felt. There could be no more cowardice. When she felt the whisper of his mouth against hers, she gasped, fell back, wrenched her hand from his.

"Don't do that," she ordered, insides in uproar.

He advanced, looking very determined. "Megan—"

"I'm in love with Lucian," she blurted.

He jerked as if struck. "In *love* with him? You hardly know the man!"

"I know him better than you think."

"Believe it or not, I understand his appeal. I do. He waltzes into town with his fancy clothes and perfect manners. He's the type of man who knows how to make a woman feel like she's important to him. Charm is bred into men like that from birth." Threading impatient fingers through his short, dark hair, he set his jaw. "Do you honestly believe he'll offer to take you back with him?"

Pain seized her. Of course Lucian would never do such a thing. She wasn't what he considered a suitable bride.

Lifting her chin, she said, "I wouldn't go even if he did ask. This is my home. My family is here. My entire life is here."

"Then why?" Lightly grasping her upper arms, Tom bent close. "Megan, please. If you don't see a future for the two of you, then give us a chance. You *know* me. You know that I'm a man of my word and that you can trust me never to hurt you. We can have a good life together, you and me and the ten kids you're so keen on having. Is he willing to give you that?"

Seeing the promise in her friend's clear green eyes, she felt tears welling up and spilling down her cheeks. This whole situation was impossible! She was in love with a man who didn't want her. And the man who *did* want her...well, her love for him was a comfortable, friendship type of love. She couldn't marry Tom or any other man. Not when her heart belonged to Lucian. Would *always* belong to him.

Thumbing moisture from her cheek, Tom picked up her hand and pressed the ring into it, curling her fingers around it when she opened her mouth to protest.

"You've a lot to sort through. Keep the ring until you've had time to consider everything I've said."

The jewel bit into her palm. "But—"

"Our friendship demands you give my proposal serious thought, don't you think? In fact, I don't want an answer until after he's gone. That way you can look at things with clearheaded perspective."

She wanted to tell him Lucian's whereabouts wouldn't

change things. "I'll keep the ring for the time being, but, Tom, I—I'm afraid you're only setting yourself up for further disappointment."

"We'll see." The light had faded to the point she could barely make out his features, the woods surrounding them brimming with shadows. "Come on, it's getting late. You know how Jane worries."

Slipping the ring deep into her pocket, she walked beside him along the path, the night noises competing with her chaotic thoughts. At the cabin, he bade her a solemn good-night. Sinking down onto the top step, she watched his retreating figure, her entire being weighed down as if a giant boulder sat upon her shoulders. He'd be crushed if he knew what she was thinking. Wishing with all her heart that the ring in her pocket was Lucian's.

Chapter Eighteen

Megan and the girls were sitting down to breakfast when Lucian's valet rapped discreetly on the door. The note he gave her requested her presence for lunch. Just her. Not her sisters. That meant she and Lucian would be alone. She couldn't deny the prospect was a daunting one. Lucian was a perceptive man. Would he notice her preoccupation? She did not want him to know about Tom's proposal. Didn't want anyone to know.

"Please tell Mr. Beaumont that I accept." She smiled tremulously at the somber Mr. Smith.

He dipped his head. "Yes, miss."

She was about to shut the door when she spotted Kate striding intently down the path looking as if she might burst with news.

"Kate? What are you doing here?"

Green eyes sparkling, the petite beauty rushed up and seized her hand. "I couldn't believe it when Josh told me Tom planned to propose! What did you say? Where's the ring?"

"Ring?" Nicole and Jane crowded in behind her. "What ring?"

Disbelief skittered across Jane's face. "Tom asked you to marry him?"

Megan held up a hand. "Settle down, everyone. Kate, Tom told Josh about this? When?"

Brushing past her, Kate advanced into the living area and whirled, her green skirts swaying. "Yesterday. He asked Josh for advice." Her gaze grew sympathetic. "I can tell by your expression that it didn't go well. You refused him, didn't you?"

Nicole sniffed. "Of course she did. Why would she marry plain ole Tom Leighton when she could have Lucian?"

"Tom is not plain," Jane hotly defended. "He'll make a wonderful husband."

Megan caught a flash of pain in her younger sister's eyes. Had she been wrong about the crush on Tanner Norton? Did Jane actually have feelings for Tom? Oh, she hoped not. Not only was he seven years older than Jane, but he saw her as a little sister. *You're forgetting the most important point—he proposed to* you.

Oh, Mama, I wish you were here. You'd know exactly what to say. How to handle this.

She met Kate's inquisitive gaze. "I didn't turn him down, exactly. He insisted I wait to give him an answer."

"Tom must be crushed." Looking pale, Jane flopped into the nearest chair.

"Because you don't love him," Kate surmised. "Is it because of your feelings for Lucian?"

Nicole clasped her hands together in a pleading motion. "Please take me with you to New Orleans when you marry Lucian! I promise to make myself scarce. You won't have to give me a single thought."

"I'm not marrying Lucian or anyone else," Megan

said with a sigh, overwhelmed with the pain she was inflicting on Tom. And possibly Jane.

"Do you have the ring?" Kate asked. "Josh mentioned Tom was going to give you his grandmother's ruby."

"Show it to us," Nicole demanded.

"Fine." They'd only nag her if she didn't relent. Retrieving it from her room, she slipped it on her finger for them to see. While Kate and Nicole oohed and ahhed over it, Jane was noticeably quiet.

"Um, my stomach's feeling a little unsettled," Kate announced suddenly, pressing a hand against her middle. She looked strange. "I haven't eaten yet. Do you mind if I join you?"

Megan led her to the table. "You're family, Kate. You don't have to ask. Sit down while I fix you a cup of tea."

To Megan's relief, the focus switched to Kate, who daintily ate her way through a stack of johnnycakes, a thick slice of ham and two eggs. Far more than she normally ate. After assuring them that she felt much improved, she went home and the girls tackled their chores. For Megan, the morning dragged. Was there a specific reason Lucian had invited only her? They had been over there every day this week. Surely he was sick of her company?

With these questions bouncing about in her head, the walk to his house seemed to stretch interminably. His smile when he opened the door seemed to her a bit forced, his brown-black eyes hollow.

"I'm glad you came." He stepped back to admit her, ushered her down the hall and into the dining room where two china place settings occupied one end of the long, mahogany table. Her gaze touched on the silver vase filled with fresh-cut pink roses and the silver-domed platters that were, judging by the rich aroma in the air, hiding something delicious.

"Isn't this a bit formal for lunch?" She waved a hand over the table, wondering if he could detect her nervousness. Tom's proposal weighed heavily on her mind. Despite the fact she and Lucian weren't involved in a relationship, she felt as if she was harboring a terrible secret. Like she was betraying Lucian somehow.

Across from her, he paused in scooting the chair back. "You should pose your question to Mrs. Calhoun. When I informed her that you would be joining me for lunch, she sprang into action."

"Well, she did a fine job." She took in his informal attire: a simple charcoal gray shirt—open at the neck—and black trousers. "You aren't wearing your sling."

"It gets tiresome." He absently massaged the back of his neck.

When he indicated the chair he'd pulled out, she rounded the table. "It strains your neck?"

He smiled, white teeth flashing. "You're very observant today, Miss O'Malley."

"Just today?" she teased, seating herself and straightening her blue skirts.

"Every day." Removing the domes from the platters, he extended his hand for her plate.

"I can serve myself, you know."

"I don't mind."

With a shrug, she gave him the plate, a little self-conscious. She'd been here alone with him many times before, but today something seemed different. The silence of the cavernous house pressed in on her, the emptiness stifling, the scrape of the serving spoons on china magnified a hundredfold.

Lucian seemed preoccupied, not fully attuned to his surroundings. Odd.

When he'd filled both of their plates and had seated himself around the corner from her, he surprised her by saying grace. The meal wasn't an easy one. Her attempts to draw him out fell flat. When he put his fork down and took a sip of lemonade, she dabbed her mouth with her napkin and, refolding it in her lap, leveled her gaze at him.

"What's bothering you, Lucian?"

Pressing his lips together, he studied the silverware, tapered fingers outlining his knife and fork. "I found something." A muscle jumped in his jaw. He pushed his chair back and stood, removing the plates to the kitchen.

Megan didn't move. Found what?

When he returned to the dining room, he went to the sideboard and picked up a wooden box she hadn't noticed before. He carried it back, set it in front of her, his hand lingering on the lid. She tilted her head back to study his face. "What is this?" she murmured, half dreading his answer.

Pain blazed hot in his eyes. "Letters. Proof Charles was telling the truth."

He slid his hand off, lifted the lid. Seating himself once more, he told her, "You may read them if you'd like."

She gazed at the stack, the elegant script on the envelopes. Lucinda's letters to Charles. Her heart squeezed. What must he be feeling right now?

"Where did you find them?"

"In the study."

She finally raised her eyes to his. "I can't possibly read all of these right now. There must be dozens."

He frowned, leaned forward and picked up the stack.

Rifling through it, he slid one out and, examining the date, handed it to her. "Try this one."

Swallowing hard, she slid out the parchment with trembling fingers, unfolding it with great care. Curiosity and dread warred in her breast.

"'Dearest Father,'" she began quietly, "'I received the chess set last week. You must understand why I had to tell Lucian it was a birthday gift from me. He was delighted, of course, but you mustn't send anything else. Gerard walked in as I was opening it, and I had to scramble to hide the packaging. I don't like having to deceive my husband and my son.'" Megan broke off to glance at Lucian, who was sitting statue-still, his expression unreadable. "Do you remember the chess set?"

"I kept it all these years, believing it was a gift from my mother," he responded with a grimace. "It's in my study. Read on. It gets better."

Sucking in a breath, Megan read, "'For now, the best thing for everyone is to keep our contact a secret. Please do not come here. Lucian wouldn't understand. Neither would Gerard.'" Her eyes smarted. Poor Charles. He'd wanted to go to them, but Lucinda had persuaded him not to. She flipped over the envelope. "Is this your address?"

"No." He spoke without emotion. "The address is that of Nannette Devereaux, a close friend of my mother's."

This iron grip on his control worried her. He needed to release his frustration, his grief. All the myriad emotions a discovery such as this must inspire.

Hurting for him and for her dear friend Charles, for their immense loss, she covered his hand with hers. "I'm so very sorry, Lucian. I can't begin to imagine how you must feel. Maybe…by willing this house to you and by adding that stipulation, it was Charles's way of reaching out to you from beyond the grave."

"Perhaps," he agreed stoically. "It's a lot to take in. I've had this fixed view of how things were for so long that I'm having trouble accepting this new reality."

She squeezed his hand. "Give yourself some time."

He glanced down at their joined hands. His gaze shot to hers. "What's this? I haven't noticed you wearing it before."

Megan gasped. Tom's ruby ring! Distracted by Kate's episode, she'd forgotten to take it off. She felt as if she might suffocate. "I—uh—"

Snatching her hand away, she stared at the ring as if it were a snake ready to strike.

Lucian visibly braced himself for her answer.

Her cheeks burned with mortification. "Tom was at the cabin when Jane and I got home last night. H-he asked me to marry him."

"I see." Lucian blinked. "I suppose congratulations are in order. When's the happy day?"

Why was he congratulating her? Did the prospect of her marrying another man not bother him? Did he care so little? Her heart broke a little at the thought. Those kisses… This *thing* between them…meant nothing to him?

"Oh, I haven't given him an answer yet." Slipping off the ring, she put it in her pocket. "He asked me to think about it awhile first. I was only wearing it this morning to show the girls."

"Tom strikes me as a fine man," Lucian said without emotion. "And it's obvious he cares about you."

Stung by his apathetic attitude, Megan lifted her chin. "He's more than fine. He's wonderful. My family adores him."

"Megan," he said, leaning forward, suddenly intense, "don't marry him simply because everyone else thinks you should. Your family won't have to live with him day after day. You will."

The tear in her heart widened, nearly rendering it in two. Lucian did not love her. His words proved it. *What did you think? He'd fall down on his knees and beg you to turn Tom down? To marry him instead? He's never going to do that. You're not his ideal wife, remember?*

The pain almost a physical ache, she shot out of her seat and glared down at him. "Don't you dare lecture me! You're the one determined to marry for duty's sake. To the least objectionable female," she mimicked, "one with all the qualifications for the esteemed Lucian Beaumont."

Feeling out of control, Megan headed for the door before she said something she'd really regret.

"Megan, wait!" He was suddenly behind her, his hand gentle but firm on her arm, halting her exit. He turned her towards him. She bit her lip at his pained expression. "I apologize. I wasn't trying to lecture you. It's just that I—" Grimacing, he made a frustrated sound, thrust his fingers through his hair. "I care about you, Megan. I want you to be happy. I don't want a love match, but you do. I want that for you, that's all."

For an instant, his guard slipped, and she thought she saw something in his eyes that said he wanted it, too. With her. But that was just wishful thinking. Lucian didn't want her love.

"I have to go." *Before I turn into a blubbering idiot.*

"Let me escort you home."

"No."

"Smith, then." Was there a desperate edge to his voice?

She stopped at the front door, her hand on the handle, not daring to look at him. "Don't worry about me. I'll be just fine on my own."

"I've upset you. Please, don't leave like this."

Yes, she was upset. He wasn't. Why would he be? His heart wasn't affected.

He was standing close behind her, close enough to feel his heat. Smell his cologne. It wouldn't take much to lean back against him. Shoving aside the temptation, she shook her head. "I don't want to discuss this anymore tonight." She opened the door. "Good night, Lucian."

And she left without a single glance back, head held high. He couldn't know that inside, she felt like a doomed heroine who'd just lost her hero.

Chapter Nineteen

Lucian gripped the porch rail, willing himself not to dash down the steps after her. She was upset. She didn't need him trailing after her like a forlorn puppy.

Too keyed up to go back inside, he strode to the barn in search of his valet. "Smith!"

"I'm here, sir." He stepped out of the stall, surprise at Lucian's tone quickly masked.

"Saddle D'Artagnan." Lucian worked to calm himself.

"But, sir, your arm…" He trailed off, clearly concerned but recognizing it wasn't his place to question his employer.

"Will be fine," he assured him, going to his horse and leading him out of the stall. "I'm not going far."

When Smith had finished, he asked, "Would you like me to accompany you?"

"No, that won't be necessary." He needed movement, a change of scenery. A chance to sort through his tumultuous thoughts.

He hauled himself into the saddle with his good arm. "*Merci*. If I'm not back in two hours' time, feel free to send out a search party." He arched a brow at the man who was a loyal employee but felt like family.

"Yes, sir." He sighed, resigned.

Lucian led his horse beyond the gardens, waving to Fred kneeling in the beds yanking weeds, and entered the sparse woods behind the Calhouns' cottage. The clouds blocked the sunlight, and the air carried the promise of a summer shower. He'd be wise to stick close to home.

Home. Since when had he started thinking of this place as home?

Since you started to care for Megan, perhaps? She was connected to this place, to his grandfather's house. Her presence was stamped in every room, the porches, the gardens. Impossible to separate the two in his mind.

Transferring the reins to his injured hand, he rubbed his chest to dislodge the pain. Only, it wasn't a physical pain, exactly. The image of Tom's ring on Megan's finger...

He growled low in his throat. What was he supposed to do? Rant and rave and beg her not to marry the man? Megan didn't belong with Tom. She belonged with *him*.

Lucian jerked on the reins, gasping as pain radiated up his forearm. D'Artagnan halted. Swished the flies away with his tail.

Cradling his arm against his belly, his gaze swept the tranquil woods, lush greens and deep browns running together. "I could marry her, you know. Well, I could offer. I'm not certain if she'd accept."

D'Artagnan dipped his head as if to agree.

"We're friends, she and I. I trust her implicitly. Megan is a special lady, different from anyone I've ever known. I care about her. A lot." *Too much.* "I should be talking to a human being about this, not a horse." D'Artagnan stamped his foot. "No offense, *mon ami*."

Who was he kidding? Megan craved a grand love to rival the most prolific romance novels. He didn't have it in him to give her that. Refused to risk repeating his father's mistakes. No. His place was in New Orleans. And she belonged here. With Tom. Or some other man who could give her what she deserved. A man who would never hurt her.

So this was what misery felt like.

From now on, she was going to stick to adventures and mysteries. No more romance. In fact, as soon as she got home from church she was going to stow them all in a crate and give them away. Why torture herself reading happy endings when she wasn't going to get one?

"Is anyone sitting here?"

Megan lifted her gaze from her lap. Tom, dressed in his Sunday best, brown hair shiny from a recent wash, waited for her permission to sit. She inwardly sighed. Tried to smile and failed.

"No. Please, join us."

With a wide smile, he sat beside her at the end of the pew. Leaning forward, he aimed that smile at her sister, seated on her other side. "Hey there, Janie-girl."

"Hi."

Tom's smile faded. Megan shot Jane a sideways glance. Her lack of enthusiasm was unusual. Off routine. Whenever Tom teased her, she would give it right back. Not today.

"Are you feeling all right, Jane?" she murmured. Megan had been so lost in her own troubles lately that she hadn't been paying particular attention to anyone around her.

"I'm fine." She lowered her gaze to her lap where her hands were tightly clasped, color surging in her cheeks. Something was definitely bothering her. Was it Tom? Could she possibly harbor feelings for him?

"What about you, Megan?" Tom said softly. "You don't look particularly happy this morning."

"I'm fine."

She felt Jane's perusal. Ugh. This was going to be a long morning.

Glancing over her shoulder, she searched for Lucian.

Tom caught her gaze. Frowned. "He's outside tethering his horse. Should I change pews?"

She blinked. "No. Lucian doesn't— That is, he wouldn't—"

"It's all right. You don't have to explain."

Flustered, Megan turned around, determined not to search him out again.

Lucian entered the church. Took one look at Megan and Tom—sitting together and swapping smiles—and turned and walked right back out, oblivious to the curious stares. He couldn't do this. Couldn't sit by and watch her with another man.

All the way home, he fought for control over his emotions. Giving in to them would accomplish nothing. He had to be rational. To plan. To leave Tennessee with his dignity intact. To leave Megan with good memories. He wouldn't cause a scene, refused to cause trouble for her. He'd meant what he said—more than anything else, he wanted her to be happy.

He found Smith straightaway and instructed him to start packing his things. They would be leaving early next week. He'd stay long enough to say goodbye to the friends he'd made—Owen and Sarah, the Monroes,

Megan's family, Fred and Madge Calhoun—and attend one more story time. He wanted to remember her that way—dressed up in a silly costume and reading to the children—forever *his* Megan.

An hour later, he was in the study trying to decide what to take with him when the doorbell rang.

"Tom?" Lucian didn't attempt to hide his surprise. "Would you like to come in?"

"No, thanks. I can't stay long. I'm headed to Sam and Mary's for lunch." He jerked a thumb over his shoulder.

Stepping out on to the porch, Lucian crossed his arms and waited. He wasn't in the mood for games.

Tom looked uncomfortable but determined. "Look, I saw you before services. I know you skipped out early, and I have to assume you did that because it bothered you to see Megan and me together. She told you about my proposal?"

"What do you want, Leighton?" he ground out. Was the man here to gloat?

"I just wanted to thank you for not challenging my relationship with her. I'm good for her, you know. I can give her what she wants."

"Are you sure about that?" Lucian challenged, not because he believed otherwise, but because the truth stung. Of course Tom would be good for her. That didn't make it any easier to swallow.

His green gaze was clear, confident. "Once you've gone, she'll see that I'm the best man for her."

"If you're asking when I'm leaving, the answer is next week. Is there anything else? Because I've got an awful lot of packing to do."

He shrugged. "Thanks for your time."

Lucian barely held on to his temper, hands curled into fists as the other man ambled off the porch and across the lawn. The pinch in his forearm penetrated the haze of anger clouding his mind and he unclenched his hands. It was wasted emotion, anyway. The only person he had a right to be mad at was himself.

Despite everything—his parents' doomed marriage, his father's cruel indifference and mother's heartbreak, his and Megan's differences—he'd foolishly allowed himself to fall in love with her.

Apparently he hadn't learned his lessons well enough… if at all.

And now it was killing him to walk away from her.

The doorbell pealed insistently just as he sat at the small kitchen table with a sandwich he'd thrown together. Tossing aside his napkin, he strode through the house. If it was Leighton again…

"Megan."

He soaked in the sight of her, silken curls tumbling about her shoulders in disarray, small hands knotted at her waist. The worry shimmering in her luminous eyes sent a shaft of apprehension through his midsection. "What's happened?"

"It's Sarah." Her lower lip trembled as she spoke, and he closed the distance between them, smoothed his hands down her arms in an attempt to reassure her. Reassurance he didn't feel. His mind conjured up a dozen scenarios…all of them dire.

"What about her?" His heart thudded with dread.

"She's sick, Lucian. Owen said the doctor doesn't know what's wrong with her. She woke up yesterday complaining of a headache and then developed a fever shortly after. They can't get the fever to come down."

Her distress a palpable thing, Lucian set aside his own concern, spoke matter-of-factly. "I'll get the wagon ready and take you over there. Surely there's something that can be done. I have resources. I'll send for another doctor, if necessary. More medicine. Whatever it takes to get her well."

None of that helped your mother, though, did it? He shook off the reminder. This was different. Sarah was young and strong. She'd pull through this. Any other option didn't bear thinking about.

Brow puckered, gaze clinging to his with a hopeful trust that twisted his insides, she nodded. He took her hand and led her through the house so that he could grab his coat. In the barn, she insisted on helping him hitch the team to the wagon.

The ride out to the Livingston farm was passed in taut silence. At one point, he surreptitiously checked her left hand, sharp relief flooding him at the sight of her bare fingers. She wasn't wearing Tom's ring. Was she still considering the matter? Or had she refused him?

It was so very wrong of him to hope she had.

When the cabin came into view, they saw Owen outside talking with another man.

"Who's that?"

"Noah Townsend," Megan replied, tension humming along her slender frame. "He's Owen's neighbor. They have something in common. Noah's wife died a year ago. They didn't have any kids, though, so he's alone."

Sadness laced her words. He glanced at her familiar profile, love for this woman expanding in his chest until he could barely breathe. A woman of infinite compassion, other people's plights touched her as deeply as if they were her own.

She turned her great big, fathomless gaze on him. "If something happens to Sarah, how will Owen go on? He'll have lost everything…" she said on a ragged whisper.

Lucian set the brake. Curved a hand about her cheek, stroking her soft skin with his thumb. "Nothing is going to happen to her."

"You can't know that."

She was right, of course. He couldn't. But clinging to that hope, refusing to accept any other alternative, kept his control in place. His fears subdued.

"At this point in time, it's best to stay positive."

"You're right."

With great reluctance, he dropped his hand. Climbing down, he came around and assisted her. Together, they approached the men.

Owen's expression, as if he bore the weight of the world on his shoulders, tore into Lucian. He'd worn a similar one last year as his mother lay dying. *Forget about the past.* Revisiting his mother's last days wouldn't help anything.

With an offer to help in any way he could, Noah mounted his horse and trotted off shortly after the introductions were made. Owen thanked them for coming.

"Has there been any change?" Megan asked quietly.

"No." He clearly hadn't slept. His clothes were wrinkled and a day-old beard darkened his jaw. "Come on inside. I don't like to leave her alone for any length of time."

With a hand at the small of her back, Lucian guided Megan inside. The curtains had been drawn closed to block out harsh daylight, and it took a moment for his eyes to adjust. The sight of sweet Sarah lying still and lifeless beneath the quilts quite literally stole his breath away. Blinking fast, he clamped down on his back teeth. *She will be fine,* he told himself. *Just fine.*

Owen paused by the head of the bed, tenderly brushed the hair from her damp forehead. Her little face flushed with fever was the only sign anything was wrong.

Megan slipped her hand into Lucian's, but she centered her gaze on Owen. "Have you been able to get her to take any fluids?" She spoke in a hushed voice.

"A bit. She fights me. Only wants to sleep."

"The medicine Doc left isn't helping?"

He shook his head. "He said to give it to her every few hours. That we'd have to wait and see if it brought her temperature down. He won't say, but I can tell he's worried. He got the same look he had right before Meredith and the baby…" He broke off, covered his mouth with his hand. After a bit, he continued, "He's coming back to check on her before nightfall." The man's grief was a palpable thing.

"I can send for a doctor in Sevierville or Knoxville if you'd like. Money isn't an issue when it comes to getting Sarah the best possible medical care. Just say the word and it's done."

"I appreciate the offer, but I trust Doc. Besides, something like that would take time we don't have." His eyes grew shiny. "And ultimately, it's in the Lord's hands. He loves my daughter even more than I do."

Lucian nodded, although he didn't understand. The man had recently lost his wife and newborn, was on the verge of losing his daughter and yet his faith in God's love held firm. Lucian's gaze was drawn to Sarah, tiny and vulnerable and precious. So innocent.

Like a powerful ocean current, sorrow tugged at him, threatened to sweep him into uncharted waters. The same sorrow he'd battled as his mother lay dying.

Memories hit him—one after another—the quiet whispers of the servants, the pungent odor of healing herbs, his mother's paper-thin hands as he cradled them in his own, urging her to fight. To get well. And for once he didn't block them. The helplessness had been the worst....

He felt pressure on his hand. "Lucian?" Megan whispered, her troubled gaze searching his face. "The doctor is here. We should wait outside."

He'd somehow missed his arrival. "All right."

Lucian appeared lost in his own world, raw anguish swirling in the brown-black depths. Megan urged him outside. In deep conversation beside the door, Owen and Doc didn't pay them any mind. Her fingers threaded through his, she continued walking until they were well away from the cabin. Unfortunately, she didn't notice the graves until too late. When she attempted to change direction, Lucian resisted, his gaze riveted to the wooden crosses.

Pale beneath his tan, his earlier confidence was gone. Seeing Sarah like that had affected her, as well, but she sensed something more was going on with him.

"What are you thinking about?"

"Death."

"This isn't just about Sarah, is it?"

He took a shuddering breath. "For so long, I've tried not to think about my mother's last days. To avoid thinking about her, period. Seeing that little girl in there..." His voice grew thick with emotion and he couldn't finish.

Her own throat knotting with tears, she placed a palm against his cool cheek. "And it brought it all back?"

His bleak gaze clinging to hers, he nodded.

"When my father died, I was in shock for days. Weeks, even. Slowly but surely, it sank in that he was never coming back. His presence was everywhere. His hat hanging on the coat rack. His shoes by the door. My first reaction was to try to avoid the memories and, in so doing, avoid the pain of his absence. But you know what I eventually realized? That by not talking about him, by refusing to even *think* about him, I was discounting his importance in my life. I was dishonoring the man that he was. And I thought, is this what I want after I'm gone? For my loved ones to pretend I never existed? That I never *mattered?* Of course not.

"Lucian, the memories will get easier to bear. And, although you might not think so now, they will eventually bring you comfort. You must allow yourself to grieve."

Trembling, he pulled her into his arms, hugged her as if he might never let go. She felt him struggling to release his sorrow, knew that it was difficult for some men to cry because they saw it as a weakness. Praying silently, she rubbed his back and simply held him.

Because she loved him, his sorrow made her own heart ache. Her utmost desire was to be there always for him, to comfort him when life got hard and rejoice with him in the good times. But he wasn't prepared to accept her in his life. All she could do was be here for him now.

Later, after he'd gone, she'd deal with the grief. Not hide from it.

When he pulled away, he turned his back, dashing the moisture from his cheeks. "I miss her. But I'm angry at her, too, and that makes me feel incredibly guilty."

"That's to be expected, considering the circumstances."

He faced her once more, his manner subdued. "Understanding why she did it doesn't make it easier to accept. I wish my grandfather had forced the issue. She couldn't have very well turned him away if he'd shown up on our doorstep."

"Look at what happened the first time he tried to force his will upon her. Perhaps Charles was afraid if he did that, he'd lose all connection with her. With you."

His brow knotted with regret, and he jerked a nod.

"You'll work through this. God will help you." She touched his hand and, because she didn't know what else to say, she asked, "Would you like to pray with me for Sarah?"

"Yes, I would." He inhaled, absently rubbing his cast. "But I've never prayed out loud with anyone before." His dark eyes were cautious, unsure, which was completely unlike him.

Taking his hand again, she suggested, "You could pray silently while I pray aloud."

"No," he said with brows lowered. "I'd like to try. After you, of course."

Bowing her head, Megan prayed for Sarah's healing, comfort for Owen and wisdom for the doctor. Lucian's prayer was short and direct. Hearing him petition God, when weeks earlier he'd questioned His love and care, brought tears of joy to her eyes.

"We should probably go." She sniffed, released his hand. "Doc is still in there. I don't want to be in the way."

"I agree."

Megan quickly let Owen know they were leaving. When they reached her place, she insisted she didn't need help getting down. He stayed seated, his gaze tracking her every move. She wished he would jump down from there and take her in his arms and tell her he was wrong. About love. About her.

"Thank you, Megan. For everything."

She nodded, unable to regret any of it. Meeting him. Loving him. "Good night, Lucian."

Looking resigned, he signaled the team to head out. She watched him go, something inside telling her his time here was short. He would leave. Soon. And she would have to find a way to live without him.

Chapter Twenty

"Megan." Tom looked at once surprised and pleased to find her on his doorstep. "Would you like to come in?"

"That's all right," she declined, determined to keep this visit short. "Do you have a moment?"

"Sure." Leaning sideways to grab his hat from a knob inside the door, he settled it on his head and closed the door behind him. Taking her arm, he led her to the single maple tree in the corner of the yard, its leafy bower providing much-needed shade. He tipped the brim up. "Any word on Sarah Livingston?"

"If anything, she's worse. I went there this afternoon to drop off some food for Owen, and she was thrashing about, her fever holding firm." At the memory, Megan's stomach hardened into a tight ball. She'd stayed only long enough to give him the food—and for him to mention that Lucian had stopped by in the early morning.

Frowning, he toed a stick with his boot. "I'm sorry to hear that."

Megan forced her mind to the task at hand. Her spirits were already low. Better get this over with before she lost her nerve.

Reaching into her reticule, she withdrew the ring. Held it out to him. "I want you to take the ring back, Tom."

His green gaze zeroed in on the ring, then lifted to her face in confusion. He made no move to accept it. "I thought you agreed to wait. To take some time—"

"Time isn't going to change my answer. I'm sorry, I—" she broke off, hating the dawning hurt spreading across his kind face. But stretching this out wouldn't make it hurt any less. She squared her shoulders. "I can't marry you."

With a sharp breath, he reluctantly took the ring from her nerveless fingers and tucked it in his pocket. "Has he changed his mind about marrying you, then?" he asked without rancor. Pain-filled eyes met hers.

"No." *This is so hard, God. All of it. Lucian. Tom. Sarah. When will it stop hurting?*

"I don't understand."

"I will marry for love or not at all. Friendship isn't enough for me. Can you understand that?"

"I understand that I love you," he pushed out. "And... you don't love me."

She touched his arm, and he flinched. "Oh, Tom, I love you like a brother. You're a dear friend. I know you don't want to hear that, but it's the truth."

Gaze riveted to the ground, he merely nodded.

"I hope we can still be friends."

"I'll need some space. Time to move past this."

"I understand." Megan felt like weeping. Felt vile for wounding him. "I have to go now, Tom. Nicole and Jane are expecting me home in time for supper."

"Tell them hello for me, will you?"

"I will."

Turning on her heel, she walked quickly through the grass and untethered Mr. Knightley. In the saddle, she chanced a glance at where he stood. Tom waved. Gulping back emotion, she waved and headed down the lane.

At home, Jane was waiting for her in the barn.

"I thought you'd be inside fixing supper." Megan dismounted, shot her a questioning glance.

"You turned him down, didn't you?" Her chest heaved, auburn hair wild about her shoulders. "You hurt him," she accused, eyes blazing.

Megan stilled, stunned by her normally even-keeled sister's outburst. "I gave him back his ring, yes."

A tear slipped down her cheek. She angrily scrubbed it away. "I don't understand how you could do that. Tom is a wonderful man! He deserves someone who will appreciate him."

"Someone like you?" Megan prodded gently.

Her eyes widened. Face crumpled. The tears began to flow in earnest, and Megan's already heavy heart splintered into a dozen pieces. Putting her arms around her sister, she stroked her hair as she cried against her shoulder. "Shh. It's going to be okay."

Oh, Mama, I wish you were here. You'd know exactly what to say to make her feel better.

When Jane pulled away, she rubbed at the moisture on her cheeks. Sniffed. "I'm afraid Tom will never see me as anything more than a pesky little sister."

"Maybe that's because of the age difference," Megan pointed out as delicately as she could. "He's twenty-two. You're fifteen."

"Almost sixteen," she protested. "Besides, lots of girls get married at sixteen."

"I don't know about *lots,* but you're right, there are

some girls who do marry young. But I know Mama would prefer you wait a few years. Maybe when you're eighteen."

"But that's two years away," she wailed. "Tom will have found someone else to marry by then!"

"Maybe not. If Tom is the man God has picked out for you, it'll work out."

"And what if he never gets over you?"

Megan closed her eyes and sighed, thinking of her love for Lucian. A love she'd never get over. "I pray that isn't the case," she said fervently.

"I know you love Lucian. Does he...?"

"No."

Jane sighed, took Megan's hands. "I'm sorry. I know how much that hurts."

Megan looked into her sister's face full of sympathy. "You're not angry with me?"

"No, not angry. I admit to being jealous. I—I've wished it was me Tom was pursuing instead of you."

"I'm sorry."

"I still love you." She managed a watery smile.

Megan tenderly brushed Jane's hair behind her shoulder. "I love you, too. I always will, no matter what happens."

"I suppose I should go inside and help Nicole with supper before she scorches it," she said with a grimace.

"Or burns down the cabin," she agreed. "I'll be inside as soon as I get Mr. Knightley squared away."

Megan watched her sister go, wishing she'd seen the evidence of her feelings much sooner. If she'd been aware, she could've been more sensitive in her handling of the situation.

Crouched in the garden picking tomatoes the next morning, Megan lifted her head at the sound of wagon wheels creaking over hard earth. Wiping the perspiration from her brow, she shaded her eyes with one hand and squinted. Lucian's unmistakable form came into view. Her pulse leaped.

Placing a tomato into the basket beside her feet, she stood and dislodged the dirt from her hands. He spotted her advancing along the row and lifted his hand in greeting. Why was he here?

Bounding to the ground, he came around to greet her, sweeping off his black bowler. He'd left off wearing his sling entirely.

"I was in town just now and noticed Doc heading in the direction of the Livingstons' place. I thought perhaps we should go out there in case there's been a change." His intense gaze swept her dusty dress, the rogue curls escaping the ribbon at her nape. "Owen might have need of some company. Do you have time now?"

"Sure. Give me a moment to take my basket inside and change. Would you like to come in for a glass of lemonade or tea?"

"*Non, merci.* Why don't you go on in and I'll retrieve your basket?"

"You don't have to do that." She glanced at his spotless boots, his formal clothes in shades of blue that made his skin glow with vibrancy.

The barest of smiles tilted his lips. "I don't mind."

"If you say so." She self-consciously brushed at the dirt on her apron. "I'll be right back."

"Take your time, *mon chou.*"

Little pastry. The familiar nickname triggered a smile. As observant as he was, had he noticed her discomfiture? Was the endearment a subtle way of telling her that, despite her untidy appearance, she was still attractive to him?

Right, Megan. Now you're being fanciful.

Inside, she hurriedly explained to her sisters that Lucian was taking her to check on Sarah.

Jane had her hands buried in bread dough. "Tell Owen we're still praying."

Nicole looked up from her sewing. "Do you think she'll pull through this?"

"I hope so." Megan hadn't stopped thinking about the little girl these past three days. She'd tried to stay positive, but doubts had crept in at times. "I'll give you a full report when we return."

Once she'd washed her hands and face, tidied her hair and changed into her apricot-hued dress, she descended the stairs to find Lucian in the living room chatting with Nicole. He'd delivered her basket to Jane in the kitchen. Spying her, he stood, his gaze lighting with appreciation.

"All ready to go?"

Her cheeks warmed. "Yes."

Bidding her sisters goodbye, he held the door for her and joined her on the porch. They walked side by side to the wagon, where she paused to regard him with open scrutiny.

"Owen mentioned you paid them a visit yesterday morning."

"Yes, that's right."

"You went alone."

His brow wrinkled in confusion, he rocked back on his heels. "I did."

Must she spell it out for him? "Why didn't you just follow Doc? Why come and get me?"

Understanding dawned. His mouth twisted. "Because it was so much easier with you."

"Oh." He'd basically confessed to needing her. Satisfaction—futile though it was—spiraled through her. "I see."

She frowned. Since when had she started talking like him?

"Sarah wasn't doing so well when I was there." He gave her a hand up and walked around to the other side, using his uninjured hand to lever himself up. The narrow seat shifted with his weight. He angled his face towards hers, his eyes shadowed by the hat's brim. "How was she when you stopped by?"

"Not good. I didn't stay long." A lump formed in her throat as she recalled Sarah, soaked with sweat and thrashing about in delirium, and Owen, looking slightly desperate.

With a grim nod, he set the wagon in motion.

Father God, please prepare us for what we might encounter. Give us the strength, the words to comfort Owen. Above all, help us to accept Your will in this matter.

Needing a connection with Lucian, Megan wove her hand beneath his arm, fingers curled about his biceps. He sent her a sidelong glance fraught with concern. He was worried, too.

The horses seemed to be traveling at a slower rate of speed than usual, the lane stretching endlessly before them. When at last they reached the turnoff, Megan tensed.

Doc's wagon was still there. Lucian covered her hand with his own, a comforting weight. "Are you ready?"

"I am."

He helped her down, his hand a constant pressure at the small of her back. A physical reminder of his support. Before he could raise his hand to knock, the door swung open and Owen stood in the doorway. Her breath stalled. Beneath his scruffiness, relief softened his features.

"Owen?"

"She's going to be okay," he said firmly, as if still trying to absorb what he was saying. "Her fever broke this morning just after dawn. Doc's checking her over."

Lucian rubbed her back in a soothing manner. "You're certain she'll be all right?"

Despite his exhaustion, Owen managed to look like a man reborn. "Come on in and see for yourself."

Moving out of the way, he went to stand beside the fireplace, his weight supported by the rough-hewn mantel. Doc's broad shoulders blocked their view. After a moment, he snapped his bag closed and edged to the foot of the bed.

"Miss Megan. Mr. Lucian." Propped up with a mound of pillows, Sarah's weak voice couldn't disguise her delight. While her blond hair was a tangled mess, she was wearing a fresh nightgown. "Did you bring me another present?"

Megan chuckled. Lucian shot her a glance, smiled broadly. Sarah was going to be fine. Just fine.

The majority of Gatlinburg's residents turned out Friday night for story time. Word of his departure had traveled like wildfire through the small town, and here they all were to bid him farewell. A sort of going-away party.

Mrs. Calhoun had outdone herself. In anticipation of the crowd, she decided to set up the refreshments in the dining room. This week she'd engaged in a baking frenzy. Cakes, pies and pastries occupied every flat surface in sight. He'd been sent to Clawson's twice for extra sugar.... No telling what kind of effect all this bounty would have on the kids.

Funny, he believed he was actually going to miss the little creatures.

He would definitely miss Megan's costumes.

He studied her over the rim of his cup. Dressed like a true cowgirl, complete with hip holster and boots with silver spurs, she stood in the archway between the kitchen and dining room. Her pale curls, restrained with a leather strip, glistened in light thrown off by the wall sconces. Cradled against her shoulder was a cherub-faced infant who strongly resembled her mother, a friend of Megan's named Rachel Prescott. The father, Cole Prescott, was playing a game with the infant, tickling her beneath the chin and making her giggle with delight.

Megan caught him staring. Her wistful smile made his gut clench with regret.

A hand clapped him on the back then, and he nearly spilled his drink. Nathan chuckled beside him. "Didn't mean to startle you, Beaumont."

"That's quite all right."

Those unreadable silver eyes studied him. "It's true, then? You're leaving us Monday?"

"I mean to get an early start." He willed his gaze not to stray to Megan. Nathan would surely notice. Had he witnessed her sad smile?

Nathan took a drink of steaming coffee, shifted to let two young men pass by. "Do you plan on coming back for a visit sometime?"

Not likely. How could he when Megan was sure to be happily ensconced in married life? "I don't know."

He nodded, considering, and glanced at Megan across the way. "We all appreciate your kindness in leaving the house in Megan's care. You don't have to worry. She won't violate your trust."

"I know that."

If Nathan noted the hint of melancholy in Lucian's voice, he didn't comment on it. Instead, he carefully surveyed the crush of people, lazily observing, "I'm surprised Tom Leighton didn't show up."

"It wouldn't be hard to miss him in this crowd." He'd been on the lookout for him since the night's beginning, dreading the encounter, seeing him claim Megan as his own.

"I don't think so. If he was here, he'd be at Megan's side." He grew thoughtful. "I stopped by his shop today for a trim. He was tight-lipped, not at all like his usual happy-go-lucky self."

Unable to stop himself, Lucian directed his gaze at Megan once more. Had something happened? Had they quarreled? Or was his absence totally unrelated to her?

The hope surging within him was wholly inappropriate. And petty. Selfish. He desired her happiness. *But not with Tom, right? You want her to be happy with* you.

That was impossible, of course. He knew it, understood it, but that didn't stop his foolish heart from yearning for the unattainable.

Another couple approached Lucian, and Nathan moved off with a quiet farewell. It took supreme effort of will to focus on their words. Megan dominated his thoughts. She was there in his peripheral vision, silently drawing him, making it all but impossible to make sane conversation. Had she decided not to marry the barbershop owner? Or worse…had Tom hurt her? His hands curled into fists. If he had…

The remainder of the night dragged. His guests weren't as eager to leave as he was for them to leave. He craved a few minutes alone with Megan. More than a few, actually. He was well aware that his time with her was growing short, every minute slipping past another minute lost to them.

It was nearing eleven when the last guest slipped out the door, and he returned to the dining room to find her assisting Mrs. Calhoun and three other young ladies he'd hired to help with tonight's festivities. Dirty dishes and cups littered the parlor and library, as well as the dining room. Cleanup would take at least an hour.

Impatient, determined to have her to himself, he stepped in front of her and took the plates from her hands, setting them aside. "Let's go for a stroll in the gardens."

"It's late."

"Fred lit the gas lamps, and the weather is fine."

She worried her lower lip, gestured to the room. "I should help with the cleanup."

"That's what these ladies are getting paid for." He tilted his head at the women watching them with interest as they went about their work. Leaning forward, he lowered his voice. "Wouldn't you like to see the gardens in the moonlight?" This may be their last chance to say a proper goodbye.

Sadness lurked in the liquid depths of her sea-blue eyes. "All right. I'll come with you."

With her hand in the crook of his elbow, he led her outside into the star-studded night. Balmy air, sweetened with the scent of magnolias, enveloped them in a warm cocoon. The fat, pearlescent moon dominated the night sky. Gas lamps situated along the path flickered, points of light in the shadows.

Their footsteps against the stones were muted. "Are you going to see Sarah and Owen one last time before you go?"

"I doubt it. I'm not good at goodbyes." This one he

couldn't escape, however difficult. Megan was too special, too dear.

"Isn't that what this is? A goodbye?" She stopped and angled towards him, one pale brow arched in challenge.

"Yes. I can't deny that it is."

Lips compressing, she fell silent. Wouldn't look at him, diverted her gaze to the wildflowers behind him. He was at a loss for words. What could he say that would convey how much she'd come to mean to him that wouldn't also confuse her?

"I heard your mother and sister are coming home at the end of next week," he said as they took up walking again. "I wish I could've made their acquaintance."

"Me, too. I'm certain they both would've taken to you as quickly as the rest of my family." She smiled faintly. "I'm eager to have my mother home again. Jessica, too. Jane needs her twin now more than ever."

His brows drew together. "Is something going on with Jane?"

Megan stopped again, her hand dropping away. "She fancies herself in love with Tom."

Poor Jane. And Megan. What a terrible fix to find herself in. "I see."

"No, I don't think you do." She lifted her chin. "I returned the ring. I'm not going to marry him."

Lucian stilled, barely breathing as relief and happiness swept through him. She turned him down. She wasn't going to marry Tom, after all.

The question was…what was he going to do about it?

Chapter Twenty-One

Megan watched the play of emotions across Lucian's face. Hope sprouted. He'd said he cared for her.... Was it possible his feelings ran deeper than what he'd conveyed?

"May I ask why?"

"I don't love him." *You're the one I love,* she wanted to shout. "Not the way a woman is supposed to love her husband. A dear friend is all he'll ever be."

Swallowing hard, he edged closer, skimmed his knuckles along her cheekbone. His eyes shone bright as the stars above, illuminating the darkened corners of her heart. "Megan, *mon bien-aime,*" he whispered, his warm breath caressing her jaw.

Capturing his hand, she pressed her cheek into his palm. Being with him like this made her dizzy with joy. "I've heard you say that before. What does it mean?"

He paused. "My beloved."

Megan could only stare up at him. Was that the same as saying he loved her? "Lucian—"

His lips cut her off, his kiss marked with a yearning that matched her own. The hands cradling her face trembled. The trace of desperation in his touch worried her, however.

When he pulled his mouth away and pressed her into his chest, his heart thundered beneath her ear. He couldn't leave. How could she go on without him?

Easing back, she gazed into his dear face, holding nothing back. "Please don't go, Lucian. I love you. Stay here. With me."

He froze. "*Non.* Don't say that."

"Why shouldn't I?" She left the circle of his arms, stung by his response. "It's the truth."

The intense regret marring his expression deflated her hopes. "It won't work."

"Why not? Because you're a polished city fellow and I'm a simple mountain girl?"

"No, of course not. To be honest, I've grown quite fond of your mountains. I consider the people here my friends."

"So it's me you don't want." Turning away, she hugged her arms about her waist, wishing herself far from here. Humiliation warred with hurt. "I thought…"

Lucian stood very close behind her. "Please forgive me. It was never my intention to lead you astray, to hurt you," he answered, self-recrimination straining his husky voice. Settling his hands lightly on her shoulders, he turned her towards him. "The truth is…I—I do want you."

"Wanting someone isn't the same as loving, Lucian."

His gaze burned into hers, and for a second, he allowed her to see the depths of his feelings. But then he threw his hands up in defeat. "What does it matter what I feel, anyway? It won't change anything. It can't."

"Because of your parents? There's no guarantee we'll repeat their mistakes."

"I can't take that risk. Don't you see? This whole thing between you and me," he protested as he motioned between them, "it mirrors my parents' situation. I won't make the same mistakes as my father. I saw what it did to my mother, and I will never do that to you."

He loved her, she was convinced, but he was fighting it. She had to try to convince him to take a chance. "You are not your father. I'm not Lucinda. We're different people, you and me. We can have a different life. You just have to be willing to try."

His shoulders rigid, implacable, he set his jaw. His eyes had lost their brilliance and were now dull. Flat. "I refuse to risk your happiness."

On this point, he was resolute. He hadn't changed, not really, was still the jaded aristocrat determined to follow duty's path.

"Then I guess this is goodbye." It hurt to breathe.

He grimaced. Stood statue-still, hands fisted at his sides. "Yes, I suppose it is."

With one last parting glance, she attempted to memorize his features. Then she turned and walked away, leaving a part of her heart behind.

"I have an announcement to make."

Looking entirely too pleased with himself, Josh sat relaxed in his chair, one arm slung about Kate's shoulders. Conversation ceased. Setting down her fork, Megan swallowed the last bite of pie, her gaze meeting Kate's across the table. A becoming blush stained her cheeks, and her green eyes sparkled.

Josh pulled his wife closer, and the two exchanged secretive smiles. "Kate and I are expecting."

Mary gasped, jumped up to bestow hugs on the happy couple. Sam patted Josh heartily on the back. Nathan shook his hand and offered his congratulations. Nicole and Jane took turns embracing Kate, and then it was Megan's turn.

"I'm so happy for you both." Megan gave Kate's fingers an affectionate squeeze. "How long have you known?"

"We've had our suspicions these last couple of weeks. I've had several dizzy spells."

"And your eating habits have changed drastically." Megan laughed at her friend's sheepish expression.

"It's true. If I keep this up, I'll be as big as a house by the time the baby comes." Her eyes went soft and dreamy. "I wonder if it will be a boy or a girl."

Megan smiled broadly, praying her friend wouldn't detect the prick of jealousy her happiness incited. "Considering Juliana just had a boy, I think you and Josh should have a girl."

"Mary would be thrilled to have a granddaughter."

"You do realize it's out of our hands, right, Goldilocks?" Josh inserted himself in the conversation, his blue eyes dancing with merriment.

In the face of this dear couple's joy, Megan blinked away the moisture gathering in her eyes. She was truly grateful God had blessed them with their heart's desire. Feeling sorry for herself in this moment was not an option.

"I'm not sure I like the sound of Cousin Megan," she said. "Auntie Megan sounds much better, don't you think?"

Josh tweaked one of her curls like he'd done when they were younger. "Whatever you're called, she or he will adore you as much as we do."

"Now you're just trying to make me cry," she protested, swatting his arm.

Nicole spoke up, the wheels in her head clearly turning. "I can go ahead and make up baby clothes in neutral colors and then, if it's a girl, I can add ruffles and overlays."

Surprised pleasure brightened Kate's expression. "That would be wonderful, Nicole. Thank you."

The raven-haired girl shrugged. "Practice makes perfect. I need lots of experience if I plan on having a successful boutique."

Kate and Megan shared a look. Typical. Nicole's purposes served herself first, others second. At least Kate and the baby would benefit.

"Once the baby comes, Jessica and I will bring food over so you can rest," Jane volunteered.

"Thank you, Jane." Kate's smile was gentle.

Megan looked at the couple, once again battling melancholy. Just because her dream wasn't coming true didn't mean she couldn't rejoice with others.

"Yours won't be the only new addition this winter," he added. "Rachel and Cole are expecting. They're due at Christmastime."

Her friend had pulled her aside at Lucian's to relay the good news.

Josh grinned. "Cole told me last night. He could hardly contain himself—he's so eager to support Rachel in any way he can."

"That's understandable," Nathan inserted, "considering he wasn't around for Abby's birth."

Megan nodded her agreement. She had a feeling Cole was going to stick to Rachel's side like glue. He was overly protective of her and Abby, no doubt due to the fact he'd nearly lost his chance with them.

The group dispersed, the men settling in the living room with their coffee while the women cleared

the table and washed dishes. Megan was quiet as sh
worked, lost in her painful world. A world without Lu
cian.

You knew a happy ending wasn't possible, a voic
accused, *yet you fell for him anyway.*

All yesterday, she'd watched the lane, hoping agains
hope he'd come to her. And this morning at church
she'd waited for him to show. He hadn't.

She wasn't certain how she was going to get throug
tomorrow. Or the next day. Or the coming weeks.

Her vision blurred. Hastily wiping the table clean c
crumbs, Megan slipped out the back door. She doubte
she'd be missed. Mary and Kate were washing dishe
engaged in a lively conversation about the baby, Jan
listening intently as she dried. Nicole had slunk o
somewhere.

With no one around to witness her breakdow
Megan allowed the tears to fall freely, the loss of h
dreams a gaping wound in her chest. She stumbled int
the barn's concealing shelter. Sinking onto the first ha
bale she encountered, she buried her face in her hand

*It feels as though my life is ending, Lord. I've a
ways considered myself an optimistic sort of perso
not often given to the doldrums, but right now...I'
lower than I've ever been and I don't know how I'
supposed to cope.*

"There you are."

Startled, she looked up to see Nathan coming towar
her. The moment he noticed her tears, he lengthene
his stride. Compassion tugged at his mouth. Lowe
ing his tall frame onto the hay beside her, he pulle
her into a hug.

Josh, Nathan and even Caleb were like brothers
her, fiercely protective and always there to comfort he

Without them, she never would've survived her father's sudden death, the hardships her family had faced afterward—financial as well as the day-to-day running of a farm—and more recently, the absence of her beloved sister Juliana.

After a while, he tilted her chin up, silver gaze assessing. "This is because of Beaumont, isn't it?"

"I love him. And I believe he loves me." When she attempted to wipe the moisture from her cheeks, he produced a handkerchief from his pocket. "But he's too afraid of repeating his parents' mistakes to give us a chance. He doesn't trust in love."

"Would you like for me to talk to him?"

"No! I'm not a little girl anymore, Nathan. I don't need you to fight my battles." She touched his cheek. "Although, I do appreciate the offer."

"I wish I could make things better for you."

"I know." She gazed at him with rueful affection.

"Would an afternoon of target practice help get your mind off things? At least for a little while?" His smile urged her to say yes.

"Yes, I believe it would," she agreed more for his sake than for hers. "I'll go home and get my gun."

He stood and held out his hand. "How about we go together?"

"In other words, you don't want to leave me alone."

He winked. "You got it, Goldilocks."

She took his hand, allowed him to pull her up. "You're a good man, Nathan O'Malley. One day, a very lucky young lady is going to come along and relieve you of your bachelor state."

"I happen to like being a bachelor," he protested. "Mark my words—you won't see me walking the aisle anytime soon."

* * *

"The carriage is ready, sir." Smith appeared in the entrance to Charles's study.

Seated at the desk, Lucian glanced out at the predawn darkness. "How bad is the rain?"

"Barely a drizzle, sir. However, it's difficult to tell at this point whether or not the weather will improve. Would you like to wait until after dawn?"

Lightly rubbing his cast in a vain effort to relieve the itching beneath, Lucian sighed. Another delay? Was God trying to tell him something?

"That would probably be best. See to the horses, will you?"

"Yes, sir." He removed himself at once.

The tick of the mantel clock mocked him, each one a strike against his heart. *You're leaving her. You're leaving her.*

He let his head fall back, closed his eyes. Beyond exhausted, he feared this weariness would be difficult to shake. Lack of sleep had little to do with it. This was a soul-deep yearning for the one woman who'd seen through his austere facade to the real man beneath, who'd challenged him, comforted him. Loved him.

He couldn't quite wrap his mind around the fact that she loved him. Her confession had shocked him; her plea for him to stay nearly brought him to his knees. How he'd longed to declare his own feelings.... Revisiting all the reasons his fears were sound had prevented him. After she'd gone, he'd sat in the garden until the wee hours of the morning, replaying their conversation. Arguing with himself. When he'd at last tumbled into bed, he'd dreamed of her, her anguish a tangible thing. He'd awoken in a sweat, trembling with the need to go to her. To fall to his knees and beg her forgiveness.

The past two days and nights of torment had shaken his convictions. If he left, he'd be leaving here half a man.

What am I supposed to do, Lord? By refusing to give us a chance, I'm doing the one thing I've dreaded doing—I'm hurting her. And myself.

Lucian smoothed the worn, faded cover of his mother's Bible. Unable to sleep for thoughts of Megan, he'd come downstairs around four o'clock and settled in with a cup of coffee to read. He'd found himself in the first book of Corinthians, where his mother had underlined an entire chapter about love, of all things. One verse in particular stuck in his mind. *And now these three remain: faith, hope and love. But the greatest of these is love.*

Was he truly prepared to live without it? To never lay eyes on Megan again?

"Sir?" Smith reappeared. "The rain has let up a bit. Shall I ready the carriage now?"

Lucian stood, adrenaline pumping through his veins. "No."

"No?"

"I want you to unload the trunks."

Smith's brow furrowed slightly. "As you wish, sir."

"Wait." He held out a hand. "Don't unload them yet. She may not accept me."

Reaching inside his coat, he retrieved a handkerchief and, laying it on the desk, peeled back the edges to reveal the disassembled bleeding-heart flower. He glanced at his servant, who was watching him with barely concealed concern. "I'm embarking on a mission of a most delicate nature, Smith. Will you help me?"

His eyes flared wide at the request. "Anything you ask, I will do my utmost to oblige."

"I appreciate your loyalty, Smith. First, I'll need a pair of rabbits..."

Megan awoke shortly after dawn to the *splat, splat, splat* of rain against the porch. She lay beneath the quilt for a long time staring out the window at the smoky gray clouds, her heaviness of spirit a perfect reflection of the gloom.

Maybe the weather will delay his departure.

What would that gain? A temporary stay of the inevitable. Better he left as soon as possible. If she were to see him again, who knew what she might do. She suspected something rash and embarrassing and totally unlike her, like begging him to take her with him.

There came a soft knock on the door.

"Come in." Shoving the hair out of her eyes, she scooted up in bed.

Jane entered bearing a small tray, still dressed in her nightclothes and wrapper, her loose auburn hair gleaming in the watery light. "I thought you might like a cup of cocoa." She smiled over at her as she slid the tray on the dresser. "There's a biscuit with strawberry jam, too."

She came and sat on the bed, empathy etched in her youthful features. "It's a pity about the rain. I'd hoped we could go for a jaunt in the woods or perhaps have a picnic down by the river."

Touched, Megan gave Jane's hand a squeeze. "You're very sweet to try and cheer me up. Perhaps the rain will let up and we can go for a ride later."

Despite her young age, Jane understood the importance of distraction.

"Are you going to be okay?"

No. Not without Lucian. "In time—" She inhaled deeply, trying to dislodge the pain in her heart. "In time, I will learn to live without him." But she'd never stop loving him.

Tears glistened in Jane's sad eyes. "I feel the same way about Tom. He hasn't been to church since...well, you know."

"We can help each other through this." Battling emotions, Megan hugged her.

Sniffling, Jane leaned away. "I should get dressed."

"Me, too. Lottie will be waiting to be milked."

Jane closed the door with a soft click. Megan made herself get out of bed, trudged over to the wardrobe, and, choosing a navy skirt, she paired it with a buttery-yellow blouse. When another knock sounded as she was pulling her blouse over her heard, she thought it was Jane again.

But it was Nicole, standing hesitantly in the doorway, teeth worrying her lower lip. Strange. Nicole wasn't the uncertain type. She typically barreled through situations with single-minded determination.

"I thought..." she began. "Well, would you like for me to do your hair? I have some combs that would look nice with that blouse."

Megan opened her mouth. Closed it. "Uh, yes, I'd like that very much."

A tiny smile lifted her lips. "I'll be right back."

Megan didn't move, struck dumb by her sister's offer. Nicole wasn't sentimental or overly sensitive to others' feelings, which made her offer all the more meaningful. Tears threatened. She quickly blinked them back as Nicole returned with said combs.

Seating herself in the lone wooden chair, Megan folded her hands in her lap. Nicole had a gentle touch, carefully combing through her curls and securing the sides with the sparkly combs. She handed her the mirror.

"What do you think?"

Megan smiled tremulously up at her. "I think you did a marvelous job, sis. Thank you."

Looking wistful, Nicole touched a curl with the tip of her finger. "It's not hard to make you look beautiful. I've always wished my hair was blond, like yours."

Standing, Megan took her hands in hers. "But you have such gorgeous hair," she protested, "as black and silky as a raven's wing. And your unique violet eyes handed down from Grandmother O'Malley are a lovely contrast."

She scrunched up her nose. "This black hair makes me look like a witch."

Megan gasped. "That's ridiculous!"

"That's what the boys at school used to say."

"They were only teasing you," she insisted. "Besides, we both know true beauty resides in the heart."

Nicole looked thoughtful. "But you have to admit that being well-groomed is important."

"Megan, you should come here," Jane called from the living room. The queer note in her voice brought Megan running. Nicole followed closely behind.

"What is it?"

She stood at the door holding a crate, her expression one of confused wonder. "This was delivered for you."

"So early? Who was it?"

"More importantly, what is it?" Nicole asked.

Peering down into the crate, Megan's breath hitched. There, huddled together in the corner of the crate on a worn blanket, were two small brown rabbits with white fuzzy tails.

"Jimmy Dixon said a stuffy-looking man paid him to

deliver these to you." Jane stared at her. "Do you think he was talking about Lucian?"

A hundred butterflies unleashed in her tummy. "I can't think of anyone else it could've been."

Nicole picked one up and cuddled it close to stop its shivering. "I don't understand. Why would he send you rabbits when he can afford to send something much more valuable?"

The bleeding-heart flower. He'd kept the one she'd used to demonstrate the story, so it meant something to him.

She took the other rabbit out and held it close, its frantic heartbeat pulsing against her finger. How darling. "We don't know for certain that it was Lucian who sent them," she said firmly, ignoring the sudden leap of her pulse.

Setting the crate on the floor, Jane took turns petting the animals, whose fur was damp from their journey in the rain. "They are so precious! What will we name them?"

They spent the next half hour debating names and where they were supposed to put them. When they heard boots thump against the porch, they stilled. Looked at each other.

"You get it, Megan," Jane urged, eyes wide.

Handing her rabbit off to Jane, Megan wiped her palms against her skirt and, sucking in a breath, opened the door. It wasn't Lucian. Swallowing her disappointment, she greeted fifteen-year-old Jimmy.

"I have another package for you, Miss Megan." Huddling beneath his slicker, he thrust a rectangular-shaped box at her. Then he dashed back out into the rain before she could question him. Her sisters crowded around the table where she placed the box. She carefully lifted the lid. Inside lay a pair of elegant, beaded ivory satin shoes lined with ivory kid and possessed of shapely heels.

"These are exquisite, Megan, and easily paired with a wedding gown." Nicole returned her rabbit to the crate so that she could admire the shoes.

Jittery with nerves, Megan explained with a growing sense of wonder, "Lucian is following the pattern of the bleeding-heart legend. I told him about it one afternoon when we were walking through the woods. He actually kept the parts of the flower."

"How romantic," Jane said with a sigh.

Megan couldn't speak. What could be his purpose? He'd been resolute in his determination to leave.

When Jimmy arrived the third time, she caught his arm. "Who sent you, Jimmy?"

"The fancy man from New Orleans."

"Mr. Beaumont?"

"Yep, that's the one."

"Can you tell me where he is now?"

He lifted a shoulder. "He left."

Megan stared. It couldn't be. "He left town? Are you certain?"

Unaware of her distress, he nodded matter-of-factly and waited for her to release him. "Th-thank you, Jimmy. You may go."

She turned back to find her sisters looking at her with sympathy.

"I—I don't understand." She spoke through her tears. Was this simply an extravagant way to say goodbye?

Utter devastation washed over her. He was well and truly gone. For good.

Needing immediate escape, she tossed the box on a nearby chair and grabbed her shawl. "I've got to go."

"You'll be soaked through within the space of a minute!" Jane called as she stepped out onto the porch.

"Don't worry," she said over her shoulder, barely able to form words. "I won't be gone long." That wasn't a promise, just a hopeful saying to allay her sister's worries. In truth, she wanted to keep going, to go somewhere new and strange and devoid of memories.

"But—"

Ignoring her, Megan hurried down the steps and raced for the woods, unmindful of the raindrops pelting her. Jane was right. It didn't take long for her to be soaked through, her hair a sodden mass on her shoulders. Entering the lush green woods, she slowed to a fast walk. The onslaught wasn't as steady here, the canopy overhead acting as a makeshift shelter.

She walked and walked for what seemed an eternity. Walked until her feet ached, the insides of her boots rubbing blisters on her toes. Walked until she was shivering. Spying a hollowed-out log, she sank down, huddled beneath her damp shawl and stared about at the woods she suddenly didn't recognize.

Did she care that she might be lost? No.

Did she care that she might have to spend the night out here? Not in the least.

It didn't matter that she'd skipped breakfast and that she didn't have her weapon with her. Nothing mattered, really, except that she was miserable. Soon, very soon, she was going to have to try to find her way back, to be responsible, but for just a little while, she would allow herself to grieve the loss of her one and only love.

* * *

"He did what?" Lucian stared at Jane and Nicole in dismay. "Why?"

"Jimmy told her that you left town, and she got upset. She tore off into the woods and hasn't returned," Jane repeated, wringing her hands.

Lucian pushed down his irritation at the lad. He had more important things to worry about…like finding Megan and admitting he'd been wrong. "How long has she been gone?"

"Over an hour." Nicole chewed on a fingernail, something he'd never seen her do.

The girls must be beside themselves with worry. He was beginning to worry, too. Running off in the midst of a rainstorm wasn't like Megan. But she'd been upset. Because of him.

"I'll find her," he promised, unable to accept any other outcome. She knew these woods like the back of her hand, and she was smart and capable. *Lord, help me,* he prayed, believing with all his heart that God cared. That He was listening. *Please lead me to her.*

He'd gone about this all wrong. By sending the gifts, he'd tried to be romantic, something he knew was important to her. He should've come here first thing and simply talked to her.

Roaming the woods, he searched for signs that someone had recently passed through. He called her name, listening for some sort of response besides the constant dripping rain. When he at last spotted her hunched on a log, wet and pale and miserable, his fears melted away. Relief weakened his knees. *Thank You, God.*

"Megan."

Startled, she whipped her head up. Stark pain twisted her features. Pain *he* had caused her. Muttering in

French, Lucian strode over to her, crouching at her knees so that he could look her squarely in the eyes.

"*Je suis désolé, mon chou.* I'm so sorry."

Megan blinked once. Twice. Lucian was really here. He'd found her somehow.

"I thought you left," she whispered. "Jimmy told me you left."

A muscle twitched in his jaw. "He was mistaken."

He looked upset. Dashingly handsome, as well, his wet hair appearing nearly black, slicked back from his forehead. She had to bury her nails in her palms to keep from lifting a hand to his dear, lovely, austere face.

"I went about this all wrong." He sighed and shook his head.

Desperate for answers, aching to launch herself into his arms, she said, "What's going on, Lucian? Why did you send those gifts?"

"That was my sorry attempt at romance," he said grimacing, then frowned as a shudder racked her body. Standing, he shrugged out of his black slicker and wrapped it about her shoulders, its warmth enveloping her. Then he sat close beside her, angling his body so that he could look her full in the face.

"I'm not a hero, Megan. I'm not a prince or a knight or a musketeer. I'm no Mr. Darcy or Mr. Knightley or any of Jane Austen's other leading men. I'm just a normal man." His obsidian eyes intense, his gaze lovingly caressed her face. "A man who loves you."

Megan didn't dare breathe or move for fear this was just a dream or a figment of her imagination. Surely this wasn't real. Lucian *loved* her?

"You're wrong, you know." She lifted a shaky hand and pressed it against his hard chest, directly over his heart. At the intimate touch, he sucked in a sharp breath. "You *are* a hero. You're a man of such deep feeling, Lucian. You possess a courageous yet tender heart. The people closest to you, the ones you should've been able to count on, betrayed you and yet despite all that, you opened yourself up enough to trust me. To care for Sarah and the other children. You forgave your mother her deception and allowed yourself to grieve her passing, a difficult, painful thing. A strong man is a man who faces his fears head-on. That's what makes a man a hero."

Ever so gently cupping her cheek, he said wonderingly, "I don't deserve your sweet words. None of that would've came about without you, my love."

Giddy with joy, she watched as he reached into his pocket and produced a flat, velvet box, held it aloft on his outstretched palm. "I have one final gift for you."

Her stomach flip-flopped. "You do?" She looked at the box for long moments before lifting her gaze to his face.

"Aren't you curious what it is?" he prompted with an endearing smile.

Heart pounding, she took the box from him, fingers fumbling on the lid. At last she was able to open it. There, nestled in the velvet folds, lay a key.

"It's the key to Charles's house."

Lifting her chin, he gazed at her with tender devotion. "I would like for it to be *our* house. Yours and mine together. Will you do me the honor of becoming my wife?"

"Oh, Lucian, I—I want that more than anything else but…what about your resolve to marry for duty?"

Cradling her face in his hands, he declared, "I only determined to marry for duty because I was afraid to be hurt again, afraid of hurting someone like my father hurt my mother. I admit, I'm still afraid. But my love for you is stronger than my fear. With God's help, I can be a good husband to you."

She covered his hands, smiled at him with all the love she felt for him shining on her face. "You are the only husband I want."

His eyes lit with happiness. "So you'll marry me?"

"Yes!" She laughed out loud, joy unlike she'd ever known filling her heart until she thought it might burst. "Most definitely."

He brought his mouth tantalizingly close. "Soon?"

"As soon as possible," she murmured, sliding her hands up to lock behind his neck.

He kissed her then, a dazzling kiss full of promise. He held nothing back, infusing all the love and affection he felt for her into the embrace. Her despair of minutes ago had vanished, replaced with a heady sense of rightness, of completeness, that only being with Lucian could inspire. This was where she belonged. With him. Her love. Her hero.

Epilogue

Three weeks later
July 1881

"**M**y dear, you look radiant."

Megan's mother, Alice, reached up to tuck a pink rose more firmly into her curls, then stepped back to observe the dress for the umpteenth time. Nicole had offered her the ivory silk confection she'd worn to the poetry recital as a wedding present. With its seed pearls adorning the scooped neck, lace overlay about the skirt and gold-and-silver stitching along the hem, it was a perfect choice for a wedding dress. Instead of the sparkly diamond pins she'd worn last time, Megan had decided to wear roses in her curls.

Tears glistened in her mother's eyes.

"Don't cry, Mama," Megan admonished with a smile "or else I will, too, and the last thing I want is to greet my groom with splotchy skin and puffy eyes."

Alice glanced about the spacious upstairs bedroom "It was kind of Lucian to offer the house for you and your sisters to get ready."

"Thoughtfulness is just one of his many endearing qualities."

Pausing in her fussing, she cocked her head to study her. "You've always been a happy girl, but now that he's come into your life, you seem…oh, I don't know the right word. Settled, maybe? At peace? Before, there was a restless gleam in your eye. That's gone now."

Megan swallowed back a tide of emotion. It was true. With Lucian in her life, she felt complete. "You do approve, don't you, Mama?"

"From what I've seen and heard, Lucian appears to be a kind and decent man. And it's plain to see he's besotted with you. I believe the two of you are a good match." She shook her head in consternation. "Just once I'd like to witness one of my daughters falling in love. First Juliana meets her true love while on the run from outlaws and comes home already married. And while I'm away attending the birth of my first grandchild, you fall for a stranger. I'm not leaving home again until your sisters are all settled."

Megan's chuckle was interrupted by a succinct knock before the door swung wide to admit Nicole—stunning in blue, her raven curls piled on top of her head in an elegant arrangement—and the twins, lovely in matching shades of seafoam-green that enhanced their auburn tresses.

Her only regret on this, her most special of days, was that Juliana couldn't be here. Evan had been firm in insisting the journey would be too risky for his wife and baby James. Megan understood. Of course her nephew's well-being was paramount. The fact that she and Lucian would be traveling there in just two days' time softened her disappointment. She could hardly wait to hold James and introduce Lucian to her sister and brother-in-law.

Nicole handed Megan her bouquet. "The ceremony starts in fifteen minutes. We need to head over to the church now if you don't want Lucian to think you've changed your mind."

Jessica gave her a quick hug. "Lucian is going to swoon when he sees you, sis. I've never seen you look more beautiful."

"I don't think grooms swoon." Jane frowned at her twin.

They debated and teased all the way to the church. Megan found it difficult to concentrate on their words, her mind on Lucian. Was he as anxious as she was? The minutes were passing in a blur, and she wished she could make time slow, wanted to savor every moment. In just a little while, she would walk out of this church a married woman.

In the alcove, Owen was waiting with a fully recovered Sarah, who'd eagerly agreed to be Megan's flower girl. Adorable in a cream confection created by Nicole, her fine hair had been braided and twisted into a neat circle about her crown. At the sight of Megan in her wedding dress, her eyes widened. Then, seeing Megan's reassuring smile, she smiled back.

The music started, and everyone hustled into place.

Before she knew it, Uncle Sam was taking her arm and guiding her through the inner doors. The faces on either side of the aisle failed to register, her focus all on Lucian, the man of her dreams, elegantly handsome in his black formal attire, his brown hair tousled like always. She smiled then, happy he hadn't attempted to tame it.

He returned her smile, an action that transformed his features and made her heart kick in recognition. She'd become quite familiar with that dazzling smile over the course of the past three weeks. That and his husky laughter. And his gentle touch. They'd spent nearly every day together, taking long walks and plotting their future.

Now she was here, about to pledge herself to him for a lifetime.

He was gazing at her with awe, as if finding it hard to believe she was his, and an eagerness that matched her own. When she at last reached his side, he took her hands in his, his thumbs gently stroking in a soothing gesture. They spoke their vows with reverence, and when Reverend Monroe announced them husband and wife, Lucian grinned, leaned over and kissed her soundly. Their guests laughed and clapped. And then she and her husband were hurrying down the aisle to a chorus of well-wishes.

He paused on the steps to lean close, a happy grin playing about his lips. "There's no changing your mind now, Mrs. Beaumont. You're mine from this day forward."

"As if I'd ever dream of such a thing, Mr. Beaumont." She splayed a hand on his chest. "I'm perfectly happy with my choice."

Chuckling, he kissed her briefly before they were swept up in the crowd as everyone made their way to their house for the reception. Mrs. Calhoun had joined forces with Alice, Aunt Mary, Kate, Jane and Jessica to produce a brunch worthy of royalty with succulent meats, egg dishes, hearty breads, bowls of fresh fruit and an astonishing array of desserts. Fresh-cut flowers, courtesy of Fred, adorned every room, scenting the air with sweet summertime.

By the time the gifts had been opened and all of the guests besides family had departed, Megan was eager for time alone with her new husband. Catching her gaze from across the parlor, he set down his cup and, with a parting word to Josh and Uncle Sam, strode purposefully towards her. His dark gaze was so full of love it made her want to weep. All of his doubts had been swept away, his misgivings given to God, and now his heart was fully hers for safekeeping.

"Care to take a stroll in the gardens, my love?"

Smiling up at him, she slipped her hand in the crook of his arm. "I thought you'd never ask."

Blushing at the knowing looks her family cast their way, she walked with him through the house—she still couldn't quite grasp it was to be her new home—and on to the back porch, where they encountered Nathan leaning against the porch railing, staring moodily out at the gardens.

He turned at their approach. Smiled and clapped Lucian on the back. "In case I forgot to say it, welcome to the family, Beaumont." Then he kissed Megan's cheek. "Congratulations, cousin. I'm glad you found your happy ending."

"Ah, but this isn't an ending." Lucian shared a smile with her. "It's a beginning."

"Right you are," Nathan conceded. "To a happy beginning, then."

Megan touched his arm. "You looked upset a moment ago. Are you all right?"

He looked surprised at the question. "I'm fine." At the quirk of her eyebrow, he continued, "This is your wedding day. Go enjoy some time with your husband."

"I didn't see Sophie today," she persisted. "Wasn't she supposed to come?"

A barely perceptible change came over him, and he fought to hide his frown. "She told me she'd be here. It could be that her grandfather wasn't feeling well. I'm heading over there soon to check on them."

"Please tell her that we missed her."

"I will."

When he'd gone inside, Lucian guided her down the steps and along the stone path they'd traveled countless times. "Who's Sophie?"

"You don't remember Sophie Tanner? My aunt and uncle's neighbor?"

His eyes lit with recognition. "Oh, do you mean the young tomboy? The one with a younger brother about ten years old? I forgot his name."

"William. And you can't blame Sophie for being a bit rough around the edges. She hasn't had a female role model in her life. Her mother died when she was very young, and her father ran off soon after. She was raised by her grandfather."

"I see." He stopped before the rose arbor, lowered himself onto the stone bench and tugged her onto his lap, wrapping his arms loosely about her. "Enough talk about Nathan's friend. I'd much rather focus on my beautiful wife. How much longer before everyone goes home?" he said wryly.

Arms draped about his sturdy shoulders, she laughed and wiggled her eyebrows. "Perhaps we'll just have to hide out here for a while. They'll get the hint eventually."

"Good idea," he whispered before he brought his mouth to hers in a soul-stirring kiss. When he lifted his head, he gazed at her adoringly. "Has anyone ever told you that you're the loveliest, most radiant bride that ever lived?"

"Actually, they have," she teased. "You're just one in a long line of people."

"What?" He reared his head back in mock horror. "That's unacceptable."

Smoothing his collar, she grew serious. "Are you absolutely certain you'll be happy here? You won't miss city living? Your work?"

His smile was patient and gentle, as if this wasn't the twentieth or so time she'd asked this exact question. "My home is where you are, *mon chou*. All that matters is that we're together. Besides, I like it here. I have a new family. New friends who don't give a fig what my last name is or how much I'm worth. As for work, Fred isn't getting any younger. I'm going to enjoy helping him work the land. I've got plans, my dear. First on the list is building your mother and sisters a new barn. Owen still needs help, and Nathan and your uncle can always use an extra hand—"

"Okay, okay." She laughed, convinced he was sincerely eager to dig into rural life. "I can see you've got it all figured out."

"And if we feel the need for a change of pace, we can visit the city anytime."

"I can't wait for you to meet my sister and Evan. They're going to love you. And I can't wait to hold baby James." They planned to stay about a week in Cades Cove before heading down to Louisiana. His father had sent his regrets—not a surprise to Lucian—along with an extravagant gift. She was a bit nervous about meeting him. "How long do you think we'll stay in New Orleans?"

"For however long you'd like. One day. One week. A month. We'll play it by ear." Then he tossed her a roguish grin that made her blood heat. "We can't stay away too long, though, if we're to get a head start on those ten kids you're set on having."

"And what if all ten are girls?"

His expression turned intense, a fiercely protective glint in his eyes. "I'll love each and every one because they'll be a part of me and you, proof of our love and commitment."

Satisfied, she caressed his cheek. "Twins run in my family, you remember. My father and Uncle Sam were twins. And, of course, Jessica and Jane."

Leaning slightly forward, arms secure about her waist, Lucian glanced around the rosebushes at the stately Victorian awash in golden sunlight, his smile brimming with joyful expectation. "Then it's a good thing we have plenty of space." His expression turned thoughtful. "What do you think my grandfather would think about us?"

"Charles would be thrilled, no doubt about it. In fact, I wouldn't be surprised if he'd considered such an outcome. He knew me well enough to know I'd fight to use the house. And I think he came to know a little about you, too, from your mother's letters. He must've suspected you'd want to hold on to the house."

"He may have willed me a house, but he gifted me with so much more." Eyes burning bright, he buried his fingers in her loose curls. "I love you, Megan."

At home in his arms, she moved in close for a kiss. "And I love you."

* * * * *

Dear Reader,

Thank you for choosing *His Mountain Miss,* the third installment in my Smoky Mountain Matches series. I've always dreamed of having my very own English-style garden like Lucian's, one with winding paths and fountains and secret hideaways where I could sit and read for hours without distraction. When I mention this to my husband, however, he points out my poor track record with plants. Maybe one day I'll have that garden... with hardy varieties that can survive my bumbling attempts at gardening!

When I began Lucian and Megan's story, I had no idea how God would work through it to help me deal with my dad's unexpected passing months earlier. Like Lucian, I chose not to face my grief. But as I wrote, God helped me to see that in doing this, I was not honoring my dad's life. I still have a long way to go, but I'm working through it with God's help. I hope that if you've lost a loved one, something in this story helped you, too.

Please feel free to write me at karenkirst@live.com or swing by my Facebook page. If you'd like to find out more information about the O'Malleys and this series, please visit my website, www.karenkirst.com.

Blessings,

Karen Kirst

Questions for Discussion

1. In the beginning, Megan and Lucian had preconceived ideas about each other's motives and characters. Have you ever made assumptions about someone that later proved to be incorrect?

2. Has anyone ever judged you unfairly? How did you handle the situation?

3. Lucinda led Lucian to believe his only grandfather wanted nothing to do with him. Has anyone ever deceived you? How did you cope when the truth came to light?

4. In Lucinda's mind, she was acting to protect her marriage. What does God's Word say about lying and deception?

5. Leaving his predictable life behind, Lucian assumes his business in Gatlinburg will be concluded quickly and without complications. When his plans go awry, he feels out of control. How do you cope with changes—both expected and unexpected—in your life?

6. Based on past experience, Lucian's first inclination is to be suspicious. How does he ultimately overcome this to trust Megan?

7. As he learns more about Megan's friendship with his grandfather, Lucian becomes jealous. And as Megan grows to care for him, she's jealous of the

socialites who possess everything he requires of a wife. How do you handle jealousy in your own life?

8. Because of Megan and Tom's long-standing friendship, she is reluctant to hurt his feelings when he declares his intentions. Do you think she could've handled it differently? How so?

9. Jane is in love with Tom, who not only views her as a little sister but has proposed to Megan. Have you ever experienced unrequited love? How did it work out?

10. Have you ever felt, like Lucian, that God was far away, distant and uncaring of your personal struggles? What happened to make you change your mind? Can you point to specific Bible verses that helped you?

11. Why do you think Charles left the house to Lucian? Do you think he was right not to insist on having a relationship with his grandson? Could he have done something differently?

12. Sarah's illness forces Lucian to deal with his own grief. How do you think refusing to deal with our losses affects us?

13. Because of his parents' troubled marriage, Lucian is hesitant to trust in love. Have you experienced a similar situation? How did you overcome your fears?

14. As the story progresses, Lucian slowly comes to suspect Megan is right about his mother and Charles'

ongoing correspondence. The letters confirm everything. Though devastated, he is ultimately able to forgive his mother. How do you go about forgiving someone who's wronged you? What does the Bible say about forgiveness?

5. 1 Corinthians 13 is often called the love chapter. What does it say about love and its importance? What are the characteristics of authentic love?

REQUEST YOUR FREE BOOKS!

FREE INSPIRATIONAL NOVELS
PLUS 2
FREE
MYSTERY GIFTS

Love Inspired
HISTORICAL
INSPIRATIONAL HISTORICAL ROMANCE

YES! Please send me 2 FREE Love Inspired® Historical novels and my 2 FREE mystery gifts (gifts are worth about $10). After receiving them, if I don't wish to receive any more books, I can return the shipping statement marked "cancel." If I don't cancel, I will receive 4 brand-new novels every month and be billed just $4.49 per book in the U.S. or $4.99 per book in Canada. That's a saving of at least 22% off the cover price. It's quite a bargain! Shipping and handling is just 50¢ per book in the U.S. and 75¢ per book in Canada.* I understand that accepting the 2 free books and gifts places me under no obligation to buy anything. I can always return a shipment and cancel at any time. Even if I never buy another book, the two free books and gifts are mine to keep forever.

102/302 IDN FVXK

Name	(PLEASE PRINT)

Address	Apt. #

City	State/Prov.	Zip/Postal Code

Signature (if under 18, a parent or guardian must sign)

Mail to the Harlequin® Reader Service:
IN U.S.A.: P.O. Box 1867, Buffalo, NY 14240-1867
IN CANADA: P.O. Box 609, Fort Erie, Ontario L2A 5X3

Want to try two free books from another series?
Call 1-800-873-8635 or visit www.ReaderService.com.

Terms and prices subject to change without notice. Prices do not include applicable taxes. Sales tax applicable in N.Y. Canadian residents will be charged applicable taxes. Offer not valid in Quebec. This offer is limited to one order per household. Not valid for current subscribers to Love Inspired Historical books. All orders subject to credit approval. Credit or debit balances in a customer's account(s) may be offset by any other outstanding balance owed by or to the customer. Please allow 4 to 6 weeks for delivery. Offer available while quantities last.

Your Privacy—The Harlequin® Reader Service is committed to protecting your privacy. Our Privacy Policy is available online at www.ReaderService.com or upon request from the Harlequin Reader Service.

We make a portion of our mailing list available to reputable third parties that offer products we believe may interest you. If you prefer that we not exchange your name with third parties, or if you wish to clarify or modify your communication preferences, please visit us at www.ReaderService.com/consumerschoice or write to us at Harlequin Reader Service Preference Service, P.O. Box 9062, Buffalo, NY 14269. Include your complete name and address.

SPECIAL EXCERPT FROM

Love Inspired HISTORICA

*Charlotte Miller has already lost her husband...she's
terrified at the thought of giving up her little girl.
The orphan Sasha is the daughter Charlotte has alway
wanted. But only married women are permitted to take
orphans. And the only eligible bachelor in town is
Wyatt Reed—the tracker hired to take the orphans awa*

*Read on for a sneak preview of
THE MARRIAGE BARTER by Christine Johnson,
the second story in the ORPHAN TRAIN series.*

"I won't lose my daughter. I'll do anything to keep her.

He flinched and looked away. "I'm sorry. I tried my be:

"I know." She boldly grasped his arm, forcing his g
back to her. "Thank you." The time had come. "Will
help me again?"

Confusion clouded his expression. "How?"

She opened her bag and pulled out the wallet. "Cha
left me some money. Whatever Mr. Baxter paid you,
pay double."

He pulled back. "It's not that simple."

"Of course it is."

"No, it's not. The Orphan Salvation Society has an ag
ment with Greenville. If the judge rules that the children n
go to Greenville, then I have no choice but to take them."

Charlotte shook her head. He didn't understand. "
not talking about all the children. I'm talking about Sas

Instead of walking away or shouting at her, he sp
firmly. "There's nothing I can do to help you keep Sash

"Yes, there is."

He stared at her. "No, there's not."

"You can marry me." The words exploded down the eet like gunfire.

He didn't blink. Not one muscle flinched except that tick low his eye. Dear Lord, he must think her mad.

"For money," she added, lifting the wallet. "I'll pay you uble, triple. I'll give you all I have." Tears threatened, t she refused to let them surface. "I don't want anything m you. You don't even have to live here. I just need to married long enough to legally adopt Sasha. Once the option goes through, you can move on." She shoved the llet at him.

He held up his hands and backed away.

"Please help me." The words came out strangled, and for moment she feared he didn't understand. She held out the llet again. "Please."

Don't miss THE MARRIAGE BARTER
by Christine Johnson, available May 2013 from
Love Inspired Historical.

In the fan-favorite miniseries
Cowboys of Eden Valley

LINDA FORD

presents

The Cowboy's Convenient Proposa

Second Chance Ranch

She is a woman in need of protection. But trust is the one thing feis
Grace "Red" Henderson is sure she'll never give any man again—r
even the cowboy who rescued her. Still, Ward Walker longs to prot
the wary beauty and her little sister—in all the ways he couldn't
safeguard his own family.

Red desperately wants to put her tarnished past behind her. Little
little, Ward is persuading her to take a chance on Eden Valley, and
him. Yet turning his practical proposal into a real marriage means
leap of faith for both…toward a future filled with the promise of lo

Available May 2013